HEAVENS BEING

Hypatia S.

Cover designer: Marta Susic

Book editing and interior layout design: Turnedpagesco.com

To those…

Who continue to gaze at the sky through the ages,

With a vast emptiness in their hearts…

Coincidence, another name for fate...

"On that day, I was surrounded by the heavy rain, and the cold gripped me, making everything worse. I was not well; my disappearance might have been better. In that moment, I continued to smile calmly. This is how I want to be, always."

— *Kenji Miyazawa*

She was running at an incredible speed... Rather, she was soaring just above the ground, so close that her feet would lightly tap the earth from time to time as if urging her flight to quicken. If these heavens being were to pass by a human, they would feel a fierce wind sweep through them for a moment, unable to see her at all.

Ahead of her lay a dense forest, its paths lit only by the faintest rays of sunlight. She glided through it, skilfully weaving between tree trunks as though she were dancing with them, a smile of pure enjoyment playing on her lips. Despite the situation she found herself in—one that offered little room for joy—this is how our companion (**Achilla**) always was... able to find, almost miraculously, delight even in the direst of circumstances.

Achilla was a slender, extraordinarily beautiful girl, as statuesque as the Greek gods. Her skin was golden, her hair the colour of the sky at sunset—ranging from a deep, wine-like red to a fiery hue, glowing like sacred flames in Persian temples. Her hair was long, flowing down to the small of her back. Her eyes were large and bright grey, like stars in the night sky, framed by thick, long black lashes and arched eyebrows matching the colour of her hair. She had a small, full mouth, a delicate nose, and two light dimples that only appeared when she smiled.

She did not maintain her appearance when blending in with humans. Like all Heavenkin, she possessed the ability to transform or alter her appearance. While she rarely made drastic changes, she preferred to darken her hair to a deep, jet-black and shorten it slightly while changing her eyes to a honeyed hue. This made her less conspicuous and more like her mother.

Achilla turned her head, scanning the surroundings for those who were chasing her. She wasn't sure whether she had managed to lose them or not. But as she looked ahead again, she was startled to see a figure moving swiftly across her path. She couldn't avoid it fast enough, and the impact was harsh, a deafening crash ringing through the air. Like two billiard balls, they collided and rebounded in opposite directions. She broke the trunk of a tree as she bounced backwards, creating another loud commotion. *Damn it,* she thought, *this will draw their attention. The sounds will bring them here.* The body she collided with left a long skid mark before finally coming to rest on the forest floor.

She lifted herself from the ground and sat up straight. Her foggy gaze fell upon her delicate white dress, which had torn along the right side. She muttered a few words of protest; it had been one of her favourite garments. It was a light summer dress, short enough to reach her knees, with thin straps that hung over her shoulders, exposing her arms. It wasn't the ideal outfit for a chase, but she had been caught off guard.

Two tall shadows appeared before her, moving swiftly toward her, making them seem as though they materialised from thin air. She had her hand pressed to her right eye, having taken a heavy blow there, feeling a slight dizziness in her head. She looked at them from the corner of her left eye as she sat beside the broken tree trunk, leaning on her other hand. She cast a quick glance at the body she had collided with and noticed two more shadows standing by it as well. Then, her gaze returned to the two figures before her. She bent her knee to stand, trying to clear the fog from her vision and focus on the features of these tall shadows. They had human shapes like hers, but like her, they were not human—nor were the other three. Otherwise, the body she had crashed into would have been reduced to pieces by now if it were human.

A warm voice came from one of these figures, asking, "Are you alright?" A voice startlingly familiar—one that had emerged from her past, shaking off the dust of years. She slowly removed her hand from her eye, her heart trembling with the memory. Before her gaze could fully rest on his face and the image become clear, he bent toward her, offering to help her stand, placing his hand on her arm—and then... the flow began.

All of this happened in seven seconds: the moving body, the collision and rebound, the shattering, the dizziness, the fog, the five shadows... and then the touch—just seven seconds.

She gasped when she saw his face, her mouth hanging open unconsciously. As for the owner of the voice, he stiffened as though his hand had been placed on a live wire, trembling in place. Memories and images rushed at him, all colliding together, all unfolding before him at once. His mind couldn't grasp what was happening to him. This accidental touch was enough to rain down all these memories at once. He collapsed onto his knees, convulsing, clenching his teeth tightly, his eyes wide open. The three distant shadows gathered around him in the blink of an eye, and the body she had collided with was still rubbing its head.

But now, she was able to see their faces clearly. There were three men and a woman, in addition to the owner of the voice.

The one beside the man convulsing on his knees asked, flustered, "What did you do? What's wrong with him?"

She didn't answer. Instead, she glanced away over her shoulder as if sensing someone's approach. With a swift movement, she rose, bending her knees, letting her legs lift gracefully and slowly into the air. Before disappearing, she tilted her face towards the one still gripped by the shock of the flood of images. With her body slightly curled, her feet slowly rising, and her face sinking in the same motion, she positioned herself directly in front of him, close enough that their faces were almost touching. She whispered softly, "I'm sorry... Karl," and lightly touched his forehead with her fingertip. A faint blue light appeared beneath her touch, and then, she vanished, continuing her escape.

The one she had collided with, named Paul, a tall man with broad shoulders and a muscular build, a youthful face, short, auburn hair, and green eyes, spoke: "Damn, what is this... What are you? What happened to Karl?"

Giovanni, who stood beside him, was the shortest among the men and much slimmer than Paulo, with unruly brown, curly hair and blue eyes; placing his hand over his mouth as if concentrating on a thought while staring at Karl, he answered in a low voice: "A flow of memories."

Abraham, who had been standing by Karl since the beginning, a man with slightly long and messy, bronze-coloured, wavy hair, medium build, brown eyes, and a somewhat long beard, asked in confusion, "A flow of memories!! What do you mean?!"

Emily, the girl accompanying them, was of medium height. She seemed shorter next to the others, with long, smooth black hair flowing to the middle of her back, thick, short eyebrows, and delicate features. She moved as if to speak. But suddenly, three figures passed through the air around them at a dizzying speed, much like the girl who had collided with them, though more violent. They cut through the air with a loud, piercing sound, shaking everything around them. They couldn't make out their faces, but they saw that they were three large, hulking men, like wild bears, dressed in black cloaks with golden rings on their heads, holding short, oddly shaped staffs in their hands. And just as quickly as they appeared, they vanished.

Emily screamed in shock: "What was that?!"

They exchanged confused, bewildered, and worried looks, still trying to process what had just happened. Suddenly, Karl collapsed, unconscious at last, worn down from what happened. They all bent toward him, and Abraham asked with concern, "Is he alright?"

Giovanni replied: "Yes, the flow was more than his mind could handle… he just needed rest. He couldn't bear it all at once."

Paul spoke up: "You do realise we don't understand a word you're saying, don't you?"

Then, they sensed a figure standing nearby. They all turned toward him at once. He was a skinny man with broad shoulders, shorter than the three bears who had passed by. His face was crinkled, showing a few signs of age, perhaps in his late forties. His dark brown hair was tightly curled, and a golden ring etched with strange symbols adorned his head. He wore a velvet navy-blue cloak, and his imposing appearance and strong presence suggested a higher rank than theirs. In his hand, he held a long staff, the top carved with the image of a strange creature, while his other hand rested behind his back. He stood for several seconds, staring at them with a stern expression.

At that moment, a young man appeared beside him—tall, strong, and handsome, with olive-toned skin and striking features. He had an air of elegance, yet his attire was different from theirs. Unlike the stern man beside him, an air of indifference and playfulness was showing on the young man's face with the light black beard and a jaw neither too broad nor too thin, eyes that were slightly wide, long lashes, thick brows that were close to his eyes, giving him a distinctive look, a beautiful nose, a wide mouth with plump lips. He seemed less a part of their group and more like someone who had joined them.

The young man flicked his gaze between the stern man beside him and the others in front of him, his amber eyes filled with curiosity. He then scratched his head, covered with thick, slightly long black hair, and appeared somewhat embarrassed.

Before anyone could speak, both the man and the young one vanished, soaring into the air.

Emily exclaimed in astonishment, "Clearly, today is the day for strange creatures with rude behaviours"—she gestured toward Karl, lying on the ground—" and incomprehensible events as well!"

Abraham replied, "We must move him quickly before anything else happens!". With that, Paul lifted Karl onto his back, and they hurried off at once.

Karl… The Sorcerer

"You are my heart, so do not fear, and answer me: Do you love her?"
And even now, her love still pulses within you?
You are not my heart, then, rather you are her heart.

The awakening of death is what I am witnessing, or do I witness the slumber of life?
In the shade, I scorch beneath the flame and the heat.
And my conscience pulls me towards a desire with no conscience of its own,

And to where? For I am lost to the unknown fate.
She destroyed me, for once, I loved her.
And even now, her love still pulses within you!
You are not my heart, then, rather you are her heart."

—*Kamel El-Shanawy*

Karl was truly a handsome man—tall, broad-shouldered, with a slender frame as white as marble. His hair was soft, light brown, and wavy if left to grow a little longer. His eyes were green, like two pieces of peridot, his lips slightly full, his nose long and perfectly straight, and his jawline clearly defined.

He slowly opened his eyes, allowing them to adjust to the light. A strange headache, unlike anything he had felt before, pulsed through his head. He pressed his palm against his forehead and let out a soft groan. A worried feminine voice reached his ears: "Oh... thank God, you've finally awakened."

He struggled to focus, the rhythmic pounding in his head filling his ears.

"What?" Karl said, attempting to sit up. They had placed him on a wide couch in the middle of a spacious living room, next to a large wooden table that could seat six people—used for meals, meetings, spellcasting, poker, and... well, almost everything. Paul, Abraham, Giovanni, and Emily were standing around it.

The feminine voice that answered him belonged to his beloved, Selene. She was blonde, with curly hair that reached her shoulders, broad-shouldered yet slender in form, tall and graceful. Freckles adorned her shoulders, and a few dotted her cheeks and nose. Her eyes, small but striking, were blue green like the surface of the sea on a summer island. Selene was incredibly attractive, with a childlike face that radiated warmth.

She extended her hand to help him sit up. "You've been unconscious for a few hours... Do you feel alright?"

Karl glanced around the room for a moment, then groaned, "Oh my God... this headache!" He fell silent abruptly as though realising something. His eyes widened in shock, his mouth slightly open as though he were focusing on something. He pressed his fingers against his forehead again and exclaimed, "Achilla... Achilla!! ... Where is Achilla?!"

He turned swiftly towards his companions, who had gathered around him, speaking urgently as though calling out to her, his gaze darting frantically from side to side. "Achilla... Where are you? Where is she?! Has she left?! ... Achilla!"

Selene tightened her grip on his hand to calm him while Abraham pressed his hands on his shoulders and said, "Pull yourself together... What's wrong? Who is Achilla?"

Karl responded, his voice breaking, "The forest... in the forest... Oh... Achilla..."

His voice faltered, the weight of distress tightening his chest. He didn't realise he was crying until Selene gently wiped away his tears. "Calm down, my dear," she said softly, her voice full of tenderness and sorrow, "Could you please explain what's happening?"

Karl fell silent, enveloped in a deep, stunned quiescence. The others looked toward Giovanni, who furrowed his brow, concentrating on Karl's thoughts, his hand resting on his mouth as he did when deep in focus. The silence hung for a while, and confusion spread across the group, growing thicker with each passing moment. Then Giovanni spoke, his tone firm yet gentle: "Why don't we leave Karl alone for a bit?"

It wasn't a question or a suggestion; it was a polite command urging his friends to step aside for a moment. Karl's state wasn't conducive to speaking. He had just realised that a large portion of his memory had been erased—or rather, restricted. Thirty years, to be precise. Not all of his memories had been locked away, only the ones tied to her... to Achilla!

This is a personal matter, and Giovanni does not believe he has the right to speak of it until Karl allows him to. In truth, Giovanni himself is also confused, for Karl's thoughts are not entirely clear to him.

The confusion deepened, and Selene looked at him with bewilderment, saying, "But how can we leave him? Don't you see his condition? He's in shock. I've never seen him so shaken!"

Giovanni replied, lowering his hands to his sides, standing upright, and shaking his head. "I don't know exactly what's wrong with him... All I can say is that he's suffering from... a flow or rush of old memories... They somehow seem... to have been erased from his mind for a long time... and I don't know why! And somehow... in the forest... they've suddenly returned."

Giovanni cleared his throat slightly, feeling, for some reason, that he had said something he should not have. He added, "He'll be fine. Just give him some time alone."

Emily, curious, asked, "Memories of what?"

Giovanni raised an eyebrow and looked at her with a glance of reproach and mild scolding for her never-ending curiosity. She blinked at him with an innocent questioning look and muttered, "What?" She saw no harm in her question.

Abraham, who understood what Giovanni meant, spoke up. He had been Karl's first and closest friend, like a brother to him, with a kind and gentle heart. "Alright then..." he began. "Giovanni said he'll need a little time, and he will..." Before Abraham could finish his sentence, Karl suddenly jumped up from among them and sprang to his feet, rushing out of the house. He was desperate to escape every sound, every whisper, every breath. He didn't want to see anyone—he only desired to run, run, and run until he was utterly exhausted, until he collapsed on the ground, with the sky covering him.

Selene sprang to follow him after a moment, startled by his sudden movement, but Abraham caught her by the arm gently, saying, "Hey... Selene... dear Selene... Let's give him some time, as Giovanni suggested, and..." Selene was about to protest, but Abraham raised his finger in front of her face and continued, "I know you're worried... we all are... but it seems... this is what Karl needs right now." He looked at Giovanni, asking, "Isn't that right?"

Giovanni nodded in agreement and Abraham added, "You know he's a very sensible man—despite his strange condition—but nothing will happen to him, I'm sure. He'll be fine."

Selene furrowed her brows in deep concern, looking around in confusion. Yet, she listened to Abraham's words and refrained from following him. She decided to respect Karl's wish to be left alone. With a sense of resignation, she silently moved to sit in a corner of the salon near the glass wall, waiting and hoping to catch a glimpse of him.

The salon resembled the lobby of a hotel in a snowy mountain resort where people go to ski. Its floor was made of dark wooden panels, and the walls were of brick, tinged with a chalky reddish hue. In the centre of the room stood a fireplace, above which hung the head of a deer with long antlers. Surrounding it were several photographs and souvenirs. From the ceiling, modern and simple chandeliers hung, casting a soft light on the room. Scattered throughout the salon were various seating areas, reminiscent of a hotel lounge, with different shapes and colours—both light and dark—yet perfectly coordinated. Some seating areas were slightly elevated by a couple of steps, while in the farthest corner of the house, between the brick wall and the glass one, the wooden floor rose by three steps to house a deep navy-blue piano. Beneath it, a round white rug made of soft, thick fur lay, its ends gently fluttering.

The glass facades surrounded the house on three sides, with the wooden front door shaped like a broad semicircle at the centre of the main glass wall. Upon entering, one would find the seating areas spread across the centre and to the right of the house, while on the left stood a wooden table. Behind it, in the farthest left corner, a marble staircase seemed to float in mid-air, its handrails absent, leading to the second floor. Various sculptures and ornaments of different sizes were scattered throughout the salon. The house consisted of three floors: the first floor housed the reception lounge, with an exterior balcony located on the right side of the house, while the second floor contained the kitchen, which was open to a living room, along with a library and a gym. The third floor had six bedrooms.

It was a warm, classic home, truly beautiful. It overlooked a large garden or a small forest filled with several types of tall pine trees, as well as flowers and shrubs of exquisite appearance, compelling anyone who gazed upon it to admire its creative design.

Selene sat in the corner of the house, between two glass walls, on a wooden rocking chair next to a small table. She had placed a small cover over her feet to shield them from the chill of the day and drifted into thought.

She had never seen Karl like this, and she had known him for eighty years! He had always been a kind, composed, patient man with a calm demeanour, gentle in his manner, and with a big heart. No matter how dire the situation was, he would always remain steadfast and confident, easy to be around, and radiated warmth wherever he went. Above all, he was the pillar of their group, the very reason it had come together.

The panic, the shock, the astonishment, the disappointment, and other emotions that Selene saw on Karl's face were beyond her understanding—new to her. *What could these memories be? What could this... named... Achilla... be?!* Selene felt a pang in her heart when she silently uttered the name Achilla. Why?

Her train of thought was interrupted by Emily's hand on her shoulder. Emily leaned over to offer her a large mug, steam rising from it and carrying the rich scent of hot chocolate. Emily winked at her with a mischievous smile and said, "Everything feels better with a cup of hot chocolate."

Selene smiled in quiet acceptance, though sadness flickered in her eyes. She cradled the mug in her cold hands, bringing it close to her face, allowing the rising steam to brush against her nose. She inhaled deeply, the warmth reddening the tip of her nose, and murmured, "Oh... and the marshmallows too... There's nothing that chocolate can't fix."

It was a line Selene had always loved to repeat, a testament to her deep affection for chocolate. This time, however, she said it as though trying to convince herself. Emily saw that in her eyes.

She had no words to offer, for she, too, was perplexed. She had known Karl for nearly fifty years, and he had never acted like this before. Still, she murmured, "Everything will be fine," as she rubbed Selene's back, kissed her on the forehead, and stepped away.

Selene sipped her chocolate in the silence of deep thought. This time, it didn't offer her the solace it usually did. Though it lightened the moment, it could not ease the weight of her worry.

****

This small group was not composed of ordinary humans, as previously mentioned. They belonged to a society of sorcerers, specifically practitioners of black magic. However, each of them had long since broken away from their original coven.

The world of sorcery was divided into two factions: the black magic sorcerers and the white magic sorcerers. Within each faction, there were various covens, each consisting of a few families. These covens belonged to one faction or the other, and this allegiance was passed down through generations, from ancestors to descendants, along with their "magical abilities," of course. It was a hereditary right, and no sorcerer could leave their coven to join another, even after marriage. If two sorcerers from different factions had a child, the child had the right to choose which faction to belong to upon reaching adulthood.

The world of sorcerers held no respect for individuals who had abandoned their covens, no matter how wicked their original faction might have been—such as the black magic sorcerers. They were always seen as traitors to the sacred bonds of their coven. The relationship between coven members was a magical and sacred bond, not easily broken. A sorcerer who left their coven lost their individual value among the rest of the sorcerers. They forfeited their titles and glory, and no matter how great their abilities were, they remained outcasts or, at best, ignored by the sorcerer community.

These traditions were even more oppressive in ancient times, and no one defected from their coven, as this small group had, except for perhaps two or three sorcerers in the distant past. The sorcerer community rejected them, and each of them lived in solitude until the end of their days.

Defection from a coven is still a highly disdained act today, but we can say that the sorcerer's world has somewhat relaxed its stance on this small group, composed of individuals who broke away from the black magic covens. They had been granted a certain "symbolic" value, so to speak. However, Karl's group did not belong to either faction of the sorcerer world; it was as though they had formed a third faction—the faction of the defectors.

Even in modern times, only a rare few individuals voluntarily broke away from their coven. Most defectors sought to leave the world of sorcery behind, desiring a normal life. These individuals could belong to either of the two factions. As for the others, like Karl's group, their defection was due to their rejection of evil magic. They specifically belonged to the black magic covens, a form of sorcery that is incredibly powerful and terrifying, containing many harmful and malevolent spells. In the world of black magic, nothing was considered forbidden. There were no prohibited spells, no boundaries, and every means was permissible to achieve power and total control, in stark contrast to white magic.

The Grand Sorcerers' Tome outlines all the spells that sorcerers are forbidden to practice, and any means that could harm another sorcerer or even a human being is considered forbidden.

The black magic factions—which are very few compared to the others—flout these rules without a second thought and show no respect for the elders of the sorcerers or the white sorcerers. However, naturally, they were forced to pretend to adhere to these rules and conceal their actions, especially after the fierce confrontation the magic world launched against them two centuries ago. Before this, the black magic factions wreaked havoc on the land. Both sides lost members in this clash, but the majority were from the black sorcerers, for the many outweighed the strength, and they learned their lesson the hard way. Despite continuing to break certain laws without evidence, the elders could not intervene.

A white magic mage is not allowed to seek ultimate power or control, for no one could truly master it, no matter how strong they became, and it would ultimately turn to dominate them, leading to disastrous destruction. This was what the old tales and teachings told them, and they must dedicate their abilities to all that is good, for the world of sorcerers is not, after all, a world of evil.

However, the one rule followed by both sides, as is the case with all mythical beings regardless of their reasons, was that: "Their existence must remain a secret." This is the absolute law to which all are bound.

It is not an ancient rule; in fact, it was specifically established after the "days of confrontation" and due to the actions of the black sorcerers. The human world launched an attack on all mages, and even though the mages had disappeared from their world, they continued to kill each other under the pretext that they were witches!

The situation calmed down, times changed, and the mages, like many other things, became mere legends, forgotten by the people.

However, the world of mages did not forget. It continued to enforce this law, with violators facing death in some cases or eternal exile to the labyrinths of the mages' elder castle of domes in others.

The reason why Karl's group was granted this respect by the world of mages, especially the elders, was due to Karl's and his loyal companion, Abraham's stance during the great confrontation that took place nearly two hundred years ago. They fought alongside the white mages against their own factions; despite the difficulty of this, they were deeply committed to stopping the evil actions of their groups, saving innocent lives, and preventing the impending catastrophe. Their special abilities were of great help during the confrontation.

The elders never forgot this, and their respect for Karl and Abraham extended to the rest of their group, who later joined them.

In addition to the high physical abilities of sorcerers, such as their sharp vision, incredible speed, and strong bones that did not break easily, along with their magical powers, which vary in strength from one individual to another. Some sorcerers possessed special abilities. This group, too, was endowed with such gifts.

Besides all of them having exceptional magical abilities, Karl was particularly gifted with an extraordinary and immensely powerful magical energy. He could imbue a simple spell with immense force. This power, as he believed, granted him control over one of the elements of nature—earth or soil, so to speak. He could cause earthquakes, create deep fissures in the ground, provoke volcanoes, and even alter the course of rivers. However, his ability was not merely destructive; he could transform barren land into fertile soil with trees, make the earth burst forth with underground springs, and accelerate the growth of plants in astonishing ways, turning a seed into a tree bearing fruit in a remarkably short time. Furthermore, he could heal the sick plants using this power. Though he never clearly recalled how he first discovered or used this extraordinary ability.

Karl was now three hundred and eighty years old. He had parted ways with his original group when he was thirty, living alone and in isolation for roughly eighty years, as he recalled. When he reached one hundred and ten, he met his loyal companion, Abraham, who was then one hundred and fifteen. However, Abraham had not separated from his group until he was eighty-five.

Breaking the bond between members of the group was not an easy matter, as we've mentioned, for it carried its own magical strength. However, the kind-hearted Abraham could no longer bear the atrocities that his group had begun committing. Despite his inability to endure the thought of solitude and isolation, he chose it over remaining and witnessing the dark deeds unfolding, even though he had never participated in any of their actions. His departure coincided almost precisely with the beginning of the forbidden acts that the black magic sects began openly practising, which continued for decades, growing and evolving, until the final confrontation occurred.

Abraham possessed the ability to control bodies, making them do his bidding regardless of the will of their owners. Initially, he could only control one body at a time, but Karl helped him develop this power, and he eventually became capable of controlling up to fifty bodies simultaneously. Of course, this ability drained much of his strength.

Ninety-two years after Karl and Abraham's reunion, they met Paul twelve years after the great confrontation. At the time, Paul was forty-six years old. Giovanni followed a month later, at fifty-four years old. Both belonged to the same group but came from different families, meaning they were somewhat related. They had learned about Karl and Abraham after the confrontation and decided to join them—Paul first, then Giovanni. Neither of them had participated in the confrontation itself.

In addition to his physical strength and expertise in martial arts, Paul possessed the *Yian Wu* ability—a high-level combat skill that allowed him to create magical weapons from the energy of Yian Wu, such as the blue sword, fiery arrows, gleaming daggers, and more.

As for Giovanni, he had the ability to read minds and predict future events, or something akin to a sixth sense, so to speak. Sometimes, he would experience visions that were unclear and ambiguous, relating to pivotal moments for him, his group, or even the world. Other times, it would manifest as a mere feeling, either good or bad.

Selene joined them much later, after one hundred and eight years, when Karl was three hundred years old, Abraham was three hundred and five, Paul was one hundred and fifty-four, and Giovanni was one hundred and sixty-two. At that time, she was fifty years old. The youngest and most recent member was Emily, who joined Selene thirty years later at the age of just twenty-one! As a result, they all considered her their beloved daughter, though this sometimes irritated her.

Selene possessed the ability to manipulate minds, allowing her to make anyone do as she wished willingly. This power, however, was limited by a certain range. If the person being controlled moved beyond that range, the effect would fade, but by then, it would be too late to resist.

As for Emily, she believed she possessed only her exceptional magical abilities. She could master any spell, no matter how complex or powerful, with ease and precision from the very first attempt without any assistance. However, she discovered her unique gift by accident ten years ago while she was competing with Paul in a spell-casting challenge. She defeated him, and he, in frustration, lunged toward her as though to grapple with her. Emily, never skilled in physical combat, instinctively raised her hands in alarm as though to push him away before he could jump on her. To her surprise, Paul suddenly collided with an invisible barrier, which threw him back forcefully the moment he made contact. It was then they realised she could create a protective shield.

Special abilities differ from magical powers in that they manifest purely through the will of the sorcerer, without the need for incantations as with magic. Sorcerers are known for their long lives; they retain their youth for extended periods, but like all beings, they inevitably age and die. Their lifespans can stretch to hundreds of years and, on rare occasions, even a few thousand. The five elders of the sorcerers are prime examples: the eldest among them is nearly six thousand years old, while the youngest has lived for three thousand. No sorcerer had ever been recorded as having lived more than seven thousand years.

****

Karl ran aimlessly for hours, exhaustion slowly overtaking him. He ran, feeling as though he could no longer breathe, gasping for air as if his lungs were suffocating. His heart felt as though it might burst, and he thought he might go mad. Thousands of memories crowded his mind, and little by little, the picture began to come into focus.

How he met her, how they became friends, how he fell in love with her, and how he hid his feelings from her for so long—why did he do that? He couldn't remember; his memories were still blurred.

He quickened his pace, his feet pounding the earth, the ground groaning beneath him. The wind struck his face, burning his eyes. He continued like this for some time until a small, rocky beach appeared before him, empty and desolate. The sun had begun to dip below the horizon, bidding the day farewell. He stood for a moment, panting, gazing at the scene, before he dragged his weary legs toward the shore. He sank heavily, struggling to catch his breath, and sat on the sand, folding his knees and resting his elbows on them.

It was sunset. How beautiful the sunlight looked, sparkling on the surface of the sea. How beautiful the crimson hue that painted the sky, just like her hair. His chest tightened further, and his eyes filled with tears. He dropped his head between his knees, his fingers tangled in his hair, and he broke down in sobs.

Yes, he loved her with a mad, indescribable love. He remembered... he remembered his feelings clearly, remembered how strong they were despite the fog in his memories. He could feel them pulsing once again as though they were alive. He remembered her face well—her mischievous, sparkling eyes, her ringing laughter, her red gypsy hair, and the scent of her hair. There was nothing like the scent of her hair or the warmth of her hands.

There she was, jumping and playing like a child in the snow. She loved the snow, and she loved fun and laughter more than anything. She laughed at any time, all the time—she could never be serious. Yes, this was Achilla, his beloved Achilla... Then another memory rushed in—him confessing his love to her for the first time. Did he confess? Then he was free from whatever had bound him, though he didn't even know what it was, and he told her... there, beneath the snow as she frolicked. How happy she looked!

She had seen the snow fall thousands of times, but every time, her face lit up as though she were a child seeing snow for the very first time. The snow covered the earth and the treetops, filling the place with pure white. A little of it had gathered on her hat and shoulders. She looked like an angel... No, she was an angel!

She smiled that wide smile, gathering snowballs and throwing them playfully. He could never see her laugh or smile without smiling himself. He had no control over it; it was a feeling beyond his power.

His feet had sunk into the snow, and he hid his hands in the pockets of his coat to shield them from the cold. The cold weather suited her perfectly; her body was always warm and accustomed to extreme cold. He didn't try to dodge her snowballs, which allowed her to continue smiling; her smile was accompanied by small giggles. He only turned his face slightly away from her, avoiding the chill she brought. She gathered a large snowball and, with mischief, threw it at his head. He squeezed his eyes shut, his face scrunching as his hair became scattered with snow. He groaned in protest at the cold and shook his head to brush it off. Then, he heard her laugh; he opened one eye while the other one was still covered in snow. She was laughing like a child at his appearance. How happy she looked! He didn't think she'd ever looked more beautiful than in that moment. He whispered, "I love you." She stopped laughing and lowered her voice to hear him better, asking, "What?" He said, as he cleared the snow from his eye, "I love you." He said it as though it were a simple fact as if he'd told her that a thousand times before. She wasn't surprised, and her smile didn't falter, but her heart tightened at that moment and then began to beat wildly. The only change in her expression was a slight flush on her cheeks.

She stepped closer to him, her face filled with mischief and began brushing the snow from his hair. "Hmm... did I hit you with a rock without knowing it?" she teased. He smiled wider than before and replied, "Maybe... but that won't change the truth."

She cupped his face in her hands and rubbed his cheeks roughly, causing his heart to leap, feeling like it had been caught in his throat, as warmth spread through his body. She teased, "You little naive child," knowing that phrase always annoyed him. She saw his eyes widen, and before he could say anything, she placed a quick kiss on his nose, which left him momentarily stunned. Then, she ran off, laughing, and as her voice grew faint, she called back, "You know it's true, little one, I'm four hundred years older than you."

In a mix of irritation, confusion, and happiness, he froze for a moment, then darted after her, holding in his laughter. "But I love old women," he called out.

From between the trees, she shouted an objection, and he couldn't hold back his laughter any longer.

She was coming back to life once more... Her presence rose within his mind, his heart, and every atom of his body. He felt the weight of her presence pressing upon him, almost pinning him to the ground with the force of its intensity. But had she truly died to come back to life? Hadn't he always felt that something was missing? That he was searching for something important... something he couldn't identify... Yes! He often felt as though he had forgotten something incredibly significant... something dear to his heart!

He now understood the reason behind certain fragmented memories, but how... how had he forgotten them? How had the memory of *her* specifically been erased from his mind? Was he demented? No, for sorcerers do not suffer from senility... So then, how?

Amidst his questions...

He remembered... Their last meeting...

He slowly lifted his head, his eyelashes wet with tears. His heartbeat slowed to the point it almost ceased, his breath stopped, and his face grew pale. Then, after a few moments, he gasped, drawing a deep breath, the sound echoing like someone lifting their head from a bucket of water after a long time.

He froze like a stone, letting the hot tears burn his eyes and face once more. He gazed at the sea before him, swallowed by the darkness.

****

He returned home at dawn. When he saw Selene awake, waiting for him, a deep sorrow washed over him. In the midst of his shock, he had forgotten about her. Now, it felt as though she were miles away from him. This sweet, giving, loving woman—whom he too had loved, though not in the same way he loved Achilla —but he loved her, and she loved him with all her heart. What had she done wrong? What could he say to her? He would never try to hurt her feelings.

Selene looked at him. He seemed lost, exhausted, and filled with anger and sorrow. Where was all this coming from? she wondered. She approached him, gently placed her hands on his face, and asked, "Are you alright?"

He answered sharply, though unintentionally, "Yes." She froze, surprised, which made him feel guilty. He took her hands, gently removed them from his face, and kissed them. With sad eyes, he apologised, "I'm sorry. I'm fine, but I need some time alone. Just a few days until I calm down."

"A few days?!" she thought, but she nodded, smiling at him with uncertainty, and murmured, "Of course."

Karl isolated himself for two days in his study, surrounded by books. He couldn't even bear to sit in his room. He was lost in his thoughts, sifting through memories, and he managed to remember almost everything.

The thirty lost years, the meeting and what came after it, and... the farewell... that treacherous farewell. Oh, how could she have done it? How was she able to do it? By what right?!

He would go out late at night, avoiding the sight of his companions, to eat when hunger pricked at him, then return to his study. No one knew what was wrong with him except Giovanni. But he denied knowing anything, despite his friends' persistent questioning, and claimed that he didn't want to listen to his thoughts. He said that when he was ready, he would speak for himself.

****

The morning light of the third day fell on Karl's face through the open glass door of the balcony, disturbing his restless sleep. He sat for a moment on the long leather couch, entirely unsuitable for sleeping, and gazed at the beautiful morning. Autumn had not yet arrived, but the last breaths of summer brought with them a touch of its chill, and the leaves began to yellow. He inhaled deeply, filling his lungs, and rose.

He went to the bathroom, letting cold water pour over his back to regain some energy. He flinched and stepped back, his body covered in goosebumps, but he forced himself to stand beneath the icy water. His breath cut short from the cold until he began to adjust to it a little.

He dried himself off and slipped into a blue shirt that beautifully reflected off his ivory skin, paired with dark grey trousers. He ran his fingers through his damp hair, then descended to the kitchen. Everyone had already eaten, not expecting his arrival as they had on the previous days, and they hadn't noticed his exit from the study. They were gathered in the living room, opposite the kitchen, watching a news report that had caught their attention for a moment, except for Selene, who was wrapped in a light shawl, lying in Emily's arms with a melancholy expression, while the latter absentmindedly ran her hand through her hair, sipping her coffee.

When Karl entered, he immediately captured everyone's attention. Their curious gazes rested on him for a moment, frozen in their positions. He stood still, one hand in his pocket, meeting their eyes in return. A moment of awkward silence followed, with nothing but the soft hum of the news report. Then, feeling embarrassed by their stares, they all simultaneously turned away, shifting in their seats, trying to act as though everything was normal, returning to the news.

A small smile tugged at the corners of his mouth as he entered the kitchen and began preparing a cup of coffee. After a short while, Selene followed him in, appearing somewhat more lively. She asked, "Would you like me to prepare something for you to eat?"

He approached her, holding the coffee cup in his hand. He gently placed his free hand on her cheek, rubbing it softly, before planting a kiss on her forehead with a sweet smile. "Thank you. Maybe in a little while," he said.

She hugged him tightly, her voice filled with warmth, "I missed you." He wrapped his arm around her neck and rested his cheek on her head, replying softly, "I know, I'm sorry."

Daughter of the Wind

"Do you know, my friend, the taste of loneliness, when the rain sobs above your head in the funeral of winter in the great cities, and you hurry alone, skating over melancholy and memories?"

— *Ghada al-Samman*

Kanaki was one of the many titles of Achilla. It was customary among Heavenkin to bestow several titles upon each other, either out of affection, which was the most common, or out of reverence. Some of these titles carried honour for their bearers, and they were based on either their traits or the powers they possessed.

Aweilda meaning "the Wild and Untamed" **Bapita** meaning "Stranger", **Inanna,** one of the names synonymous with "the Goddess of Beauty", **Alala** meaning "the Goddess of War", **Alika** meaning "the Protector", **Amazonia** meaning "Warrior-like", **Ella** meaning "Whirlwind", **Khalycon**, "the Legendary Birds and Storms". But **Kanaki**, meaning "the Daughter of the Wind", was the title that most closely resonated with Achilla.

The reason behind these titles, which would soon become clear in our story, could be traced back to an ancient incident that changed her significantly. It was rare for one person to have more than three titles, yet our dear Achilla held eight. Well, as you would come to understand, she was a very special being!

She was given the title **Kanaki**, or "Daughter of the Wind," because of her temperament and unpredictable mood. Much like the wind, you never know from where it would blow nor to where it would go. Like the wind, she had no home—roaming the earth endlessly, never ceasing to wander. Moody, sharp, and unexpected, she is a tempest of mischief. Sometimes, she is a gentle, pleasant spring breeze, and at other times, she is a fierce, howling storm. She lingers for a while but cannot help but run like the wind... No wonder she is the Daughter of the Wind!

Achilla lost her parents at a young age. Her father, **Nanar**, passed away when she was only thirty years old. If you knew the Heavenkin well, you'll realise that this was an incredibly young age for them, equivalent to a seven-year-old child in human terms—though only physically speaking.

He died a natural death at the age of twenty-three thousand years. Achilla inherited his golden-brown skin. Although he was a bit older in years, heavens beings do not age and wither like other living creatures. Their appearance may change slightly over time, but even at their oldest, they resemble humans in their mid-fifties—assuming those humans are in the prime of their lives!

They do not bend, sag, or wrinkle. Ageing, it seemed, was not such a bad thing for them after all!

The lifespan of Heavenkin stretched across thousands of years, but sometimes only hundreds, depending on the strength of their spiritual energy. The greater their energy, the longer they lived.

The death rituals of Heavenkin were truly remarkable and beautiful.

The heavenly would die only after receiving three prophecies or visions. Unlike humans, they did not sleep. Instead, they entered what was known as a **meditative slumber**, a state that resembled yoga meditation, or more accurately, yoga resembled it, if we were to be precise. Every day at dawn, they entered this meditative slumber to regulate their spiritual energy and bring comfort to their bodies. It also helped them develop and sharpen their energy.

The heavenly do not die until they had received three prophecies or visions, which they experience while in a state of meditation. Sometimes, between each vision or prophecy—or whatever you wished to call it—there are centuries, years, months, weeks, or even days! But most often, it is years.

When the heavenly sees the third prophecy, they journey to the oracle of the **Urbahra Temple** to prepare for the death ritual over the course of three days. On the third day, the one destined to return to **Mata** would go to the temple, and the entire population of the **Fala Island**, including the king or queen, would gather to witness the ritual of death, or as they called it, the return to **Mata**.

The one returning to Mata would be immersed three times in the sacred **Clotho Lake** by the oracle, and hymns would be recited during this process. Then, they would ascend to a small cliff overlooking the lake, where all the gathered attendees would chant the hymns of departure or return together. Their voices would sound like the hum of a beehive. At the end of the hymns, they would release their spiritual energy in the form of threads of multi-coloured light that fill the sky above, creating a brilliant and stunning scene for the eye. The departing soul would then begin to rise, soaring from the cliff, carried by the immortal souls rising from Clotho Lake. This lake is the gateway to the realm of the eternal souls. It is not **Mata**, but the heavenly would first have to pass through it with the help of the immortal souls, who would guide them through the lake and carry them to **Mata**, or sometimes to **Kieris**, the realm of evil souls—or in other words, **hell**.

The souls would also appear in magnificent colours, formed as threads of spiritual energy, to help guide the departing soul and control its troubled energy as it left the body, ensuring it did not stray from **Mata**. You could see their hands, heads, and bodies clearly and distinguish their gender, although their exact features might remain difficult to discern. Each soul had an independent form that Heavenkin could easily recognise and tell apart from one another.

The number of immortal souls is thirty, but only between three to five souls would usually appear in the rituals of departure. The number would vary depending on the spiritual energy of the one departing, and the souls themselves would differ according to the abilities and deeds of the soul in life. Eleven souls would emerge when the protector of the kingdom departs, whether it be the king or queen—whoever was chosen by the souls—due to their immense spiritual energy. Three, five, or even seven souls could not control such powerful energy alone.

It was said that in a very ancient time, seventeen souls were required to manage the energy of one of the kingdom's guardians, **Aleeka**. But all the souls only emerged under one condition—when a new immortal soul was to join them. There was no greater honour than for the immortal souls to choose one of the Heavenkin to join their ranks. This signified that the chosen one had unmatched spiritual energy, on par with the souls themselves. Moreover, it implied that this being possessed a unique and noble character, a wise mind, and a giving heart. But there was no task more difficult than this.

To enter the realm of immortal souls meant to live in their intermediary world, **Clotho**, situated between **Fala**, **Mata**, and **Kieris**. There, one guards and protects the lives of the heavens beings forever, helps them find their way to **Mata** and ensures their souls do not wander after death. One does not return to **Mata**... ever. This is what the ancient legends tell.

It is for this very reason that Heavenkin hold the immortal souls in the highest regard for their immense sacrifice. To remain a soul trapped in an intermediary world for eternity for the sake of your people was no small feat.

The thirty souls had gathered over millions of years. No one understood the price of their choices more than they did, yet they were proud and content with their fate. The immortal souls did not take lightly the idea of accepting a new member into their fold. In fact, they might never have even considered it... They tried to avoid it at all costs, as their primary mission was to protect the souls of the heavens beings, care for their future, and guide them to the realm of **Mata**, not to trap them in the intermediary world of **Clotho**. However, their task is incredibly difficult, and sometimes, when a soul with rare energy would appear, it would become their duty to offer this possibility to them. But, in any case, it was never a compulsory act.

Let us return to **Achilla's** father, **Nanar**. **Achilla** saw him go through all the rituals we had mentioned. Finally, he began to rise, little by little, carried by seven of the immortal souls. Gradually, he began to transform into a statue of quartz. Then, a brilliant light shone, and something glittering and restless emerged from the statue. The immortal souls surrounded it gently in a scene so breathtaking it stole one's breath away. They then took this soul into Clotho Lake. The quartz statue shattered into pieces of varying sizes, scattering behind them into the lake. Some of the pieces fell onto the small cliff, and the Sibyl picked them up and threw them into the lake.

This was **Achilla's** first time witnessing the ritual of death or of crossing over.

As for her mother, she was killed forty years after this event. The only way to kill a heavenly is through the **amethyst stone** extracted from the shattered quartz statues of the Heavenkin whose souls had returned to **Mata** or been banished to **Kieris**. For this reason, the sibyl always made sure to dispose of the remains. Now, only one amethyst stone remained, carefully kept by the sibyl herself due to the sacred law of **Shishak**.

****

Achilla sat on that branch, hesitant, for hours. That fleeting encounter had stirred emotions she had tried to suppress for so long. She thought to herself, *How small the world is! Especially for those who live for such a long time...* How much time had passed since their last meeting? She began to count the years in her head. *Fifty... Seventy... One hundred... One hundred and thirty... Two hundred... Two hundred and fifty... Two hundred and eighty years?!!* My God, more than two and a half centuries... It felt like an eternity. She had stopped counting the days after their farewell, for time had stopped the moment her hands cradled his face as if it were a fragile work of art she feared would break. She had touched him with the gentlest tenderness and told him she couldn't continue with him, that there was no hope for a happy ending, and that she was sorry for allowing their relationship to go on for so long and reach this point.

He had looked at her, stunned, his eyes wide in disbelief, his heart sinking into a deep abyss. *"Why?!"* he whispered.

She smiled, hiding her sorrow, though she could feel every ounce of pain squeezing his heart, as well as her own, which made it all the more difficult for her. A tear escaped her eye, forced out by the pain, while his eyes froze, unable to shed a single tear. With a broken voice, she spoke, *"It's okay, my love. You won't have to suffer anymore... You won't... remember... It's enough for one of us. This is my burden alone."*

His eyes blinked, confused by her words. *"What do you mean?"* he asked.

She answered, almost as if speaking to herself, *"You don't need all this pain anymore."* Then she smiled, a wide smile, battling her tears, and kissed him deeply—their first and last kiss. It was strong, profound, but brief. He staggered from it, unsure of what he felt—should he be happy or should he mourn? Then she pulled away slightly, letting her fingers run through his hair, and murmured, *"Forget... Leave the burden of remembering to me."* A blue light gleamed beneath her fingertips.

Achilla had bound all of Karl's memories of her—thirty years of love and friendship vanished, erased. At that time, she was not yet adept at using all of her spiritual powers on others, so she resorted to the weakest method of memory binding, one that she could execute with precision. The flaw of this binding was that it would unravel the moment the person under the binding touched the one who bound them, even unintentionally. Otherwise, they would remember nothing. She told herself then, *"It's alright, I will disappear from his life entirely. I will never cross his path again, never touch him..."* She bound his memory and left, never telling him the reason for their parting.

It was enough for one person to suffer for the sake of two. He was too stubborn to have allowed her to do anything like that if he had known—he would never have agreed to part, never have accepted the binding of his memories. She did it for him...for his sake, so he could continue his life without the torment that would bring him no relief.

So, he could live, so he could be happy as he deserved...so he could have a family, a warm home as he had always wished. But fate had other plans.

Achilla sighed as she returned to that memory, still vividly remembering how she felt afterward—how she still felt! Two hundred and eighty years had passed, yet it had not diminished her love in the slightest, as though she had bid him farewell just yesterday. She recalled how she had left her island for years, how her hatred for her own kind had grown... *Hadn't they been the cause of their separation?*

She shook her head, as though trying to rid herself of these thoughts, and turned her memory back to the very first day she had seen him.

He was a young man, just a child, only seventy years old! – This was how she saw him. He was there, sitting under the shade of a tree, isolated and alone, lost in melancholy thoughts and feelings that she could sense and feel herself. He had spent forty years of his life neither belonging to the world of ordinary humans nor able to return to his own kind, much like her. At that time, he had reached the deepest point of his solitude and sorrow, and her heart ached for him. She felt an overwhelming curiosity toward him, so she approached him and sat by his side under the oak tree. He flinched, and she smiled at him mischievously, saying cheerfully, "Hello... Would you be my friend?"

She extended her hand to shake his. His eyes widened in astonishment, captivated by her beauty. Who was this mythical creature, so exquisitely beautiful? She appeared out of nowhere, and she wanted his friendship? Friendship with such a miserable being? She read his thoughts and said, "Oh... I'm Achilla... a heavens being!"

She said it so casually, shrugging her shoulders. Karl, breathless and stunned, wondered if this was a dream. He couldn't be blamed, for Heavenkin possessed a commanding presence, dazzling beauty, and an irresistible magnetism. Sorcerers can distinguish such beings from others by the energy that emanated from them, and around her was a strange aura unlike anything he had ever seen.

She waved her hand in front of his face and said, "Are you planning to stare for long? You should know, that's an awkward and strange behaviour that doesn't please girls, especially when you leave your mouth hanging open like that." She let out a soft laugh.

Karl blushed, deeply embarrassed, shaken from his awe by her words. He cleared his throat, lowered his head in shame, and flushed. He took off his hat, turned his body to face her, and said, "I apologise, my lady... it's not every day I witness... such a magnificent sight!" He took her hand and kissed it, adding, "I'm Karl... a forsaken sorcerer."

She smiled broadly and replied, "I know!"

And from that day on, they were never apart... for thirty years.

They had ventured across the world together, exploring every corner of it. With him, she felt she had finally found her home, her family—the mother she had lost when she was young. How could she forget him? How could her feelings for him change, even after a thousand years?

He was the one who made that bitterness in her heart vanish with his presence, the bitterness she had long hidden behind her neglect, her mischief, and her laughter.

Suddenly, Karl appeared behind the glass wall in the kitchen. Her heart skipped a beat when she saw him. She was sitting on a branch of one of the pine trees overlooking the house, hidden among its leaves. She had wandered around the house just hours before... and had seen him there, asleep in the library. She had studied him until he woke, and from his thoughts, she knew he intended to head to the kitchen, so she beat him to it.

She watched as he stood frozen, hesitating, wondering what to say. She heard the whisper of his thoughts, his friends'—no, his family's—thoughts: *"Ah, damn me... may the heavens curse me... he has locked himself away for three days because of me... Hmm, seems someone's reading thoughts too... what a kind people!... they really do care about him... Finally, Karl has a family... He's no longer alone..."*

A blonde girl approached him. *Who is she? ... Hmm, Selene... Her name is Selene... and... she is... his... girlfriend.* Something inside her shattered as the echo of those thoughts reverberated in her mind. *Should I leave? What am I doing here? Will my presence change anything... What would I say to him, anyway? I'll just complicate his life... He's suffering now...*

Selene embraced Karl, and how much Achilla longed to be in her place. She had never felt envy toward anyone until now. *She truly loves him... deeply... She seems like a good girl... he... loves her too... but... is he feeling guilty? Why does he think he has hurt her? No, you are not selfish... and none of this is your fault, it's mine, my fault... but I can fix it... yes, I can... I can do it again... bind his memory once more, and them too... My abilities have developed now, and I'll cast a powerful bond that no silly, accidental touch will break. There's no need for all this pain... no need to disturb his life for... memories.*

Karl sat alone at the round kitchen table, while Selene returned to the rest of her family so as not to pressure him further, happy to see he was beginning to return to his old self. As for Achilla, her heart twisted and writhed under the weight of her conflicting thoughts and emotions. Who could relieve this crushing pain in her chest? Who could bind her memory?!

She sighed deeply, her gaze wandering over the garden around her. She smiled, speaking softly to herself… *It must have been that little gardener's doing.* A fleeting flash of another memory passed by… when she had helped him unlock his ability. In truth, she had given him the power to control some of his mental faculties, using her own spiritual strength. She had granted him the power to control earth; since he was fond of forests… he adored plants and flowers… he loved nature to be present in everything around him. So, was there a better gift than this?

Then she heard her name—Achilla—and turned, startled. "Achilla… Achilla… I will never forget you…" he was repeating it to himself. Her muscles relaxed, as she thought he must have seen her.

She felt it—his love, his anger, his confusion, his pain, and his sadness. He was once again reliving the painful experience of goodbye, as if she had only said farewell to him yesterday. Surely, only days had passed since the memories and all the emotions that had bound within him erupted once more… still fresh, still powerful, as if they had truly happened just the day before. Binding memories meant binding the emotions attached to them as well, as if they were frozen in time, locked away with all their strength, only to surge forth with unrelenting force when the chains were broken—attacking him with pain, as if they were roaring angrily at his forgetfulness. Achilla had never allowed him to live with or adapt to those feelings over the years… but it seemed that it was his fate—to endure this pain with a double dose of disappointment.

She had left without a word, stealing his heart with her. Had she become so indifferent? He still remembered the chaos and confusion that overwhelmed him for days after his memory was bound, how he woke up one day feeling an immense emptiness, how he stood frozen for what seemed like hours, disoriented, glancing at his watch over and over again, rubbing his eyes, unable to grasp the time, the duration of his sleep, or whether it was morning or evening, or even what day it was. He now realised that this state had been a result of his mind's resistance to the binding. As the days passed, he found himself surrendering to it, trying to ignore the unsettling feeling.

He began repeating her name inside his head, over and over again: *Achilla... I won't let anyone, not even you, steal my memories from me... Achilla...* And as he gazed at the coffee cup before him for a few moments, a cold breeze wafted through the large open window in the glass wall. Something urged him to look to his right, and he turned... There, behind the glass barrier, he saw her.

She was standing, floating in mid-air... rising and falling slightly in place with a serene movement. The breeze tousled the strands of her red hair in all directions.

She was smiling... her usual mischievous smile. *Oh, she hasn't changed... that smile... how it still melts my heart, like a fool.*

For a few seconds, he remained frozen, staring at her, convinced she must be a figment of his imagination.

A sweet melody echoed in his mind—a tune he had once played for her on the piano, long ago.

She was listening to that same old tune with him...

How can she seem so real? he wondered, gazing at her, his eyes filled with weariness. Then, suddenly, he sprang to his feet, knocking the chair behind him with a loud crash as he stood, his eyes never leaving her. She was slowly approaching the large open window, wide enough for an adult to pass through without even needing to bend.

She stood gracefully on the tip of her left foot, the other suspended in midair, her right hand gripping the window frame. She wore a pair of blue jeans that revealed one of her knees, a matching denim shirt with long and rolled-up sleeves. Her fragrance, carried by the breeze—the scent of her hair—wafted toward him. How he had missed her scent! It felt as though cold water had been poured over him, as though his body had gone numb. He couldn't move.

"Are you planning to stare for long? You should know, that's an awkward and strange behaviour that doesn't please girls, especially when you leave your mouth hanging open like that," she said with a broad smile, before letting out a soft, amused laugh.

At that moment, the family gathered behind the short stoney barrier of the kitchen, astonished!

He blinked... this time, his mouth wasn't open, rather he clenched his teeth tightly. Yet, when she uttered that phrase, it was as though it roused him from his daze.

She walked into the kitchen with ease and cheerfulness, picked an apple from the fruit bowl on the table, and took a large bite, as though she were an old friend— someone who was used to visiting them all the time. *This was Achilla, just as she always had been!*

With the bite still in her mouth, muffling her words, she said, "Henno... Mynum ig Akila... ahh... oh... my bad." She covered her mouth with her hand and giggled like a child, swallowing the bite before continuing in a voice as light and melodic as birdsong, like tiny bells ringing: "Sorry, I'm so hungry... hello again, my name is Achilla... Karl's old friend... do you have anything to eat?"

She spoke quickly, as she always did, finishing her sentence while taking another bite, opening the fridge door, and sticking her head inside.

Karl couldn't believe his eyes. Just like she had always been—unchanged, still the same reckless, indifferent, carefree girl, acting as though everyone around her were her closest friends. She barged into their homes, rifled through their things without a second thought, knowing that no one could ever resist someone as enchanting as her. She knew she could capture anyone's heart in an instant. Hadn't he seen it with his own eyes?

Hadn't he seen the wild lions scratching their hides against her legs, pleading for a touch as though they were mere house cats?

Hadn't he seen the deer playing with her?

And the birds landing around her wherever she went?

And the bears sitting beside her in the forests?

Hadn't he seen all this—and more?

What a conceited, foolish, reckless and indifferent creature she was!

What a beautiful, sweet, and gentle being she was!

She pulled her head out of the refrigerator, finding nothing of interest. The family froze for a moment, all except for Paul, who began speaking with the same ease as her, for he shared some of her playful nature. He shrugged and said, "There's some creamy chocolate if you'd like?" He gestured toward the right, where it sat on a shelf next to the coffee can and kettle. Achilla let out a delighted exclamation, saying, "Chocolate!"

She pressed the kettle's button, set the half-eaten apple down, grabbed the chocolate tin, opened the dishwasher drawer, took two small spoons, and a coffee cup. Then, she sat cross-legged on the marble table's edge next to the kettle, scooping a large spoonful of chocolate and without a second thought, placed it in her mouth, savouring it as if it were a precious treasure.

She didn't seem to notice—or rather, didn't care—about the four stunned individuals or the one frozen in place beside the chair on the floor.

Paul leaned against the short stone wall of the kitchen, breaking the thick silence as he spoke to her. "So, you said you're a friend of…"

She didn't let him finish his sentence. Interrupting him with a quick nod of her head, she said, "Yes." Then, she placed a second bite into her mouth and wiped the chocolate off the corner of her mouth with the back of her hand.

"Weren't you the girl who bumped into me in the forest?"

She nodded while looking at the chocolate tin, reaching for a third bite. "Yes."

"How did you find our house?"

She raised her head, waved the spoonful of chocolate in the air, and answered, swallowing the previous bite, "Oh, that's easy. I touched his forehead and knew where you lived."

"You can find where people live just by touching their foreheads?"

She put the spoon into her mouth and left it there, staring at the ceiling for a moment, as if pondering how to give an easy answer. "Hmmn… I can know anything I want by touching their foreheads!"

The conversation began to capture the attention of everyone. She didn't seem a sorcerer like them, nor human... What could she possibly be?

Paul asked, "Anything, anything?"

She repeated with a smile, "Anything, anything, dear Paul."

Paul's mouth dropped open in astonishment. *How did she know his name?* She winked at him, and just as he was about to ask, Abraham interrupted, his tone composed, saying, "Excuse me, to which species do you belong?"

The kettle clicked off, and she placed two spoons of coffee into a cup before pouring the hot water over it. Then, she answered, "Heavens beings."

Emily gasped. "Really? Didn't you all go extinct long ago when your islands fell from the sky?"

She took a sip of her coffee before replying, "No, not exactly all of us... I mean, the fall of the islands led to the extinction of most other tribes of Heavenkin after their islands were destroyed, and time helped in the extinction of the rest—since we aren't exactly a species that reproduces quickly, as you might know—but three islands remain, if you will, with three tribes, and we are one of them."

Paul said, "Heavens beings... I've never heard of them!"

A sly smile spread across Achilla's face as she raised an eyebrow and said, "Haven't you heard of the gods of Babylon, the Greeks, or the Pharaohs?"

Without giving Paul a chance to reply, she turned to Giovanni after picking up the small spoon from the chocolate tin again, filling it, and pointing it at him. "Don't strain yourself, dear Giovanni...

you won't be able to read my thoughts." She placed the spoon in her mouth, followed it with a sip of coffee.

Paul exclaimed, deducing, "You can read minds too!"

She winked at him again, "Bingo! ...and feelings as well."

He asked, puzzled, "But why do you need to touch people's foreheads if you can read their thoughts?"

With her mouth full, she answered, "Isn't it obvious, dear? If I want to know something you're not currently thinking about, all I have to do is touch your forehead and look for it."

At that point, Karl reached his breaking point. His chest was boiling, and if he were a kettle, they would have heard the whistle! His blood was bubbling, and a vein in his forehead almost popped.

He shouted, "Enough! What is this farce?! You jump into my kitchen out of nowhere, chatting with my family!! After all these years… after everything you did… and you act like we were having dinner together last night!! Like nothing ever happened!! Can you really be *this* heartless?!"

His family froze at the sound of his shout. They had never heard him yell like this before.

As for Achilla, she turned her head and said, waving her hands through the air as though she hadn't heard the shouting, her voice cold: "Ah… you're such a drama queen!" She stepped down from the table, tossed the spoon into the sink from where she stood, placed the chocolate tin aside, and picked up her cup, leaning her back against the table, sipping her coffee.

"Drama queen? I'm the one being dramatic?" he said, pointing to himself, his anger flaring. "You call my fury over your sudden departure, with no reason, mere overblown drama?! You call my rage over you taking thirty years of my memories, without justification, without my consent, without even the decency to tell me, just excessive drama?!"

"By what right? Who gave you permission? By what right?!" He repeated, his voice shaking with intensity.

She replied, her eyes on her cup, her voice dropping slightly as her expression began to shift: "It was for the best... for your own good."

His voice rose again, louder now: "For the best?! Ha ha ha... Please! Were you with me when I wandered alone, lost and aimless, not caring about anything? When I walked with a gaping hole in my chest—" He struck his fist against his chest, hard. "—wandering in confusion, searching for something I'd lost and had no idea what it was?! For years and years, I carried that hole, a hole that killed me! It nearly consumed me! It made me feel incomplete! Like a huge part of me had vanished! There was always something unfinished... Always this sadness, even when I was happy! All those emotions, I couldn't understand them... I couldn't grasp them! I felt like I might lose my mind!"

"Do you understand what I'm saying? Can your crazy, arrogant mind even comprehend my words? By what right do you decide for me? Am I nothing to you?!" His voice broke on the final sentence.

She had placed the coffee cup down in the middle of his speech and began fidgeting, pulling her hair back with her hand, and glancing around as if his words were painful slaps. When he finished speaking, she took a deep breath, trying to control her anger, but her voice came out sharp and her words rushed, gesturing with her hand:

"Do you blame me for sparing you unnecessary pain?! Do you complain because you suffered less than you should have?! Oh, for heaven's sake, don't act like the victim." She turned her back to him and leaned on the table with her hands. "Here you are now, you've moved on with your life... You have a beautiful home," she gestured sarcastically, "a loving family... and a beautiful girlfriend!"

He interrupted her, shouting, "After two hundred years!!!" He was specifically referring to her last sentence, not even knowing why he said it, boiling with anger. A fleeting thought crossed his mind (After eighty years with her... I couldn't even marry her... now I know why!!) He didn't say it. But she heard it anyway - and so did Giovanni. She turned to him with a scowl and said, "If I hadn't done that, it would have taken you two thousand years... you stubborn, crying, foolish child."

Gray clouds began to gather in the sky, obscuring the sunlight...

He shouted again, "I am not a child!! Who do you think you are?! You arrogant... You're always right, aren't you?! We're all foolish children!! And even if we are... It's my mind... This is my life... My memories... These are my decisions... Me, not you!! Where do you get all this confidence from?!"

He was screaming like a madman, not just out of anger at her, but because he couldn't comprehend all the emotions weighing him down. He had completely lost control; his hands were trembling, he felt a strong pulse in his head and ears, and he thought his heart would explode... for her and because of her. All this love erupted as anger, and all these emotions and thoughts reached her, permeating her bones.

The darkness outside grew denser with each passing second...

Finally, she screamed back with the same crazed tone, "She would have killed you!!!"

A powerful thunderstorm roared in the sky, deafening, accompanying her scream. Darkness enveloped the house suddenly, even though it was eleven in the morning. Karl stood still for a moment, his scowl softened by shock, and a hint of questioning appeared in his eyes.

After a second of silence, she continued: "That old hag would have killed you! If... if she had only intended to kill me, I wouldn't have cared... But that icy woman would kill you in cold blood... just like she killed my mother!!"

The sky growled again.

"Did you want me to let her get to you?! To allow her to lay a finger on the one thing that brought life back to me... No!"

Still angry, he said, "I wouldn't have cared if I died for you!"

The thunderstorm roared again, as if it too was angry, screaming along with her. The sounds of thunder continued to shake the place, accompanying Achilla's fury...

She shrieked, "I know... and that's exactly why I did all this!! Because you wouldn't leave it alone... Because you wouldn't listen to me with that stubborn mind of yours!! You would have followed me to the ends of the earth no matter how far I went. You would have searched for me until your last day because you're stubborn... because you're a foolish, stubborn child!"

Her voice cracked at the end of her words, and just as her eyes glistened with the urge to cry, the rain began to fall.

A sudden downpour from this strange thunderstorm... but Achilla did not cry.

As if the rain had extinguished Karl's rage, he spoke in a low voice, like a child confessing a sin: "I would have... and I would have carried you away."

She replied with some sharpness: "To where?! Do you think I haven't thought about this? Don't you understand... There is no place that hag can't reach! Is that how you wanted us to spend our lives?! Running until our inevitable execution?! Oh, please! I've been running from that stubborn old woman for fifty years! And she's still following me... that cursed witch!"

In truth, no one knows who is the most stubborn among these three! Karl, Achilla, or that "cursed hag," as she calls her.

She leaned back against the marble table again, running her hands through her hair, pulling it back, then crossed her arms over her chest and exhaled deeply, trying to calm her nerves.

Karl looked at the open window and the puddle of water starting to fill the kitchen from the rain. He walked over and closed it, now standing just two steps away from Achilla. As he tightened the window latch, he spoke in the same voice as her old friend, "Are you still doing this?"

She looked at him curiously, staring directly into his eyes, and they exchanged glances. Amidst that deep sadness, she glimpsed a tender look... a look of longing, and she smiled at it.

She said, "I think we need to calm down now... before I destroy your house with a lightning bolt or an earthquake..." and turned her face away from him.

He asked, hiding his worry, "Why are you running from the Queen?"

She replied, looking ahead... at them: "Maybe you should start by explaining to your family first."

He turned to them. How could he have forgotten them? Suddenly, he no longer felt anyone's presence except hers. Where had they appeared from? No, more importantly, how had they disappeared? He scanned the group, their faces etched with confusion, misunderstanding, anxiety, and fear. No one seemed to grasp the reason for all the shouting, the anger, the pain, the sorrow, and the woman standing beside him! Except for one among them, who had his hand pressed to his mouth, the other clutching his chest, brow furrowed with intense concentration.

Finally, he looked at Selene, who stood like a steadfast rock in the middle of a rushing river, her curly blonde hair framing her gentle, beautiful face and falling in front of her eyes. She stood clutching the shawl around her shoulders tightly against her chest, her eyes like springs of water... crying.

Damn it... how could he have done this to her... He had hurt her again without meaning to. He shouldn't have lost his temper in front of her like that. Selene wasn't a fool; she might not know their story, but she understood everything. She saw that love in his eyes and the agony of their separation, the way he looked at her. He had never looked at her that way in eighty years, and how he forgot their presence in hers! You can't block out the sun with your hand—he adored this stranger... and she adored him too.

(Ah... curse me... I shouldn't have opened my mouth... I should have continued that ridiculous charade with Achilla and controlled myself. We should have been alone. I should've at least pulled her hand, and we'd have walked away. I'd vent my anger far from here, not in front of her.

Should I have raged and fumed like a madman... what's wrong with me? Since when do I lose control like this?)

He was crushed under the weight of all these thoughts, his face twisted in guilt and pain. Beside him, Achilla kept her head lowered, her expression vacant as she stared at her feet, one crossed over the other. She remained as she was, leaning against the table, hands tightly clasped.

The storm's growl outside had quieted, and the rain had lightened, while the sky slowly shifted back from black to gray.

Abraham took a step closer to Selene, wrapping his hands around her arms, gently rubbing one of them, silently commanding her body to relax. And so, it did. Her muscles loosened, the grip of her hand—pale from the force she had pressed it with—eased. Her ribcage expanded as she inhaled deeply, a breath that had been shallow and stifled now flowing freely, as though someone had finally pulled her from the depths of a well.

Abraham spoke quietly, his eyes casting a reproachful glance toward his old companion: "Yes. She's right. You should speak."

Karl shifted uncomfortably in his place, wanting to step forward. He began, *"I..."* but then paused, reconsidering, and turned toward Achilla, his eyes asking a silent question that betrayed his hidden worry. Achilla understood his unspoken query and murmured reassuringly, "Don't worry, I won't disappear again."

It was clear he feared her leaving once more. Nothing about this moment seemed real to him. The past three days had passed like a whirlpool of memories and foggy emotions, blurring the line between fantasy and reality until it seemed as fragile as a thread.

Suddenly, Paul blurted out, "Hey! Wasn't your hair black the last time?" Only Paul could be distracted by something so trivial at a moment like this! Only Paul could be so oblivious!

All his friends turned to him at once, their eyes wide, unable to believe he had said something so foolish. Emily snapped at him, "Really!! That's what bothers you now, you empty-headed ox, after everything that's happened?!" She slapped the back of his neck, and he scratched it as if he'd been bitten by a mosquito.

Achilla let out a booming laugh, throwing her head back, a sweet, resonant laugh that filled the space with a new, comforting warmth, seeping into their hearts. Her face lit up, and the grey clouds parted slightly, allowing sunlight to stream through, brightening the entire place. Birds began to chirp, and the rustling of the trees became a soft melody. Suddenly, everything seemed better!

What was all this?!

When Achilla finished laughing, she remained with a broad smile that revealed her sparkling teeth and faint dimples. Then, she gently shook her head from side to side, as if to indicate a "no.", Gradually, the colour of her hair began to change, with a stream of black spreading from the roots to the ends, transforming the sunset hue in her hair into the depths of a starless night. Her eyes then sparkled, turning the two stars into twin suns.

Paul gasped, "That's amazing!" only to receive another slap from Emily! He was right, it was indeed a magical sight for everyone, but Emily considered his comment insensitive to Selene's feelings.

Karl approached them, crossing the stone barrier, and placed his hand on Selene's elbow, while Abraham still had his arms around her.

"Let's talk," Karl said. Selene blinked, her eyes now dry of tears, and weakly nodded. Abraham loosened his hold and lowered his arms. They all made their way to the nearby sofas, except for Achilla, who remained leaning against the marble table. She picked up half of the apple she had eaten and took another bite.

Selene sat beside Karl, with the others gathered around him and before him. Karl cleared his throat, pondering where to begin. He took a deep breath and spoke hesitantly, "Well... uh... as Achilla said... she... is... an old friend of mine... and... well, we knew each other two hundred years ago... we were... friends," —he emphasised the last word, forcing it out for the second time— "close... very close... Achilla helped me greatly after my years of solitude... She was my first friend back then... and the only one."

His face darkened at the last words, Achilla sighed, saying in a slightly louder voice, "Ah... you've always been terrible at telling stories!"

Karl grimaced slightly and objected, "Oh really? Well, why don't you honour us with your presence and tell 'the story' yourself, since I apparently don't know everything after all!"

She shrugged nonchalantly, moved from her spot, and tossed the apple she had finally finished into the trash as she approached them casually. She sat in the only empty seat next to Karl, causing his heart to skip a beat.

She leaned forward, parting her legs slightly, placing her elbows on her knees, and interlocking her fingers. "Well," she said, "I hope you'll all close your eyes... it'll be less distracting that way."

Before they could understand her intent, a series of images began to unfold within their minds, startling them. It was truly strange and distracting. The images and sounds played out like a film reel—brief, successive scenes... laughter and sighs... joy and sorrow... strange places... Here, Karl was laughing... here, he sat alone beneath a tree, wearing an old outfit from over two hundred years ago... and here, Achilla poured cold water over his head, startling him awake as her laughter echoed. They closed their eyes instinctively to focus, and Karl's heartbeat began to race.

She brought them back to the first scene... to the first memory. Karl under the reddish yellow oak tree... a cold autumn day... a lonely, sorrowful man. She remarked, "This is where we met." She wasn't showing the entire scene, just snippets—cut dialogues, faint sounds. Had she wished to, she could have formed a circle with them, holding hands, and shared her emotions too, but she never desired that. Then, she shifted to other scenes, showing different moments and times they had shared, both happy and sad.

"As Karl said... our friendship grew stronger over time... and he was also my only friend."

She showed a brief scene of that snowy day...

"Our relationship evolved and became... deeper than friendship."

A new series of scenes began to unfold, ones that seemed more intimate. Karl's loving gazes... Karl kissing her hand... holding her close and spinning her in the air... laughing with her, the most beautiful laughter they had never seen before.

"I acted foolishly... and allowed this to develop."

Karl flinched and opened his eyes, his brows furrowed. She paid him no attention and continued, her voice darkening, "There is but one law among us, a law we never allow our kind to break... *Shishak*."

Different scenes began to emerge, a magnificent island, fantastical, unlike any island that could exist on Earth, inhabited by magical, legendary beings who seemed like ancient Greek or Egyptian gods.

"Our kind is peaceful... and forgiving... but we are very protective of our survival, especially now with extinction looming over us. The killing of any one of us is a grave matter... forbidden... sacred, untouched. But should the law of *Shishak* be broken... death is the fate of the violator."

Massive stone tablets appeared, engraved with strange characters, resembling more drawings than letters. The scenes were displayed as Achilla had seen them through her own eyes.

A dignified man appeared, dressed in a green robe. Achilla looked up at him; this memory distant and ancient, over seven hundred years ago, from her childhood.

This venerable master was recounting the legend of *Shishak*, a tale that stretched back thousands of years, his gravelly voice resonating in an incomprehensible language. Achilla, acting as a translator, echoed his words:

"These tablets tell the story behind the greatest and most sacred law of our kind. Thousands upon thousands of years ago, a heaven being named *Shishak* fell in love with a man of the Earth and married him. This act was met with disdain by our kind, though it was not forbidden at the time. It simply did not align with our nature or the survival of our race. Moreover, the ancients did not hold much respect for the Earth-dwellers. They saw them as ignorant, primitive, limited in intelligence, violent, and excessively greedy. Yet, no one stood in her way... procreation between our kinds was not considered likely, for the genetics of the Earth-dwellers are weak, unable to withstand our own. But this time, a miracle occurred... *Shishak* gave birth to a being, half-Earthly, half-heavenly. But... it was different! New... strange... and dark. It grew at an astonishing rate, unlike us, but still slower than the Earth dwellers. And after twenty-five years, it reached adulthood. Some of its behaviours were more akin to predatory animals than to either Earth-dwellers or Heavenkin. One day, it killed its father, drank all his blood, and fled!

Shishak gave birth to a vampire! It adored human blood, wreaking havoc on the earth and slaughtering them in enormous numbers. Possessing some of the powers of the Heavenkin, it was too formidable for humans to resist. Somehow, its venom had the ability to transform humans into bloodthirsty beings as powerful as it was, spreading them far and wide. This union between a heavenly and an earthly being produced such an evil entity—a strange mutation between two species that should never have merged.

The Earthlings called upon the ancient Heavenkin for help, and the Heavenkin couldn't remain silent about this, whether they liked it or not; this strange being was part of them as well. They hunted it down and killed it, then began to chase its kin, managing to kill many of them. They thought they had eradicated them. But centuries later, they discovered that they still existed, hiding in the shadows, fleeing and keeping their existence secret for fear of the Heavenkin's wrath. They moved cautiously and didn't produce large numbers.

Due to this strange creature and the devastation it caused, the ancients established the Sacred Law of Shishak: Heavenkin are forbidden to mate with any other species. Otherwise, their fate is the amethyst stone.

The Heavenkin do not fear death, but this punishment is severe, for a Heavenkin who dies unnaturally faces the doom of their soul being lost in an eternal realm, unable to cross the sacred lake of Clotho to the second life in Mata." The venerable teacher fell silent.

The scene transformed. Before them appeared something that resembled a small lake, shimmering with strange, mesmerising colours. It was circular with a diameter of three meters, surrounded by rocky ground. Directly behind it rose a stone cliff about four meters high, with a wide, flat surface ending in a cave. The cave had a large, very wide, square-shaped entrance. The entire place was composed of white stones veined with light, vivid hues in delicate patterns. The sight was breathtaking, and there, gathered around this sacred place, were groups of Heavenkin waiting for one of their own to emerge from the cave. This memory, too, was old... and sorrowful.

Outside, the grey clouds had gathered once again... but none of the sorcerers noticed. They all had their eyes closed, immersed in the flood of images, entranced... enchanted by the magnificent scenes... as though they were in another world!

A woman emerged from the depths of the cave, dressed in white. Her flowing white gown was adorned with a thin gold belt at her waist, engraved with various designs and decorated with a few small gemstones. Beneath it, the gown cascaded in wide, uneven layers, its sleeves left bare and held in place by two golden clasps on her shoulders similar to the belt. Behind her, a large white cloak hung down to the lower part of her back. She wore a golden circlet on her head, resembling the ones worn by the men they had seen in the forest, but this one was thicker, more resplendent, and embellished with three vivid gemstones, the middle stone was slightly larger than its companions. In her hand, she held a golden staff, its top crowned with a large amethyst stone, nearly thirty centimetres long. The edges of the stone were unevenly shaped, tapering to a sharp point in the form of a pyramid, gleaming with shifting hues of violet, purple, pink, and azure as the light caught it.

The woman had an enchanting appearance, with a delicate body and face. Her face was small and oval, her lips were also small and rosy, with a slender nose and drowsy, grey eyes. Her hair looked just like Achilla's hair, and it was pulled back and gathered loosely behind her head, allowing several short locks to fall gently over her face and long neck, which bore a rectangular tattoo at the base on the left side. The tattoo was adorned with incomprehensible symbols, drawn vertically. Her skin was as pale as a snowflake, and so were the features that adorned her face, despite their beauty, conveyed a certain coldness... a coldness devoid of emotion. She did not appear young, nor was she looking old; no wrinkles marred her face, yet she appeared as a woman in her early forties—at her best—although she was actually over five thousand years old.

When the woman appeared, the sky was overcast. She walked with dignified steps, and low murmurs were heard from those present, all of them chanting a single word, "Bissilia", while raising their hands toward their faces, touching their foreheads with their fingertips and bowing their heads slightly. As she stood at the edge of the cliff, she tilted her eyes skyward for a moment, her expression betraying no discernible emotion. A strong, cold gusts began to blow, stirring her gown and locks of hair, and the distant rustle of trees was heard, coming from the forest of Fala that surrounded this place.

The woman spoke in a calm, deep voice, in the same incomprehensible language.

Achilla said, "This is the temple of Urbahra... and this is Queen... (Etliea)... and she says, 'O Good people, it is a sorrowful day... like this unusually cloudy sky... It seems the immortal souls are as angry and mournful as we are today. Yet, if there is one thing we cannot overlook, it is the committing of the greatest sin—the sin of Shishak.'"

A second woman emerged from the depths of the cave.

A muffled rumble of thunder was heard outside the house, making Emily shiver slightly.

The woman wore a white velvet robe, similar to the garments they had seen before. She resembled the queen greatly, with her pristine white skin, although her complexion had a slight blush. Her hair was jet black, long, and flowing down to her lower back, and her bright hazel eyes gleamed with an enigmatic light. She lifted her slender nose with clear pride and smiled a gentle smile, allowing her faint dimples to show, her face radiating confidence and ease. She did not wear a circlet on her head as might have been expected. She stood two paces behind the queen to her left. Achilla's heart began to pound like war drums before the onset of battle when her eyes fell upon this woman.

The sky grew darker in the memory...

Behind her emerged a third woman, appearing older than the others, seemingly in her fifties. She wore a deep crimson robe and stood solemnly at the cave's entrance, maintaining considerable distance from them. Her skin was a rich, deep brown, and her striking violet eyes matched the colour of her hair. Her hood was drawn up, covering the upper half of her head, and a golden circlet encircled her brow rather than resting atop her head. Her face bore three small tattoos: one above her left eyebrow, another below her eye on her right cheek, and the third on the upper right side of her forehead, slanting with her hairline.

This scene was incredibly vivid, appearing very real, unlike the other fleeting glimpses they had seen.

They experienced it as if they were at the heart of this moment, feeling the cold air hitting their faces, the presence of the people, the forest and the rustling of the trees, and the fragrant scent that now tickled their noses surrounding them from every side. Everything unfolded at a natural pace, as if they had been magically transported to the island of Fala, to the heart of that memory.

Achilla was older in this memory than in the previous one, though she appeared younger than her current form; she was seventy years old at the time.

Achilla began to scream with a broken voice, wanting to go to the woman in the white robe. She stood in the front row of the gathering, separated from her by only a few steps and the lake of Clotho, which she could easily cross, but she could not move. Something held her firmly in place, pulling her back, and she looked at it helplessly. She looked down and they saw heavy white stone shackles on her hands and feet, from which chains extended, held by three men as large as bears in black robes standing three steps behind her. Achilla turned to them, screaming at them, then looked at the man with the stern, wrinkled face in the dark blue robe, who had appeared to them in the forest. He stood a few steps to the left of the three men. She spoke to him loudly, raising her hands toward her face as if asking to be freed, but he did not look at her and seemed not to hear her.

She looked back at the two women on the high cliff, blood boiling in her heart and her face flushed with anger and sorrow. She felt her head seething and her ears ringing.

Achilla screamed! The sky darkened, and the sound of thunder was heard...

She screamed incomprehensible words, her voice deafening and shattering stone with the weight of her grief. For the first time, a nearly imperceptible look of fear appeared in the eyes of the emotionless queen. She glanced briefly at the sky, then at Achilla who stood at the bottom of the cliff... and that look quickly vanished!

The second woman cast a tender, captivating glance at Achilla, one that penetrated her heart in moments and soothed it. She smiled at her, a wider, warmer, gentler smile, and spoke to her without opening her mouth.

Karl and his family could hear this woman's voice inside Achilla's head, speaking to her telepathically. None of the others present could hear her words except Achilla... and the queen.

They listened to her delicate, bell-like voice, like a beautiful melody, very similar to Achilla's own voice. They did not understand what she said, but Achilla froze in place after she spoke, as if a cold bucket of water and ice had been poured over her. She stopped screaming, quieted down, and they began to hear the sound of her laboured breathing.

The woman winked at her mischievously... then the scene before them blurred with tears.

Achilla said in a muffled voice without translating the woman's words, "This is my mother... (Hanila)." Their hearts sank upon hearing this, knowing something terrible was about to happen.

The queen turned toward Hanila and stood upright. Hanila stepped forward confidently, still wearing a look of calm assurance. She stood face-to-face with the queen, only a step away.

The queen spoke in her calm voice, and they heard her pronounce Hanila's name. Achilla said, "She says, 'My eldest daughter, Hanila, has committed the greatest sin. Though members of my family, above all others, should uphold our laws, protect our people, and preserve our rituals. This makes her crime all the graver. But the punishment, in any case, remains the same.'"

The queen paused for a moment, looking into her eldest daughter's eyes, who still smiled gently and exchanged glances with her mother, the queen. Hanila whispered inside Queen Etliea's mind, only audible to Achilla. Karl and his family could also hear it. Achilla said in a choked voice, "She is telling her, 'I hope this does not haunt you for the rest of your life.'"

Hanila was forgiving, calm, and resigned, knowing that she had made a grave mistake for the sake of love, yet she did not care and was ready for her punishment. She did not see her breach of Shishak's law as a sin, unlike the queen and all the Heavenkin. She believed her only guilt was causing the queen to kill her earthly lover. She knew her mother's nature well. Queen Etliea was a woman of unyielding sternness and gravity, with no tolerance for anything that violated the laws of Fala, harmed her people, or threatened their survival, purity, or continuity. She executed her decisions with icy resolve, concealing every emotion behind a mask of frost. There was no room for sentiment in her judgments.

They heard a muffled sob, and Achilla turned to the source of the sound on her right. There was a woman kneeling, covering her mouth with both hands to stifle her cries, her hair falling over her face, and her eyes brimming with tears. Her back was hunched, and her neck bent as she looked down at the ground. She was embraced by a girl who seemed to be her daughter, biting her lips in silent weeping, with red-rimmed eyes looking painfully away from the cliff. The man standing beside them stood frozen, his neck stiff and his fists clenched, his jaw tight and teeth gritted forcefully.

This man also seemed familiar to them; he was the young man who stood beside the one in the dark blue robe in the forest that day, although he looked slightly younger in this memory.

Tears glistened in the man's eyes, though he did not allow them to fall. His brows were furrowed in intense anger, causing his smooth forehead to crease, but he kept his head held high, looking at the queen. Achilla observed their situation for a moment as if she were in a dream, then the queen's voice echoed once more, so she turned toward her again. Achilla continued translating her words, 'Because the sinner is a member of my family, I have decided to deliver the punishment myself, not through the Sibyl of the temple of Urbahra (Wert-Hakaou), as is customary.'

Thunder roared... and a strong wind swept through the place...

Queen Etliea stepped back with her left foot, leaning on it, and raised the staff in her right hand horizontally, placing her other hand on it and gripping it firmly. She directed the pointed amethyst stone towards her daughter Hanila's body... towards her heart.

The stone pierced Hanila's chest with a swift motion from the queen, pushing her backward. Hanila's eyes widened, and a tear escaped, her face expressing pain she struggled to conceal. She groaned softly with closed lips. The queen blinked and clenched her teeth tightly, staring into her daughter's eyes, and Hanila's smile returned.

Gradually, she transformed into a statue of quartz...

Achilla gasped sharply, as though she had finally broken free from the suffocating depths of the sea, drawing air into her lungs after holding her breath for far too long.

And then, everything suddenly became still!

The wind's howl ceased... the thunder's roar silenced... and the rustling of trees stilled. The queen raised her gaze to the sky, released her grip on the staff embedded in Hanila's body, and let her empty hands fall to her sides and turned her eyes toward Achilla.

No sound... No breath... Nothing... For a few moments, an eerie stillness enveloped them, that was exactly the calm before the storm.

Achilla unleashed a deafening scream... loud so loud, like a cry of a feral, mythical furious beast—and heartbroken. The sheer volume of her voice was indescribable, reverberating with a majestic echo that compelled everyone to cover their ears tightly, fearing their hearing might be stolen.

Simultaneously, the sky rumbled with a terrifying sound that shook their hearts, and lightning bolts struck all around. The vast crowd began leaping away from the descending bolts.

Several fire tornadoes formed, carrying away anything in their path—trees, stones, and even living beings. The gale-force winds threatened to hurl people away, torrential rain poured from the heavens, and the sky turned pitch black.

Achilla's eyes glowed with a grey light, her wild, gypsy hair flared around her like tongues of flame. She easily broke the shackles on her wrists as an overwhelming force suddenly possessed her. She extended her arms beside her body, her fists clenched tightly, and lifted her head, screaming with her mouth wide open, revealing newly emerged fangs. Strange, dark-coloured threads of light emanated from her body, twisting and stretching far.

The terrifying sound continued to pour from her throat, her entire body straining with such intensity that the veins in her neck and forehead bulged. The louder her screams and fury grew, the more intense the thunderous storm became.

As the ground beneath her feet began to tremble and small cracks appeared, both under her and in the cliff before her, Achilla slowly rose into the air. The massive men leaped at her, trying to hold her down, and the man in the dark blue robe jumped to restrain her. The Sibyl Wert-Hakaou moved swiftly from the cave entrance, standing before Achilla, placing her hands around her face. Her eyes gleamed as a faint blue light radiated beneath her fingers.

The last thing Achilla saw was her grandmother, Queen Etliea, kneeling on the ground with her mouth agape in astonishment. The image gradually faded until it disappeared.

Everyone opened their eyes slowly, tears welling up. Emily and Selene were quietly sobbing. They all looked toward Achilla's empty seat, searching for her. She stood by the glass wall, looking outside, her hands in her pants pockets, her back turned to them.

A light rain resumed its fall, the sound of the raindrops hitting the leaves and ground, combined with the gentle movement of the branches, evoking a sense of relaxation, sorrow, and longing all at once.

Achilla said in a quiet tone, that did not suggest any feelings: "The queen killed my mother because she loved a non-Heavenly being and broke Shishak's law... She killed her in front of her family's eyes... in front of my eyes... and forced me to witness it... That wretched old woman murdered her own daughter without a flicker of hesitation... I hated her, and I hated all my kind.

After that incident, they held me in the sacred cave with the Sibyl Wert-Hakaou for several days until my anger subsided. I was on the verge of destroying the island of Fala at the time, for that day my ability to influence the nature around me manifested... a destructive power if one does not master their temperament.

Afterwards, I left the island for about one hundred and fifty years. The only ones of my kind I saw were my mother's younger sister (Beth-Nahra) and her children (Echor) and (Dasha)... They are the three you saw earlier. The kneeling woman is my aunt, embraced by her younger daughter Dasha, and the one standing beside them is her eldest son, Echor.

After their many persistent and annoying attempts, I finally agreed to return to Fala... It is incredibly difficult for us to live outside our islands for long periods, but my relationship with the queen remained perpetually strained.

Shishak's law does not forbid us from forming friendships with non-Heavenly beings, nor can it prevent us from loving them. It is clear: 'No mating' only... no physical relationship that could lead to a mixed-species being. When I met Karl, I never expected our feelings to develop, but that's how things unfolded. I never forgot what happened to my mother... and I made sure it would never happen to Karl. Though we never crossed the forbidden line, the queen disapproved of my relationship with Karl once she learned about it. She issued many warnings, but I always ignored them. I knew she could not do anything to me unless I committed Shishak's sin. Then one day she came to me and said, 'I won't let him cause your fate to be like your mother's. This time, I will not be late...'

I understood then what she meant... it was a clear threat. She would kill Karl before anything happened that would force her to kill me too. She wouldn't easily lose me after all the signs that had appeared on me. At that moment, I decided to distance myself from him, to let my friend live in peace... to not drag him into something he had nothing to do with, something none of us could change."

Achilla turned to face them, they saw a small vein visible between her eyebrows. A dignified expression spread across her face, and her eyelids drooped slightly. Then she added, "And the rest you know." Moments of silence passed.

Suddenly, as if someone had changed the channel, Achilla's expression transformed completely. She broke into a wide grin, and the carefree spark returned to her face. She walked lightly until she stood behind the double sofa where Karl and Selene sat. Leaning on it with her elbows between them, she addressed everyone, "But that is in the past... and it no longer matters now."

She looked at Selene, and their eyes met. A single tear still clung to the corner of Selene's eye. Achilla reached out and gently wiped it away with the tip of her finger. Selene blinked, and Achilla added, "Not anymore... right?" Achilla then looked at the tear on her, and gradually it began to crystallise, turning into a small, gleaming shard of crystal. She remarked, "Some tears are too precious, and by not shedding them, we preserve their value... and the value of what you weep for."

They exchanged glances for a moment, as if a silent conversation was taking place between them. Achilla's words carried many meanings, most of which Selene perhaps did not fully grasp. It was as if Achilla was indirectly telling her there was no need for her worry, sorrow, or jealousy. Nothing mattered now; the past was gone. Never to return. The silent words settled in Selene's heart through Achilla's gaze and warm smile.

But Selene did not know that the last words Achilla had spoken to her were the very same words her mother, Hanila, had whispered in her mind on that sorrowful day.

Her mother had always repeated this phrase to her, "Some sorrows should not be wept." And Hanila did not cry when her beloved was killed by the Queen; she preserved his value. Nor did she cry, rage, or scream when the Queen decided to send her to eternal exile; she preserved her value, her pride, her dignity, and the worth of her decisions.

Once, Achilla asked her, "What do you mean by that? Isn't not crying over sorrow a form of cruelty? Isn't it hard not to weep for your grief?"

Hanila replied, "My dear, I never said that I do not cry... Some tears are too precious, and by not shedding them, we preserve their value... and the value of what you weep for. I do not cry in front of just anyone, nor do I cry in front of those who do not care about my tears, and I do not cry in situations where tears are of no use. At times, the person that you are weeping for or because of, your tears might diminish the reason for your tears and degrade it. Some sorrows should not be wept; some you should hold your head high with pride, some you can meet with a quiet smile, and others you might greet with laughter or silence. A look can sometimes be more potent and eloquent. Crying is not always the best or only way to express sorrow; sometimes it is the weakest form of expression."

When her mother whispered those words to her during that final meeting, Achilla understood what her mother wanted from her—no screaming, no anger, no tears. She was to preserve her value and the value of that sorrow, deep within herself, showing it to no one. Although Achilla might not have been able to fulfil her mother's wish on that day despite her attempts, she certainly abided by it afterward.

She never cried in front of anyone again, except for two instances—if we can call the escape of a single tear crying—one was during her farewell to Karl, and the other will be mentioned later.

Achilla opened Selene's hand and placed the crystal tear in it, making her close her fist around it. There wasn't a man or woman who could resist Achilla's charisma or her compelling presence. A truly beautiful person inside and out, a distinguished lady of the highest calibre. You couldn't help but admire and respect her. Something told you that behind all the merriment, mischief, recklessness, and daring lay a very special and profound character, fully aware of what she was doing, despite her lack of seriousness, her freedom and rejection of everything her people believed she should adhere to.

Something within Selene, despite the pain gripping her heart, felt sympathy for her. After what she had seen in her memories, she realised that the woman standing before her had suffered greatly, alone for a long time, ill-fated. Despite all her remarkable qualities, she seemed like a wanderer in a world where she felt she didn't belong to any side... How sad!

Paul, pretending shyly that he did not cry, said, "Well, you really are a better storyteller than Karl!" Achilla laughed cheerfully at his comment, returned to her single seat, and sat down in the same position as before.

As for Karl, he was lost in an entirely different world. All of this, Achilla had lived through alone, all this pain, and he knew nothing of it. For thirty years, he had only seen one side of her—the cheerful, carefree side. She always found humour in everything. He had seen her anger, seen her go mad at her grandmother, the Queen, but he never knew about her mother's story. She had once briefly told him about the sacred Law of Shishak. Over time, he thought it was just an ancient legend, outdated traditions that no longer held value. And though that legend—along with his feeling that a wretched creature like him could never reach a being as exquisite as her— had kept him from expressing his love for her in the beginning. But nothing like this!

Giovanni asked with interest, "You said you can influence nature? —He gestured towards the rainy weather outside the glass barrier— Are you doing this now?"

The rain had become a drizzle...

Achilla nodded affirmatively and then closed her eyes. Within seconds, the drizzling ceased, the clouds parted, and the sun shone brightly. She said, "The weather is affected by my mood, but not always; only my strong or clear emotions of anger, joy, distress, and tension."

Before the incident with her mother Hanila, the rare power that Achilla possessed lay dormant. It manifested when Achilla released an immense spiritual energy in her utmost rage. This power was sacred among the Heavenkin, a rare gift held by only a few guardians and some immortal souls. It had been missing for thousands of years. On that day, when Queen Etliea saw the cloudy weather, she was marvelled! As were the other Heavenkin; clouds never gathered over the island of Fala, and it never rained there. No one understood what was happening, but the Queen realised, when thunder roared alongside Achilla's screams after her mother emerged from the cave, that it was Achilla who was causing it. She couldn't believe the destructive and formidable force her granddaughter possessed when she almost destroyed the island. It was the first time the Queen lost control of her emotions in front of others.

Heavy rains and the sounds of thunder and lightning continued for three days after the incident, though less intensely. The Sibyl, Wert-Hakaou, the great Sibyl of the Heavenkin, tried for days to teach Achilla how to control her mental state. It was not an easy task, given Achilla's severe psychological condition and raging anger. But Wert-Hakaou, with her eleven thousand years of wisdom, used all her abilities and spiritual energy to calm her, reminding her of the enormous responsibility she bore. It wouldn't be pleasant to destroy their island or kill thousands of earthlings in a day due to an outburst of anger over a trivial prank!

This was very difficult for Achilla, especially considering her highly unpredictable nature. However, she knew that the first step she needed to take was to leave Fala, to distance herself from the Queen, whom she had come to despise intensely. She felt that her homeland was no longer her home. She had lost her sense of belonging to that place forever.

In the first months after Achilla returned to Fala, the weather was mostly cloudy, especially when she met with her grandmother. My God, how she hated her! Seven hundred years and more had not lessened the intensity of her feelings towards her, but she had learned to control her mental state better in her presence.

Abraham asked with hesitation, "You mentioned something about signs that appeared on you? What do you mean by that?"

She replied, "Oh, well... The Guardian of the Kingdom of Fala is chosen by the immortal souls, through signs or symbols that manifest from a young age, usually special abilities or high spiritual energy. But the distinguishing sign is when the king or queen finds someone among the Heavenkin whose thoughts they cannot hear." Knowing that Giovanni would follow up with a question, Achilla continued, "Our people are born with unique abilities; we can all read thoughts and emotions, and we can all fly, for instance. There are basic spiritual abilities that a heavenly is born with and can practice without any training—they are as natural to us as breathing! But, as in the case of reading thoughts and emotions, we learn how to mute or block them, to stop reading each other's minds most of the time. We consider it rude for someone to use it all the time, like eavesdropping on people's conversations without their knowledge!"

Giovanni remarked in wonder, "Mute them! Like muting the television?"

Achilla smiled at the humour of the comparison and his expression. "Yes, like a television, we mute the sounds coming from others' thoughts, so we no longer hear them. Those with high spiritual energy can place mental barriers around their thoughts, so others with equal or lesser spiritual energy cannot listen to them.

However, the Guardian of the kingdom, the king or queen, can listen to the thoughts of all Heavenkin, except for one person." And she raised her index finger in the air in front of her face.

Giovanni and Abraham muttered together, "Their heir." She nodded with a slight smile.

Giovanni added, "So, I cannot listen to your thoughts because my spiritual energy is less than yours?"

She raised an eyebrow, correcting him, "Because your spiritual energy is less than any Heavenly. You wouldn't be able to hear the thoughts of even a baby among us."

Giovanni pursed his lips and furrowed his brows, feeling somewhat insulted... about his abilities.

Emily asked, "So, you are the heir to the Queen?"

Achilla replied, "Not yet... at least not officially."

Emily questioned, "What do you mean?"

She replied, "Certain rituals must be performed; it's like a coronation ceremony among the earthlings, well, with a few differences." She scratched her neck slightly, as if hiding something, and it seemed she was deep in thought.

Karl snapped out of his reverie, recalling something, and asked, "You said you've been running for fifty years?!"

She replied, a hint of boredom in her voice, "Yes, that's exactly what I've been running from." She leaned back, placed her hands behind her neck, and relaxed, stretching her legs and crossing them as if in repose.

Emily exclaimed in astonishment, "The coronation?!"

She answered nonchalantly, "Uha."

Emily asked, "Why?"

Achilla replied in a distracted voice, "Who would want such a heavy chain... That old woman is really stubborn!"

Abraham commented, "Is it mandatory? Can't you refuse?! You said that not reading thoughts is a distinguishing sign, but not the only one. Are there no others with similar signs, like you?"

She replied, "A heavenly cannot shirk the choice of the immortal souls and the responsibility placed upon them, doing so would dishonour them... Well, they can all go to hell."

Abraham asked, "Is it a hereditary right? As I understand, the Queen... is your grandmother?" He said the last part hesitantly.

She answered indifferently, "No, although it often is. My family has carried the duty of protection for a long time, and it has rarely gone outside the family."

Paul asked, "Is it that bad?"

Achilla adjusted her posture, raised her eyebrows high, and said, "Are you kidding me? I... the heir to that old hag; join hands with her and help enforce those ridiculous ancient laws on those worn-out tablets. I don't think you can find another Heavenkin who has as little respect for those customs and laws as I do. Oh, for heaven's sake, it would be somewhat comical if it happened!" She turned her face away.

A brief silence followed as they all contemplated the predicament this miserable one was trapped in.

Achilla cleared her throat as if considering how to phrase her next sentence, which was unusual for her, as she typically spoke whatever came to mind, however and whenever she pleased.

She turned her body towards Karl, placing her hands on the armrest in front of him. She looked at him hesitantly, choosing her words carefully, "You... you know you don't have to... suffer... or burden yourselves... with this... this story. You can go back to... your previous state." She turned her hand over, palm up, as if holding something to show him, and continued, "Easily... You wouldn't need to be troubled... by this chaos again... No need... to feel sadness or let your emotions get tangled over... nothing."

Karl remained in his place for a moment, turning her words over in his head. Then he understood, and his eyes flashed with anger. He sprang up, moving away from her quickly as if afraid she might grab him. Standing by the kitchen, he shouted, "No... no... not again. I won't let you this time." He gestured forcefully in the air and paced nervously. Selene jumped behind him to calm him down.

Achilla let her hands fall between her legs and said without looking at him, "Think of your family, Karl."

Karl said, "We are not children... we can manage our own affairs... Don't you dare, Achilla... don't you dare..."

"Alright, alright, calm down... I don't intend to repeat my first act, at least not against your will this time. It was just a suggestion," she said, standing from her seat and gesturing with her hand for him to calm down.

Paul asked, "What's the matter with you?"

Emily replied, "Really, Paul! How much stupid can you be? She wants to erase all our memories!"

Akila interjected, "Restrict, not erase. Nothing can erase memories entirely unless something rips out your brains or damages them. You just wouldn't be able to access them, and it would only be those related to me. Wouldn't it be great to wake up tomorrow as if nothing had happened, and all this chaos disappeared?"

She said the last two sentences with a sarcastic tone, but she was addressing Karl indirectly. Karl growled, "No!"

Selene wished for it... and Achilla knew that.

Achilla sighed and rolled her eyes, "Alright, alright, relax, man, or you'll die soon from high blood pressure or a heart attack!" Paul laughed.

Achilla suddenly turned towards the glass wall on her right and muttered, "Damn it!"

The Coronation Ceremony

"Do not be saddened, my friend.
I have grown used to weeping alone,
burying the lump of sorrow within my chest.
I have grown used to slip away, drowning in the flood of sorrow,
leaning on the cane of my pride to rise once more,
with my eternal dignity."

— *Beshara Al Khoury*

Suddenly, the sound of shattering glass echoed loudly as the three temple knights burst through the glass wall like a bullet or faster, causing chaos all around them. They pinned Achilla down violently on the wooden floor. One of them pressed her shoulders forcefully, making her left cheek stick to the ground. The second had gathered her arms behind her back, holding them in an uncomfortable grip and kneeling on her. The third had grabbed her legs. The sorcerers were startled by this sudden and swift entry and instinctively jumped back, except for Karl, who leaped forward but stopped when he realised what he saw.

He had seen them long ago with Achilla, the three temple knights, massive like bears, each standing about two and a half meters tall and nearly a meter wide. He wondered why they were pinning down this delicate, fragile creature, who seemed so small compared to them, even though she was 183 cm tall. Her height had never been an issue for Karl, as he was 192 cm tall. This slender, beautiful woman didn't seem to pose such a threat! One of them would have been enough to hold her down. Why were they restraining her like American police officers arresting a Black man, whether he carried an AK-47 or not? Whatever the case!

What are they doing here anyway?! The temple knights rarely, and I mean rarely, ventured out. Achilla had once told him so. And where... where is their leader?!

We must remember that Karl had not seen the temple knights in the forest three days ago, while under the overwhelming flow of memories.

Achilla, with her features crinkled from the force of her face being pressed against the wooden floor, spoke with difficulty, her words coming out strained and muffled. As always, she managed to make a terrifying situation appear comedic: "Astro... Aristocles... Behemoth... It's been a long time, my dear ones!"

The three murmured with wide, friendly smiles, "Greetings, Kharissa!"

The scene could imply anything but a friendly reunion between old friends, despite how they made it seem. Unless, of course, this was the Heavenkin way of greeting each other! What strange creatures! Was this their version of a hug?!

The sorcerers were confused, unsure whether to attack them or greet them in the same way.

Then, drifting in with quiet grace, came the man with the grim face, landing on the right side of Achilla, in the space between her and Paul, Giovanni, Abraham, and Emily. Karl and Selene were in front of him. The other sorcerers moved slowly towards Karl, but he paid them no attention, his eyes filled with satisfaction as he looked at the scene before him. Behind him, Echor followed closely.

Achilla said, "Oh... Hello, Ahikar-Abigail! It seems that the old woman has finally lost her patience to send you all."

Abigail, with dignity and a thick voice, replied, "Speak respectfully of the queen. How are you still so reckless? You can't control your temper even when you're trying to escape from us. You know it's not very common for thunderstorms to form and disappear in two minutes! Oh, how careless you are!"

Echor, with nonchalance and a hint of humour on his face, said, "Is this necessary, Ahikar-Abigail?"

Achilla intervened jokingly, "What's the matter, Kharis-Echor? Have you joined the Templar Knights now?"

Echor replied sarcastically, "They wish!"

Behemoth, who was holding her shoulders, spoke in a light, casual manner, "You know how mischievous Kharissa-Achilla can be at times, Kharis-Echor."

Astro, who was at her feet, commented, "Just blink, and she'll be on the other side of the world!"

Aristocles, who was perched on her back, laughed.

Echor shrugged with the smile of someone who knows the matter of fact, slipped his hands in his trouser pockets, and oh, how handsome he was!

Abigail murmured as he scanned the sorcerers before him, "It seems we've interrupted an intimate meeting here." He finally fixed his gaze on Karl. "It appears the queen has been far too lenient after all!"

He turned his eyes back to Achilla, his gaze now carrying a very unsettling meaning. His dignified features had become irritating and provocative.

Suspicion and doubt began to show on Echor's face as he looked at him.

Achilla's eyes glinted and sparked with clear threat and challenge. She raised her head and bared her fangs, which slowly began to emerge in a broad smile that reflected boldness and mirth, her hair beginning to shift back to its crimson hue.

She knew that Abigail was provoking her just to make her take this step. It was easier for him than trying to restrain her himself, which would be a difficult and destructive task. Nevertheless, she responded to his provocation because she knew Karl would be severely hurt if she didn't.

She said, with a voice that began to rise gradually, and strong waves coursed through her body as she writhed slowly, making the three above her struggle to hold her down, their hands trembled violently from the intense pressure on her. She said, "Kaaaarl... I'm sorry for thiiis."

Karl looked at her, unsure of what was happening or what she was apologising for.

Abigail pulled out four small, thick, pentagonal rings from under his robe, each the size of a bracelet, adorned with strange engravings and coloured like rusty iron. He tossed them into the air, and they opened on their own as he threw them, soaring like flying saucers toward Karl, like crab's claws ready to close in on him.

In the blink of an eye, the three men were flung in different directions, smashing through the house as they fell. Achilla leapt nimbly into the air, somersaulting to intercept the pentagonal rings, making them clamp onto her wrists and ankles, then, she landed forcefully on her feet, she stood upright, positioning herself sideways between the sorcerers and Abigail, looking into Abigail's eyes with imposing determination.

Echor had grabbed Abigail by the collar, baring his fangs and shouting angrily in a booming voice, "How dare you, you scoundrel! Have you forgotten who she is? Have you forgotten what she will become?"

Abigail looked to Echor and calmly said, while gripping his hands, "I did nothing that Queen Etliea did not command."

Echor's eyes widened in astonishment, then he added angrily, shaking him forcefully, "Did she order you to bind her with the Avernus bracelets, like a criminal?!"

Abigail calmly lowered Echor's hands, despite Echor's strong resistance, and said, "Yes, and she ordered me to keep them on her until she reaches Fala."

Echor pulled his hands free from Abigail's grip and delivered a powerful punch that sounded like two large stones colliding. The punch made Abigail stagger back, but he managed to steady himself with effort before falling. The knights leaped at Echor with lightning speed, surrounding him; one pushed him from the chest, while the others grabbed his arms. Behemoth, who was pushing him from the chest, said, "Have you gone mad, striking the Grand Knight?!"

Echor shouted angrily, "Let me go, damn you all! You're the mad ones; how dare you do this to Achilla!".

Achilla screamed, "Echor, stop!"

Echor looked at Achilla in great alarm. She stood there with a smile on her face, as usual! But small tremors were emanating from her body. She was struggling immensely to control herself and remain standing despite the evident suffering. She clenched her body tightly, with veins bulging in her fists, neck, and face, which had turned a purplish red.

Echor knew the immense pain Achilla was enduring now. No one could bear even one of the Avernus rings from hell without collapsing in writhing agony, screaming from the excruciating pain. Let alone four!

How was she able to hold herself together? To stand firm?

Echor's face was etched with guilt, and his voice was filled with deep regret as he said, "I swear, Achilla... I swear I knew nothing about this! I accompanied them hoping to persuade you to return... so that... I swear I had no knowledge of this."

He approached her after breaking free from the knights' grip, then placed his hands on her shoulders. But as he did, he tremored and fell to his knees before her; from the intense pain caused by the waves emanating from the rings coursing through her body. His face contorted with sorrow as he looked up at her.

Achilla let out a small, difficult laugh and spoke in a trembling voice, trying to sound playful, "You gentle fool, Echor, there's no need to swear. I know how cunning that old hag can be."

Karl ran to her, his face flushed with blood, unable to bear the painful scene. He wanted to free her from that hellish grip, even at the cost of his own life. He shouted, "Achilla!"

She jumped away from him, raising her hand as if to say "Stop!" and said, "Don't come closer, I'm fine... I think the escape journey has ended."

Abigail, who didn't care about Echor's punch, said, "Shouldn't you have ended it before things reached this stage?"

She replied sarcastically, "You know I wouldn't leave without a fight." Then she let out a muffled groan and clenched her teeth tightly to suppress it.

The three knights stood behind Abigail, also unaware of the Avernus rings. Their faces bore expressions of awe and reverence for the immense power these heavens being possessed before them. No wonder the queen had been pursuing her for fifty years to force her return and crown her as her heir. Who else could be more competent for this? They were witnessing an unparalleled spiritual energy. Each time, she surprised them with more and more of her abilities hidden behind that nonchalant demeanour. Surely, she would be a great queen one day, immortalised in the history of Heavenkin.

The three knights bowed their heads in deep respect, touched their foreheads with three fingers of their right hand, then moved their hands to their hearts as if drawing a half-circle in the air. They then clenched their hands into fists and struck their chests forcefully, before bending their wrists as if pulling something from within their chests. They extended their arms towards Achilla, palms open, from which thin, shimmering threads of light emerged, spreading into the air and stretching until they disappeared after a while.

This gesture among the Heavenkin signified the utmost reverence and profound respect for the person before them, declaring their deep humility in the presence of such immense spiritual power and high status. It was the first time the knights had performed this gesture.

Echor repeated the same gesture, while Abigail remained silent.

She smiled at them with a feigned lightness and looked at Karl, saying in her trembling voice, "I repeat my apologies for what happened to your home. I will ensure you are compensated."

So, this was what she had apologised for earlier!

Before allowing him to respond, she took off swiftly, followed immediately by the three knights and Echor. Abigail cast one last glance at them before taking off after them. Within mere seconds, they had vanished, as if they had never been there at all, leaving only the wreckage they had left behind!

The sorcerers looked around their home. One of the chairs was split in half, the inner padding of the sofa scattered like feathers everywhere, a stone statue was broken in another corner, and a large crack had formed in the wall behind it. In another spot, the wooden floor was damaged, and a single chair that had been there was flung far into the air through the large hole where a glass wall once stood, landing shattered in the garden. A cushion hung from the sharp edge of the broken glass, like a knife blade, dangling outward, and the shattered glass glittered on the ground, scattered all around.

Most of this chaos happened in a second... and it will take weeks to repair!

Emily said in a breathless voice, "That was terrifying!"

Paul commented excitedly, "Wooow... that was thrilling!"

He jumped away before Emily's hand could reach him to slap him.

Selene said despondently, "Oh, it looks like we have a lot of work here." She clapped her hands, announcing the start of a major cleaning campaign, and everyone groaned.

There was no time to reflect on what had happened; they had to take care of this dilapidated house first. As for Karl, he returned to his own world. Giovanni tapped him on the shoulder, and Karl turned to him. Giovanni said, "Go if you want, we'll take care of the house." He smiled at him. Abraham stood behind Giovanni and nodded in agreement, while Selene smiled at him gently when he turned to her. Then, he turned her face away, pretending to be busy with the cleaning.

The next day, they found a large leather bag at the door of the house, containing a letter and a large sum of money. The letter, written in elegant handwriting without a name or signature, read: "I hope the amount is sufficient to repair the house. My apologies."

****

Four months and several days had passed since that incident, and Karl spent them like a ghost among his family. Despite his attempts to appear normal and act as if nothing had happened, his distant gaze most of the time and his diminished vitality betrayed him.

He was preoccupied with Achilla's fate. What had happened to her? Had she finally been forced to take the throne?

He was lost in his memories with her, still sifting through those thirty years and what they held. Sometimes, they would find him smiling to himself without realising it, and sometimes a tear would glisten in his eye. No one knew what was going through his mind—though it wasn't hard to guess who it was about—except Giovanni. But Karl didn't care about him; all that mattered to him was not hurting Selene. No one would be affected by his old-new love except her. For her alone, he exerted all his "failed" acting skills.

How difficult his situation was, to suddenly realise that his feelings for the woman he had loved for eighty years did not equal a quarter of what he felt for Achilla, with whom he had no hope. What should he do? Should he abandon his current companion just for a woman from his past whom he loved?

Was Achilla right? If she hadn't bound his memory, would he have moved on and loved Selene? Or would he have remained alone forever?

Or was Achilla the cause of what he was going through now, because of what she had done? If she hadn't, he might at least be living with the consequences of his conscious choices!

But she protected him! He understood that. He knew she was telling the truth. He would have followed her even if he didn't know where this island of Fala was; he would have found it somehow. He was not a quitter or a coward! He would never abandon her... ever.

But now his situation was different. He had lived a full life since then, forming a family of which he is the cornerstone. The bond between them had grown as strong as the ties of a sorcerer's coven. He couldn't leave them behind, couldn't abandon them, and they wouldn't abandon him. He wouldn't hurt Selene or make her feel like an outsider or wounded among them. She had no place other than this family, outside this group. He wouldn't allow it. He would not be the cause of tearing his family apart. He would do his best. He would love them... and he would love Achilla, always.

His heart was big enough for all of them. Selene would give him the time he needed to return to his old self—he knew that. He would do his best to make everything normal again, if there was anything normal in this life!

Karl looked through the glass wall at the falling snow and sighed. Everything seemed to conspire against him, even nature. He took a sip of his hot coffee and returned to contemplating the blanket of snow that covered the garden and the leaves. When he heard the doorbell, the men were either playing cards or bickering! The women were out of the house, and it didn't seem like any of them were thinking of opening the door for that visitor! Paul shouted, "Karl, open the door, it's the delivery guy!"

Karl muttered, "You glutton, didn't you devour an entire pizza by yourself an hour ago? It seems you really do have two stomachs, as Emily said!" Paul chuckled at his comment, unbothered.

Karl walked to the door, still holding his cup. He opened it to find two tall, handsome men in elegant and unusual attire, wearing pins shaped like wings adorned with blue and green agate on their chests. One of them appeared more cheerful, with a broad smile, while the other seemed more formal and smiled gently. The man on the right, who seemed more cheerful, said, "Hello, Mr. Karl!"

Karl replied, "Hello!"

The man said, "We are pleased to meet you. I am Tarah," he pointed to the man on his left, "and this is my companion, Adnos. Kharissa-Achilla has sent us to deliver this invitation to you," he extended a small box he was holding, "to attend her coronation as heir to the throne. It would be our honour to escort you to the island of Fala."

Karl felt a shiver run through his body when this stranger mentioned Achilla's name. He stood there, staring at the two men in front of him in bewilderment. Abraham nudged him with his elbow, as the three of them had moved beside him as soon as they heard Achilla's name, driven by curiosity. Karl handed his coffee cup to Abraham and took the small white stone box. It was a rectangular box with a large black opal stone set in the centre of its lid. The four of them lowered their heads to admire this exquisite stone, its colours dancing like a rainbow.

Tarah cleared his throat to prompt Karl to open the box, which he did. Inside, he found six small pins made of a precious stone that looked like tiny, spread-out obelisks, with a distinctive light blue colour, resembling... ice crystals. They were all arranged on a burgundy velvet lining. The stones were truly magnificent!

Adnos said, "This is the jeremejevite stone of Kharissa-Achilla. Every Heavenkin of high rank chooses a special stone that represents them..." he hesitated slightly before continuing, "Kharissa-Achilla sent this invitation to no one but you."

Karl, with a look of suspicion on his face, asked, "Inviting us to the island of Fala? Isn't it forbidden for non-Heavenkin to enter, or something like that?"

Tarah replied, "It's precisely forbidden for you to know the way there, but entering it is fine, especially with a special invitation like this!"

Paul commented, "What? Are you going to cover our eyes with clothes the whole way?"

Tarah burst out laughing at the image he saw in Paul's mind. Adnos gave him a warning look, urging him to be more serious. Tarah cleared his throat apologetically and said, "No, we won't need that. We'll use instantaneous teleportation. You'll be in your home and... voilà! In a second, you'll be in the middle of the island of Fala."

Paul exclaimed, "Whoa, that sounds awesome, man!" He clenched his fist and raised it towards Tarah, who did the same, and they bumped fists like friends. Adnos couldn't believe the farce happening before him. They were official envoys from the heir to the throne. He still didn't know why she chose Tarah to accompany him, knowing his nature well. Well, it wasn't entirely surprising, as he was as reckless as she was. The question was, why did she choose him to go with Tarah?

Meanwhile, the two women arrived, got out of the car, and stood by the door next to Tarah and Adnos. Emily glanced at them with admiration. Tarah, with his broad smile, commented, "You must be Miss Selene and Miss Emily. It's a pleasure to meet you. I am Tarah." He extended his hand towards Emily, who placed her hand in his. He lifted it, bowed, and kissed it, then winked at her, causing Emily's face to turn red. She felt a warmth in her ears and neck, and began fanning her face with her other hand, saying, "Oh, what a charming man!" Adnos felt an overwhelming urge to punch him.

Giovanni, observing the scene before him, muttered to the men on his right, tilting his head towards them without looking at them and placing his hand over his mouth, "Is this guy flirting... what's his name, the tall one?" Karl answered, "Tarah." Giovanni continued, "Yes, is this Tarah flirting with Emily as it seems to me?" They all shrugged in amazement and answered simultaneously; Karl said, "Yes." Abraham said, "Definitely." And Paul said, "Without a doubt."

Tarah also kissed Selene's hand, but thankfully, without a wink.

Adnos, firmly placed his hand on his companion's shoulder, said, "Well, gentlemen, we will return tomorrow at four in the afternoon. The celebration will last for a week. Now, please excuse us. We must leave before my companion commits more foolishness." He laughed nervously, a short, awkward chuckle, then smiled at them, nodded, and dragged Tarah away while he was still flirting with Emily. They then flew off.

Emily looked after them foolishly, placed her hands around her flushed face, and said, "Wow, he's so handsome!"

Giovanni commented, "What! That clumsy tall guy is handsome?! I can't believe your taste is that bad!"

Emily gave him a look of someone who had fallen in love and sighed, "Jealousy is eating you up, shorty."

Giovanni fumed, "Me! Jealous of that ship's mast?!" and began arguing with Emily.

Selene paid them no attention and asked Karl, looking at the box in his hands, "What's going on?"

Karl answered gently, fearing the news might upset her, "Achilla sent them to deliver her invitation for us to attend the coronation ceremony." He opened the box for Selene.

Emily ---who hadn't noticed Adnos's earlier words because she was too busy with Tarah, screamed with excitement, "Did they invite us?! Really!! Wow, these stones are amazing, what are they?"

Giovanni replied, "It's jeremejevite, you ignoramus." If Adnos hadn't mentioned the name of the stone earlier, Giovanni wouldn't have known it.

Emily took a brooch from the box and turned it in her hand, saying, "So this is how Heavenkin send their invitations. I must admit, it's exquisite and luxurious." Then she gasped and put her hand over her mouth, "Oh my God, what will I wear?" She looked at Selene to ask her, and when her eyes fell on her, she realised she had gotten carried away, forgetting her friend's feelings. Emily muttered with clear disappointment, "Oh, I'm sorry, or are we not going?"

Karl said in a gentle tone, though there was a firmness underlying his words, "Achilla extended this special invitation to us alone. This is a very important day for her, and for her to honour us with such a gesture is a great privilege and honour."

(Certainly, Karl would never disappoint Achilla. He would never hesitate to go to her whenever she asked. He would never abandon her. She would always be the first, with no one to rival her.) This is what Selene thought, but she said calmly, without showing any annoyance, "It's okay, Emily, I'll help you choose your clothes. But—" she turned to Karl, "I hope Achilla won't consider it rude if I don't want to go with you."

Karl, placing his free hand on her shoulder and looking directly into her eyes, asked, "Does this bother you? I won't force you to go, of course... but are you sure about this? Achilla might be a little disappointed, but I hope our going doesn't upset you. I'm going as an old friend, that's all."

Selene nodded, "I know that. Achilla is a nice girl, but..." she pursed her lips as if trying to hold something back, then decided to speak frankly, "I don't think I can handle this!"

Karl hugged her and kissed her forehead, while Paul grabbed the box from his hand and ran inside, followed calmly by Abraham. Emily and Giovanni resumed their bickering and went in after them. Selene smiled at the scene, though her eyes hid tears.

Karl asked her without looking at her while still holding her, "If... if this... bothers you a lot... then..." Karl struggled to make his suggestion, not wanting to say something he couldn't commit to, "If you don't want us to go..."

Selene interrupted him, "There's no need for that. I know how important this is to you. Don't feel like you have to do something for my sake. Don't make me feel like you're obligated to do anything for my sake." Karl looked at her with both relief and sadness and said, "You are a great woman."

Her words were clear and sharp in meaning, though her tone was gentle. Selene was not a weak woman or one of those who might wither away behind a man. She simply loved him deeply and was in pain, for his sake and hers. Karl was not just her lover, but a member of her family and group. She wouldn't allow herself to be a burden to him. She fully understood his position; it wasn't his fault, nor anyone else's. It was just their misfortune, the bad luck of the three of them.

She would give him this chance to say goodbye to Achilla in the proper way. It was time for this story to have a good ending after all this time. The first time, Achilla ended things on her own without consulting him or taking his opinion. The second time, well, half the house was destroyed before they could have a serious conversation together. Now, if he went, maybe... after they talk, after they pour out their hearts to each other, after he truly understands the situation, maybe he could return to his old self. Perhaps, he would find peace and come to terms with his fate.

****

Emily was on the verge of breaking down as she sat in the living room on the second floor that evening, with Giovanni and Paul beside her. She placed her hands on her face, looking exhausted, leaning forward with her hair scattered in all directions. "I feel like I'm going to throw up. I'm not okay, believe me!"

Selene, who was standing in the kitchen with Abraham, helping her prepare a late dinner, replied, "Oh, come on, take it easy. I think you're overreacting a bit!"

Emily turned her head towards her with a tense tone, responded, "Oh really!! Am I overreacting!! Didn't you see how the Heavenkin women looked like Greek goddesses in their... strange... bizarre outfits!! What is a poor ordinary girl from the human world supposed to wear there!! So she doesn't look like a wild boar among them, or at best, a vagrant!!... Oh, I really think I'm going to throw up!!" She buried her face in her hands again.

Giovanni, lying on the couch, snorted and said, "Darling, you'd look like a wild boar even if you wore the same clothes as them!" Paul laughed along with him.

Emily, angry, said, "Damn you both, you idiots... you're laughing now? Let's see how you'll laugh tomorrow when you look like stray insects among them... especially you, shorty, in your clothes that stopped evolving since the last century! And you, bull, are you planning to go to the party in your sportswear? You don't even own a formal suit!! Is there a man in the world who doesn't own a formal suit!!"

The argument between the three of them flared up, and Abraham said calmly, "Hey, guys, there's no need for all this shouting."

Selene addressed Emily to stop the argument. "Have you taken out all the dresses in your closet? You must find something, and you can look in my closet too... I think you'll find something suitable there."

Emily, distracted from the men in front of her, said, "Which dresses? Which dresses? The classic ones or the modern ones? Long or short? Is it appropriate to wear bright colours or stick to light and dark ones... loose or tight... what kind of events will we attend during the week... dance parties or dinner parties... should I wear high heels or low ones... all my clothes are on the floor, the bed isn't enough for them anymore!... Damn those two guys, how did they leave without giving us the event schedule? And they expect us to prepare for such an occasion in one day! I don't even have time to shop..." She groaned in pain and furrowed her brows. "Oh, I have to go shopping tomorrow morning."

Giovanni replied, "Have you gone mad, woman? You just came back from shopping today." He commented sarcastically, "But we know the real reason for your stress, tomorrow will be a big hunting day for you!"

Selene said calmly, "Take it easy. I think classic dresses will be perfectly suitable, and light and dark colours are fine, too!" But Emily had already ignored her and resumed arguing with Giovanni again.

Abraham, chopping vegetables in a low voice only Selene could hear, commented, "Since when has Giovanni been jealous over Emily?"

Selene, stirring the chicken with onions in the pan, looked up to observe them with a bit of curiosity to confirm Abraham's words. She cast a brief glance at them and saw that Emily had completely lost her patience with Giovanni's unusually sharp comments. She began hitting him repeatedly with a pillow, while he raised his hands in front of his face and laughed heartily, which only made her angrier. We could imagine that Paul had started cheering immediately.

She said, "Hmm, do you think so?" Abraham didn't answer, only shrugged.

Karl was in his room on the third floor, contemplating the Jeremejevite pin. He could hear his friends shouting on the second floor, even though the record player was playing soft classical music. He had finished packing his light suitcase. Ah, how easy it is for men to choose their clothes!

It looks like a snowflake... definitely... that's why she chose it, it's like snowflakes, he thought to himself as he held the pin, which was about half the length of a finger, feeling immense joy that he would see her tomorrow. He had calmed down after all this time had passed and after venting his anger that day four months ago. But what would happen after he saw her? *It doesn't matter, it's enough to make sure she's okay and see her well,* he said to himself, then sighed. He put the brooch back in the box, which was empty except for one other pin, and closed it. He turned off the record player and headed downstairs. As he descended the stairs, the delicious smell of food made his stomach growl. "Alright, alright, what's all this shouting about, guys?" he asked.

Paul shouted, "Emily says she looks like a wild boar!!" and laughed.

Emily retorted, "Shut up, pumpkin head."

Giovanni laughed and said, "Oh... oh, it seems Emily gets more creative with her comparisons when she's angry. Your head does look like a pumpkin, how did we not notice that before?!"

Emily added slyly, "And you look like a poodle with that frizzy hair of yours, shorty."

Paul laughed heartily, "Hahaha... you deserve that, you fool... a poodle, hahaha, how cute and adorable you are." He then began to ruffle Giovanni's hair roughly.

Selene muttered, fidgeting, "Oh, they're going to start wrestling again now!"

Karl, entering the kitchen and eyeing the food while rubbing his stomach, asked, "What's all this about?"

Abraham, like a patient grandfather tired of his grandchildren's noise, replied, "Who knows, my friend, what their fight is really about!"

Selene, knowing that the light punches would soon turn into kicks, holds, and free jumps, which would make the place look like a wrestling ring, commanded, "Go outside to the garden if you want to wrestle, or you'll go to bed without dinner!"

No further threat was needed; the fight could wait, as Paul was, of course, starving. Besides, it's bad to live with someone who could mess with your mind and make you do anything willingly and against your will at the same time! It seemed like a difficult equation. It's good that Selene doesn't often use her powers on her family members, 'only in times of crisis' as she says, or so they think!

Finally, dinner was served. After a while, when Emily grew tired of thinking about the models of dresses she would wear, and while a serious discussion was taking place between Giovanni and Abraham about who was expected to win tomorrow's football match, she said, "Selene, will you come with me to the mall tomorrow morning?"

Selene replied, "Oh, Emily, I..."

Emily interrupted her with pleading eyes, "Please... please... please!"

Selene shook her head in weary resignation, "Alright, but on one condition!"

Emily's face lit up with joy, her eyes widening like a puppy wagging its tail in happiness, "What? What?"

Selene, in a motherly tone, said, "First, we'll go through your clothes after dinner. If we don't find anything suitable, then we'll go to the market."

Emily agreed, "Alright, deal." Selene knew this condition was futile; Emily would go through half her clothes and still insist on going to the mall.

Karl, knowing Emily's nature well, commented, "Please, Emily, there's no need to take more than one large suitcase. I think one suitcase will be more than enough for a week!" How Karl wished he hadn't opened his mouth.

Emily exclaimed in astonishment, "Are you crazy?! How will one suitcase be enough?! Do you realise there are clothes for the day and others for the night? Plus, there are evening wears, backup clothes, mood-based outfits, and those two pieces you can't decide between, so you take both, including sleepwear, underwear, accessories, jewellery, makeup, beauty products, body and skincare items, bath and hygiene supplies, and... shoes. Do you know that shoes need a separate suitcase?! Each outfit needs its own specific shoes, I won't repeat anything for sure!! Plus, you can never know what you might need there, so you have to take some extra items, just in case!" She finished her sentence, raising an eyebrow at him.

Karl, surrendering, replied, "I know, I know, but we're not taking a plane, I don't know how the luggage will be transported, and we don't know the location of their island to use one of our spells."

Emily responded in the clipped words, "My. Luggage. Will. Arrive. Before. Me. On. That. Island."

Karl didn't think of arguing further. Who in their right mind would argue with women about the amount of clothes they might need for a trip?!

Paul whispered to Karl after Emily resumed talking with Selene, not wanting her to hear him, though she was too busy to notice anyway. "Hey, Karl, do you have an extra suit?"

Karl whispered back, "Yes, but it won't fit you; you're broader than me!"

Paul muttered, "Oh," and shrugged nonchalantly.

Karl whispered, "Why don't you go with them to the mall tomorrow since you need a suit?"

Paul's eyes widened, "Are you crazy?! Do you want me to die of boredom?! That shopping fanatic won't leave me alone. She'll make me her puppet, forcing me to try on and take off clothes for hours until she finds something that suits her taste. Then I'll turn into a bag carrier. No thanks, I've been through that before!"

Karl smiled, stifling his laughter. Right! How could he forget that miserable day in Paul's life? He didn't think he'd ever seen him in a worse state. It was the first and last time he went shopping with Emily. He had learned his lesson well.

****

Karl couldn't sleep well that night. He woke up a bit late and took a hot shower to relax his nerves. As he stood in front of the mirror, he noticed the light stubble on his chin. When he put the razor to his face to shave, he remembered one of those times when Achilla would rub her hands against his cheeks whenever his stubble grew. He used to think she did it to remind him to shave, so he commented, "I know, it's gotten long, I need to shave it." She replied, gently tugging a lock of his hair, "I like it this way, you little boy!"

****

"My God, Emily, do you plan to stay there forever?!" Giovanni exclaimed in disbelief as he saw Emily's three suitcases flying behind her as she descended the marble stairs. There were two large suitcases and one medium-sized bag.

Selene, showing signs of exhaustion from the arduous task, remarked, "I swear I did my best, guys. She was going to take five bags."

Emily groaned, placing her hand on her head, "I don't even know what the weather is like on that island."

Despite not having slept well, as they had stayed up late choosing clothes and went out early to shop, her face looked radiant.

She was wearing a white dress made of polyester fabric similar to soft organza, with a wide V-neckline at the front and back, and loose sleeves reaching mid-arm. The dress was gathered around her waist under a wide piece of fabric tied into a nearly vertical black bow, accentuating her slender waist. The dress extended below her knees, and she wore high-heeled black lace shoes. She carried a short black fur coat in her hand and let her black hair cascade comfortably down to the middle of her back, with a Jeremejevite brooch attached to the right side. She looked truly elegant.

Giovanni commented, "Aren't you overdoing it, Emily? What's with all these clothes and that dress?"

Emily retorted, "What do you know about elegance with that traditional suit of yours?" Giovanni was wearing a very traditional black formal suit, with the brooch fixed on his chest.

Paul stood beside him, wearing a white shirt with the brooch attached and blue trousers he somehow found in the corner of his closet. Not the best outfit, but the best of the worst. Abraham, on the other hand, wore a modern navy blue suit with a matching vest, a shiny navy tie, and a white pocket square folded into a rose shape.

Karl groaned as he saw Emily's suitcases, looking stunning in his black suit. Underneath, he wore a vest in a shade between silver and sky blue, with one end wrapped over the other, forming small sharp angles pointing downward. He replaced the traditional tie with a more modern cravat of the same colour as the vest, which flowed elegantly from under his white shirt collar, gathered with a fabric tie at the top, and folded neatly into his closed vest. He opted for a simple pocket square that appeared as a white line, and pinned the brooch, which was of a similar colour to his vest, on his right chest. His light brown hair was slicked back with a slight wave, and he kept his beard light and neatly trimmed.

Emily looked at him admiringly, "You are the only man with good taste in this house." Abraham cleared his throat, and she added, "And you, your taste is not bad, at least you stay on the safe side. But these two are a disgrace to fashion!" She pointed to Giovanni and Paul.

The doorbell rang before another argument could start among them; it was four in the afternoon.

Emily rushed to the door and opened it, revealing the handsome Tarah and Adnos standing like Michelangelo's marble statues. They wore matching outfits that closely resembled Indian Punjabi attire: sky-blue coats reaching their knees, embroidered with shiny silver threads along the inner edges and sleeve cuffs, adorned with light-coloured gemstones around the high collars and upper chests. Beneath the open collars, white ruffled shirts with high necklines peeked through. A large piece of soft, natural grey linen was draped over their left shoulders, covering the entire left sleeve and hanging down to the waist, where it was secured with a large pin shaped like the head of a strange animal, its eyes set with yellow agate stones.

They wore the same Jeremejevite brooch on their exposed left sides, over their hearts, and loose-fitting matte white trousers.

Emily sighed involuntarily at the sight before her. Adnos bowed in greeting, and Tarah seized her hand, planting a kiss on it while still holding it, he said, "Signora bella, is it possible for you to grow more beautiful with each passing moment? "She placed the fingers of her other hand over her mouth and laughed nervously, her face turning red as it had the last time.

Giovanni muttered, "What a flatterer! Come and look at her suitcases, and you'll change your mind."

Tarah heard him and wrapped her arm around his elbow, stepping forward confidently with a broad smile, and said, "Of course! Necessity knows no bounds" he gestured towards her dress, "A lady of such beauty must take care of her elegance. A woman never knows what she might need, right?" Then he looked at her and winked.

She sighed with a silly smile, "Not all men understand this; only the smart ones do."

Tarah added, "Allow me to express, Signora, how much I admire your exquisite taste—though, of course, it is you who enhances its beauty."

She replied shyly, "Do you think it's suitable?"

He took the fur coat hanging on her elbow and tossed it onto one of the sofas, saying, "Very suitable, but you won't need this coat; the weather is always beautiful in Fala."

Adnos interrupted the flirtatious conversation, accompanied by Karl, as they entered and said, "Hello, gentlemen, I hope you are ready." He glanced at Selene, who sat far away on the rocking chair.

She waved at him with a tired but gentle smile. He bowed his head to her; having listened to her and Karl's thoughts, he did not ask.

Emily asked, "What about the suitcases?"

Tarah replied, "No problem, my lady. Now, shall we form a circle if you are ready?"

Tarah and Adnos stood facing each other, and the sorcerers joined them, linking hands to form a closed circle. Tarah looked at the suitcases piled next to the marble stairs, and they jumped on their own into the centre of the circle.

Adnos said, "Alright, gentlemen, it's best to close your eyes to avoid nausea. The instantaneous transition might be a bit strong since it's your first time but hold on tight; it will be over quickly."

Everyone closed their eyes and then felt as if Earth's gravity was gradually decreasing. Suddenly, there was a strong pull from behind them, as if someone was grabbing the tops of their backs and pulling them backwards and upward forcefully. They tightened their grips, and then everything stopped as quickly as it had started. As for Selene, all she saw was that she blinked, and they were gone.

Tarah said, "Gentlemen, we have arrived."

They opened their eyes to a scene that could only exist in dreams. They were suspended in the air, and far below their feet, they saw an island from a fantasy world. Trees and plants of various colours, sizes, and shapes. Rivers flowing in white, honey, and greenish-blue hues, all originating from the peak of a majestic mountain. Houses carved from white rock dotted the landscape. They began to descend in a slow, circular motion, their hearts dancing at the breathtaking sight. The closer they got, the clearer the island's features became, reflecting the sun's rays off the shimmering stone houses adorned with delicate, vibrant colours. They saw smaller, multi-coloured, polygonal stones in shades of green, blue, red, purple, black, and other unnamed colours scattered here and there, some decorating the house facades, most strewn across the ground. These were the island's ordinary stones, not the grey stones of human lands.

Is this what the Sky Island Fala looks like? It must be an island from paradise! Nothing here resembled anything they had seen before on this planet. No wonder it was in the sky!

They landed on a flat, circular, white rocky ground engraved with lines, drawings, and strange letters, followed by their luggage.

On two sides, they were surrounded by gardens filled with flowers, blossoms, small plants of various colours, and some statues carved from colourful stones in the shapes of mythical creatures. They could also see the blood-red soil mixed with a shiny copper hue.

The circle led to two opposite paths: one was a mahogany wooden bridge adorned with golden arms, arching over a greenish-blue river like lapis lazuli, leading to a grand arched gate of white stone with strange engravings encrusted with gemstones and gold. The other path was of white marble, which, although very similar to the white rock, lacked veins of different colours and did not sparkle like tiny diamonds. This wide marble path led to a magnificent and enormous white palace with high, pointed towers, all carved from a rocky mountain or constructed from rock pieces—who knows?

The palace featured tall, pointed, purple-tinted glass windows. In the middle of the palace stood a high, very wide semi-circular balcony, with short stone columns around its outer edge entwined with light blue and green climbing plants bearing pink, yellow, and reddish-white flowers. The balcony had an arched glass door open, with sheer white silk curtains gently dancing in the soft breeze. Small bell-like pieces of golden colour hung between the folds of the curtains, dangling from the top with thin red silk ribbons, reaching about a quarter of the balcony door's length, perhaps a bit longer, producing a delicate chime as the curtains swayed.

Tarah said cheerfully, "Welcome to Fala!"

The sorcerers were still breathless; this was not a sight easily overlooked. They murmured, "Thank you."

Suddenly, the curtains opened, revealing a figure with a broad, radiant smile. She appeared between the swaying white curtains like a mythical character, perhaps resembling Aphrodite, Ishtar, Inanna, Khikhi, or whatever was the name of the goddess of beauty. Her red hair was styled in a loose, wavy braid adorned with tiny diamond pins matching her earrings. The hairstyle allowed some wavy strands to fall freely around her face. She wore a thick golden band engraved with strange drawings and words, as they were accustomed to, placed just above her hairline, with her hair covering the rest.

She wore a dress that accentuated her slender figure, made of silvery-white silk, fastened at her shoulders with pleated silk ribbons from the same dress, revealing her arms. Around her waist, she tied a long, dark silver silk ribbon with a bronze sheen into a medium-sized bow on one side, with the rest of the long ribbon cascading down to mid-thigh. The semi-fitted silk dress flowed from her hips to just below her knees. She pinned a Jeremejevite stone brooch to the chest of her dress, near her heart, and wore slightly elevated shoes resembling snakeskin, with colours ranging from dark grey to light grey and shiny silver.

She was a sight to behold.

She seemed to have come in a hurry upon learning of their arrival. A voice from behind her called out anxiously, urging her to return and finish what they were doing: "Kharissa-Achilla... Kharissa-Achilla," then mumbled incomprehensible words, but she ignored it.

Achilla, with a joyful expression on her face, pushed the curtains aside and began to walk with dancing steps. She lightly leapt from the balcony, almost landing on the stone railing but tapping it gently with her toes. Then she bent her knees slightly and began to float towards them, descending gradually. The hem of her silk dress, the ribbons, and the strands of her hair swayed with the air as she flew, appearing to hurry but with lightness and grace. She landed on one foot and smoothly stepped forward with the other, continuing her walk with short, quick steps.

Tarah approached her with open arms and a wide stride, saying, "Kharissa-Inanna, is there anyone more beautiful than you?"

She slapped him gently on the head when he stood before her and continued on her way. Rubbing his head, he muttered, "Oh, what did I do wrong this time?"

She replied playfully, "That was for flirting with Emily." Giovanni and Adnos smiled in satisfaction.

Adnos approached her, greeting her with a gentle smile, "Kharissa, good day to you..."

She slapped him on the head as well, saying, "And this is for tattling on your friend." Tarah laughed, "You deserve it, you snitch."

She approached the sorcerers with open arms. Emily was the closest, so she hugged her warmly. Then, she took Emily's hand and made her spin around to admire her dress and said, "Wow, what exquisite taste, Emily!"

Emily remarked in surprise, pointing to Achilla's dress, "I didn't expect you to wear... a normal dress!"

Achilla laughed, "What? Did you expect me to wear those old-fashioned clothes you saw in my memories? She leaned towards her and said, "They date back to seven hundred years ago!"

Emily replied shyly, "I know, but I didn't expect clothes... like ours!" and laughed.

Achilla said, "We live on Earth too and buy most of our clothes from your stores. But don't worry, we won't disappoint you. The parties haven't started yet; these are just everyday clothes."

She said it so casually that Emily swallowed hard. If these were "everyday clothes," what would the party outfits be like?!

Achilla read her thoughts and wrapped an arm around Emily's neck, and said, "By the way, I've prepared wardrobes full of clothes that might suit your tastes in your private rooms, just in case you need them or something like that." Then she glanced at Emily's suitcases, while Emily's heart soared with an endless happiness at this news. Achilla added, "Though, I doubt you'll need them, my dear." Emily hugged her tightly like a child, repeating, "Oh, thank you, thank you! That's so kind of you!"

Paul exclaimed cheerfully, "What luck! Did you hear that, Karl? Clothes filling the wardrobe without the hell of shopping. You tortured poor Selene all night for nothing!"

Emily glared at Paul with a small scowl, then stuck her tongue out at him and muttered, "Shut up! Pumpkin head!"

The sorcerers gathered around her, and she embraced everyone warmly as if she had known them for a long time, welcoming them with genuine affection. When she reached her old friend, she extended her hands, and Karl clasped them in his, smiling gently as she said, "Selene?!" He didn't speak, but she heard him, nodded and added with a broader smile, "Wow, I must admit, you look very handsome, little one!" She began to rub his cheeks as she used to do in the past, then turned to walk towards the palace and said, "Alright then, let me show you your rooms first, and then..."

Karl pulled her back forcefully, making her turn towards him again and collide with his chest. He wrapped his free arm around her slender waist while still holding her hand with the other, lifting her slightly off the ground and whispered, "I haven't had my hug yet."

Everyone averted their eyes, perhaps to give them some privacy or out of embarrassment.

She smiled and wrapped her arms around his neck, and he encircled her with his other arm, pressing her back tightly as if afraid she might slip away. He swayed gently in place, closing his eyes and burying his nose in her hair, taking a deep breath and drowning in its fragrant scent. Her cheeks flushed with overwhelming happiness and contentment. Both had missed this warm embrace for a long time and finally, they found it after more than two hundred years!

Karl was not usually bold with women, but he was always bold with her. She brought out everything in his heart and the beautiful, shy corners of his personality.

She said in a playful, gentle voice, "Do you know that everyone in Fala can hear your thoughts right now?" and let out a soft laugh.

He reluctantly loosened his arms around her but still held her gently, kissed her forehead and said, "I'm sorry..."

She looked directly into his eyes with a tender and gentle expression, "Don't be, but I'm glad you're not angry with me anymore."

He replied sweetly, "You know I've never been angry with you."

As usual, her expression quickly changed back to her playful, mischievous, and charming demeanour. She rubbed his cheeks vigorously and said, "You sweet child with a big, beautiful heart," and began to pinch his cheeks.

Karl protested a bit loudly, "Damn it, Achilla, I'm three hundred and eighty years old. This is really... embarrassing!"

She laughed and commented, "Eh, you're still four hundred years younger than me!" She then pulled him along by the hand and said, "Come on, everyone, let's head to your rooms first."

She walked a bit quickly, pulling Karl by the hand, and soon they all found themselves a few inches off the ground!

Giovanni exclaimed, "Oh, oh, who's doing this?"

Achilla said, "I am. Isn't this better than walking?"

Paul said, "Whoa, this is amazing! Flying spells have always been exhausting, so I never enjoyed flying. But this is truly delightful!" Everyone expressed their satisfaction and joy.

They all moved forward, led by Achilla, who held Karl's hand, followed by the sorcerers, her assistants, then Tarah and Adnos. They passed through the palace's long gate, which seemed to open on its own. They flew through the wide, long corridors adorned with large and small artworks, colourful stone statues, marble sculptures, and large doors leading to spacious rooms, some resembling reception rooms, others like libraries, some like banquet halls, and various other rooms. They passed through a glass corridor overlooking an inner garden with beautiful fountains and scattered seating areas. The palace corridors felt like a maze, making it difficult to remember which path led where. Whenever they encountered one of the Heavenkin in the corridors, they watched them greet Achilla by placing their fingers over their hearts, then extending their palms towards her with a bow of the head, murmuring "Sarai," and she greeted them by name.

Finally, they reached a wide white stone staircase, standing in the middle of a spacious, circular, heptagonal hall with a very high ceiling, like the rest of the palace. Above it was a glass dome that looked like a mosaic due to the multi-coloured glass pieces, allowing the fractured sunlight to bathe the circular hall in magical colours that reflected on the stairs and the floor, which was a true mosaic forming beautiful depictions of mythical creatures. Thirty life-sized white stone statues of immortal souls were distributed in the corners of the hall and front of its walls, surrounding them from all directions. The stone staircase, with its mahogany wooden columns and golden arms encrusted with gemstones, split into two from the middle, one winding up to the second floor and the other to the third.

Emily let out a sigh of awe she couldn't hide as Achilla hurried them through. She was struggling to contain herself amidst this unparalleled beauty, not wanting to wander around the place like a fool with her mouth open! How she hoped this awe would soon pass.

On the second floor, the path was divided into five corridors. Achilla led them through the first one on the left, into a long corridor with high windows on their right, similar to those they had seen at the palace's facade, overlooking another part of the palace they had seen earlier and below, an outdoor garden. On their left were several reddish-brown wooden doors, spaced a bit apart, each with a different coloured stone fixed on it. A golden, ornate carpet ran the length of the corridor. They all landed on the ground, and Achilla called out, "Tarah, Adnos!" They responded, "At your service."

They stepped forward, leading the group of sorcerers. Adnos said, "Please, gentlemen." They began to guide each person to their room. Achilla walked with Karl, clinging to his arm until they stood before a door roughly in the middle of the corridor, preceded by the doors of his companions' rooms. On the door was a sparkling peridot stone that caught Karl's eye. Achilla turned to Karl and whispered, "Just like your eyes!" He felt his heart skip a beat as he looked at her angelic face.

She opened the door, revealing a spacious room with high ceilings. Most of the furniture was in shades of dark and light green, with a few pieces in yellow and others in red, arranged in an elegantly innovative harmony. To the left was a wide wardrobe, and directly ahead, a large window that looked like a glass wall occupied most of the opposite wall. It was divided into large squares by thin wooden panels running vertically and horizontally, and it had a door leading to a balcony furnished with a table, chairs, and potted flowers everywhere. The balcony overlooked a lush garden followed by a beautifully coloured forest with tall trees. Long curtains descended from the high ceiling to cover the entire glass window; the first layer was white and lacey, while the second layer was green velvet, drawn back to allow the sunlight and the beautiful view to shine through. In front of the window were several chairs, and to the right, in a corner raised by two steps, was a cosy bed. On the wall opposite the window, next to the room's door, was a small classic wooden desk and chair. Needless to say, the room was filled with paintings, vases, flowers, and artefacts, which gave it a warm and intimate feel despite its spaciousness.

Achilla pointed to the bed and said, "This is a new addition to the room. No guest who needed a bed has ever stayed in this room before. Usually, we host them in other corridors equipped for that, but I felt this room was the most suitable for you, and it has the best view." She winked at him with a smile.

He smiled at her gently, not caring where he was as long as he was near her, and joked, "How lucky I am! I apologise for any disruption to the room's beautiful design due to my urgent need to lie down for several hours a day. What was in place of the bed?" She pointed over her left shoulder to the area behind the door and in front of the wardrobe, which he hadn't noticed.

A musical instrument resembling a piano but slightly different and larger, in turquoise colour, was placed at an angle. Karl commented, "What a beautiful instrument!" and began to admire the gemstones encrusted on it.

As she walked him to the middle of the room, she said, "Although its place isn't suitable now, I didn't want to remove it from the room, knowing how much you love the piano. This isn't a traditional piano; I think you'll enjoy trying it, and... I hope you like staying here."

He wandered into the space of her sparkling eyes and didn't speak; He questioned whether her eyes reflected the entire universe or if the universe itself had been contained within them.

His leather suitcase floated into the room on its own, moving as if an invisible person were carrying it and swaying it back and forth playfully. This distracted him, and he took a deep breath to help him focus. He commented, "Even though I'm a sorcerer, this makes the place feel like a haunted castle!"

She laughed and said, "You'll see wonders from that fool, Tarah! But he's very entertaining."

Karl replied, "No doubt!"

He placed his fingertips on the golden band, "Is this like a crown for you?"

She said, "Hmm, something like that, but not exactly. It's more like military ranks. Every person of status among the Heavenkin wears a similar band, varying in thickness and engravings from person to person. Only the Guardian and his heir have stones in their bands."

He noted, "Your band doesn't have a stone!"

She replied, "Because I haven't been officially crowned yet."

He asked, his voice deep with concern, "Are you okay?"

She answered, "I'm always okay, don't worry about me."

He asked, "But didn't you run away from this for fifty years?"

She replied, "Yes, but I no longer want to run, not anymore. I've been fleeing for eight centuries, and nothing has changed. Maybe... it's time to face it!" She smiled broadly at him, the kind of smile that always made him smile back, even against his will.

Tarah cleared his throat as he stood at the door with Adnos and said, "Kashirta will kill us, Kharissa!"

Kashirta was Achilla's maid, responsible for her appearance. Achilla ignored her on the balcony when Karl and his family arrived.

Achilla sighed in annoyance, "I have to go get ready. The reception for guests arriving from outside Fala will start soon. Tarah and Adnos will stay with you to explain the arrangements, the schedule of celebrations, and the rest of the boring stuff, as you know."

She let go of his arm, stood on her tiptoes, and kissed the tip of his nose. Then she walked away, and before disappearing, she pinched Tarah's cheek, saying, "Behave yourself!"

The sorcerers all gathered in Karl's room. Emily's eyes sparkled, on the verge of tears from happiness, as she said, "A room inspired by black opal! Do you understand what that means? It's like a room from a rainbow! Like a room at the bottom of the sea surrounded by beautifully coloured coral reefs! I swear my heart can't handle all this beauty at once! Oh, I have a painting by Da Vinci!! Da Vinci painted several pieces for this palace, can you believe that?! You're not lying to me, Tarah, are you?"

Tarah said, "No, and the paintings in this room are by Michelangelo, who also has several statues in the palace, along with works by Van Gogh, Pablo Ruiz, Picasso, Salvador Dalí, Francisco de Goya, Frida Kahlo, Claude Monet, Najib Beloufa, Mustafa Al-Hallaj, Chaibia Talal, Shakir Hassan Al Said, Mahmoud Saeed, Mustafa Farroukh, Sesshū, and Emaki Azumaya, among many other earthly painters and sculptors, in addition to Heavenkin artists. The reason for the meeting of Heavenkin and Earthlings has always been art in all its forms. If there is a reason for the recent recognition of earth dwellers by the new Heavenkin, it is their artistic and technological development. Before that, the ancients saw them as a primitive species with limited intelligence."

Adnos cleared his throat and said, "My colleague means no offence; you are not just earth dwellers to us."

Tarah, realising the rudeness of his words, said, "Oh, of course, of course, I meant ordinary humans, not you. There's no need to mention the mutual cooperation between us and the sorcerers' elders and the friendly relations between our worlds."

The sorcerers nodded, pretending to understand what Tarah was talking about.

He explained the week's schedule: the first day was dedicated to welcoming guests from outside the island, which certainly included them. The second day was for welcoming guests from the island. On the third day, the coronation ceremony would take place at the sacred temple of Urbahra. After the queen performs her rituals, Achilla reveals the "Dia" energy, which will be granted to her by the immortal souls —Dia, by the way, is the gift or blessing given by an immortal soul, and it is a special power possessed by that soul —the souls would take her into the Clotho Lake in the intermediate world for three days to perform their rituals. She would emerge on the third day at three in the afternoon.

Tarah commented, "We are all eager to see what the souls will grant her. Kharissa-Achilla already possesses very unique abilities, so we believe the Dia granted to her will be rare as well. Usually, the souls grant the power of foresight, wisdom and knowledge, or control over fire or light. Among the rare powers is control over one or more elements of nature, which Kharissa already possesses. It is said that rare powers are only granted in times when the tribe is threatened by some danger or to a great soul of the guardians."

Abraham asked, "What Dia does Queen Etliea possess?"

Tarah replied, "Bissilia-Etliea possesses the power to control fire."

Giovanni asked, "What does Bissilia and... Kalissa mean? I don't know how to pronounce it."

Tarah replied, "Bissilia means queen and Kharissa—" he corrected Giovanni's pronunciation, "means... umm, there's no literal translation, but it means 'the dearly beloved' in our language."

He then continued explaining the ceremonies: "After Alika-Achilla emerges from Clotho Lake, the Sibyl Wert-Hakaou will accompany her for the rest of the day into the Urbahra Cave to conclude the coronation ceremonies, recite the previous guardians' commandments to the Heavenkin, and perform the sacred vows. On the sixth day, there will be a celebration marking the end of the ceremonies, and on the seventh day, there will be a farewell celebration for the guests from outside the island."

Emily asked, "Who are the guests from outside the island?"

Adnos answered, "They include prominent figures from the remaining two Heavenkin tribes, elders from the sorcerer's world, leaders of the Amazonian, some delegations of shapeshifters, mountain giants, sea dwellers, cave monks, and delegations of senior vampires."

Emily exclaimed in surprise, "Vampires! Didn't you hunt them down in the past to eradicate them?"

Adnos replied, "Yes, they are attending for the first time. Bissilia-Etliea decided to reconcile with them before Kharissa-Achilla was born. She saw that they had become a reality and a recognised species, and they have become more disciplined and civilised."

Karl said, "I didn't know that the elders also attended the coronation ceremonies!"

Tarah replied, "As I told you, we have close relations with the sorcerer's world."

There was a knock on the door, and then a food cart pushed by very small creatures, like children's dolls, entered. Emily exclaimed excitedly, "I didn't know that the Borrowers lived on your island. Here's another mythical creature proven to exist. How wonderful!"

Tarah replied, "Yes, dear, they are good people and excellent workers. They came to our island after it descended to Earth. Before that, it was impossible for any non-heavenly creatures to live on it due to the extreme cold. They were severely harassed by humans despite being peaceful people. We welcomed them among us, considered them part of us, and they became trusted members of our community. Now, they handle all the tasks we do in the palace, from care, management, and arrangement to construction, renovation, gardening, and all other crafts, as well as many scientific, medical, and artistic tasks. Over the years, some have even become advisors and assistants to the queen and the guardians."

Tarah and Adnos left the sorcerers for their light meal, promising to return and escort them when the ceremony began.

Emily didn't eat; she went to prepare and choose from the clothes Achilla had laid out for her. She was eager to try one on. Karl, on the other hand, had no appetite and preferred to play that piano-like instrument. He struck the keys, producing a sweet, resonant, and profoundly deep sound. At first, he played random notes, but once he grasped how to play and the sounds it produced, he decided to play a tune close to his heart—a recent piece by an Italian composer he adored. The enchanting melody that emerged was indescribable, making one's heart melt and mind reel from its sweetness. It made one believe that no beauty could surpass this and that no instrument could produce such a heavenly sound. Wasn't it a shame to keep such a magical instrument hidden in a corner of a green room, in a magnificent stone palace, on a legendary mystical island?

He followed the piece with Schubert's *The Miller and the Brook*. When he finished, feeling something he had never felt before while playing, he turned to his companions and found each of them with their mouths agape, the extraordinary sound having captivated them. They had forgotten the food before them and were frozen in place, even Paul! And that, as you know, was no ordinary feat.

It was time for the celebration. Emily donned a light pink silk dress from the array of clothes in her wardrobe. Karl was never fond of being received with the pomp of a VIP, being paraded with his family before all the Heavenkin into the hall to stand before the queen and her successor for greetings. But he resigned himself to the reality; these were their traditions, and he had to respect them. Besides, they were the only ones personally invited by Achilla, while the rest of the attendees were invited by the queen.

Tarah and Adnos escorted them to the grand hall of the palace, which had a towering gate that opened after a trumpet was blown to announce the guests' entrance. Their names were then recited as they began to cross the gate, which closed again immediately after they passed through, and so on with each guest.

Karl and his family were the last to enter, indicating they were the most important guests—one could easily imagine whose favour they enjoyed.

The trumpet was blown, the door opened, and Karl's family lined up like a flock of migrating birds, led by Karl, followed by Abraham and Paul, then Emily and Giovanni. As they crossed the gate, the names were announced: "The great sorcerer, Lord Karl, special guest of the heir Kharissa-Achilla, the future Alika of the Fala people and our source of pride, arriving from the American continent with his companions, the great sorcerer Mr. Abraham, the great sorcerer Mr. Paul, the great sorcerer Mr. Giovanni, the great sorceress Miss Emily. They all responded to the special invitation as close friends of the Crown Princess Kharissa-Achilla and wish to offer their greetings and congratulations to the queen and her heir."

They walked through the long marble corridor, drawing the curious and astonished gazes of all present. Who were Karl and his companions to hold such a place of honour with the future Alika of Fala? Karl could even see the surprise on the faces of the sorcerers elders, who had not known of their existence until now.

The corridor was slightly elevated and bordered on both sides by flowers of exquisite colours, shapes, and fragrances. The hall was filled with flowers, even cascading from the grand, beautiful chandeliers intertwined with red ribbons, making the place resemble the Hanging Gardens of Babylon. Like the palace, the hall was adorned with jewelled stones, strange statues, mosaics here and there, artworks, sparkling glass, and so much more. Yet, what was truly worthy of description was the magnificent throne.

The back of the throne was vast, like a monumental mural, crafted entirely from pure gold, upon which the Milky Way was etched in its entirety—its core and its spiralling arms. The stars, planets, nebulae, and the black hole were all studiously inlaid with varying colours, their locations pinpointed with remarkable precision. The stars themselves were embedded with individual gemstones, with a distinct colour separating the large stars from the smaller ones. There, on the edge of the galaxy, in the arm of Orion, our solar system stood out, each celestial body marked by a gem—one for the sun, one for the earth, one for the moon.

The planets were set apart from the stars with different stones and their moons with others. Their orbits were drawn in silver; even the comets and meteors were not forgotten in this grand mural. Beneath this glittering galaxy, a jewelled golden seat was placed, covered with green velvet. Below the seat extended a white stone staircase of thirteen wide steps in a semicircle, narrowing as they approached the throne.

The queen sat on the throne. It was the first time they saw her in reality, looking just as she did in Achilla's memories from seven hundred years ago, but her actual presence was more radiant and imposing. She wore an off-shoulder, velvet burgundy dress, cinched at the waist, then flaring out wide and long. Its train was so long it spread out in waves, covering the golden seat and two steps of the stone staircase. She looked like a white rose emerging from among the petals of red roses or like a magnificent marble statue. Achilla must have inherited her stunning beauty from her grandmother. What a grandmother!

Achilla knelt beside her on her right knee, raising her left in front of her, placing her palm upon it, and holding a golden staff with a gemstone head shaped like a spear with many sharp teeth in her right hand.

She wore a long silk dress of two colours, white and yellow. From below the chest to the waist, it resembled old-fashioned corsets but was a thin, engraved gold belt. The dress covered the chest and shoulders with two interwoven fabrics, yellow and white, like braids. Wide ribbons fell from the shoulders, covering the arms to the midpoint. The dress flowed wide from below the broad belt, with long slits hidden under multiple wide folds. The white fabric beneath the yellow only peeked out slightly from between the folds and varying lengths of the dress. She let it fall spread out on the ground, some parts overlapping. Her left knee protruded from one of the wide slits, revealing her leg, which looked like a piece of golden velvet. Her hair was all let down in broad waves, with only the front of the golden circlet visible above her forehead and the Jeremejevite brooch fastened over her heart.

As Karl entered, Achilla's smile widened, revealing her molars. The queen's expression remained unchanged as usual when she saw them, but Karl, who knew Achilla's face by heart, understood those features well. Her smile indicated mischief and enjoyment, with bright and cunning eyes. Karl understood; Achilla must have forced Queen Etliea to comply with her request to summon them to the island. Why did Queen Etliea agree? Did Achilla bargain that she wouldn't accept the crown princess title unless she was allowed to summon Karl and his family?

Karl saw Achilla's smile widen further as if she was about to laugh when she listened to his thoughts, and then she winked at him. It must be true, then! But (*damn, everyone here can hear the echo of my thoughts, I need to stop this now*), Karl thought. Achilla was on the verge of tumbling from her place due to her suppressed laughter. She wouldn't miss any chance to annoy that old hag. How she enjoyed that night, knowing that the icy queen had conceded against her will. She would enjoy annoying her, no matter how small the opportunity.

The queen shot her a warning glance. Finally, the sorcerers reached the queen and greeted her as Adnos had taught them: "Place your fingertips on your forehead with a slight bow of the head, then extend your arm and open your hand towards the queen, saying 'Bissilia' After that, greet Kharissa-Achilla by placing your fingers on your hearts and extending them towards her, saying 'Sarai', which means princess."

The greeting was completed peacefully, and the guest reception time ended. Achilla rose from her place and mingled with the guests, welcoming them. Then she approached her companions, accompanied by her aunt Beth-Nahra and her children, Dasha and Echor. They all looked elegant and beautiful, like a living piece of art.

Beth-Nahra said kindly, "Ah, finally, we meet the old friend. I've heard so much about you, dear Karl."

Dasha commented, "So, you are the ones who took Kanaki from us today! Kashirta almost lost her mind; Kanaki was avoiding her all the time. She managed to finish her work in record time."

Achilla said, "She loves to exaggerate. I hate that. If I hadn't escaped from her, I would have become like that fossil." Beth-Nahra pinched her ear, reminding her to mind her words.

Echor laughed and added, "But she did well in the end. You look very beautiful, Kanaki." Then he turned to the sorcerers and said, "Allow me to welcome you properly. I know we met in a... bad way." He shrugged.

Everyone smiled, feeling relieved that those strange days were now in the past. Who could have guessed that such a night would come to them?

Beth-Nahra and her daughter withdrew and mingled with the rest of the guests, leaving Echor with them.

Echor, in his wit and some of his mannerisms, resembled Achilla, but he was calmer and more serious. He acted as if he were her personal guard or caretaker, very protective of her, following her wherever she went. Karl felt a strange sensation he tried to suppress.

Karl whispered to Achilla, "That was quite an awkward moment when we entered! Did everyone hear my thoughts?"

She replied, fidgeting, "Oh, don't worry. The queen didn't allow your thoughts to spread. As soon as your thoughts started to lean in a direction she didn't like, she put a mental cover on them immediately. That old woman knows how to protect her image well."

A melancholic melody filled the air, one that Karl did not recognise, but it seemed to be one of Achilla's favourites as she immediately turned to the orchestra, completely in tune with the music. Most of the instruments were familiar to them, but some appeared strange. A tall, broad-shouldered woman with a full figure entered and stood beside the orchestra. She wore a black, off-the-shoulder dress, and her curly hair was styled in a seemingly chaotic yet beautiful and distinctive manner. The woman began to sing, her voice resembling opera but with a unique twist. Her voice was magnificent, filled with music, reaching heights no human could achieve and descending, taking hearts with it. The audience swayed, and so did Achilla. In her intense enjoyment, she clasped her hands in front of her chest, then opened them, extending her arms as if to release a dove into flight. Bright lights in blue, fuchsia, purple, and yellow burst from her hands, and the audience did the same, filling the hall's ceiling with that strange aurora, a sign of deep admiration, like applause.

Achilla said, "Ornina, you are a marvel," then turned to Karl, "I don't think any living being has a voice as beautiful as hers."

Karl, enchanted, replied, "Without a doubt!"

She finished her first song and began the second. Echor turned to Achilla, saying words that were incomprehensible except for "Kharissa," but the meaning was clear. She placed her hand in his outstretched one, and they headed to the empty dance floor.

Karl watched the strange dance, akin to an acrobatic performance! Who dances while flying in the air?!

They spun together, soaring and descending. He lifted her with one arm and set her down, spun around her while hovering, held her hand, making her spin around herself, then fly away only to return! What a strange dance! Their dance was just like them... fantastical and wonderful. They were so in sync with their peculiar dance, so... perfectly suited for each other! Karl felt a pang in his heart and tried to suppress his feelings and change his thoughts as much as possible.

Dance requests poured in for Achilla after this performance. She looked at Echor as if threatening to kill him; he was the reason for this, and she would now have to indulge everyone. Echor stifled his laughter and approached the table where the sorcerers were seated. He sat down, joking, "Only she gets dance requests, while poor me, no one even looks at my face!"

Abraham consoled him, "It's the custom; the man asks the woman to dance!"

Echor replied, "Not here, my friend."

The dance floor gradually filled with others. Finally, Karl moved from his spot, tapping Achilla's companion on the shoulder, "May I?"

She was finally in his arms. He joked, "I couldn't let your torment continue any longer!"

She laughed gently and said, "Thank you. I was really dying of boredom. I'll kill you, Echor!" Echor laughed, even though she hadn't spoken loudly; if her voice didn't reach him, her thoughts would.

Karl cleared his throat, "Well, although I can't fly with you as he did," he wrapped his arm around her waist, lifted her, and spun her around a bit, making her laugh, "I can always make you laugh like this!"

He said his last sentence in a tender, soft voice, his eyes brimming with a great flood of longing, love, and care.

She gazed at the face she had missed for so long, the one that made everything else disappear in its presence. Everything around them vanished, as it always did when they met. There was no one else in this world, just the two of them dancing to a melody that came from within their hearts. She told him in that dance, "I love you," a thousand times without speaking, and he echoed it a thousand times more. If only this moment could last forever!

The song ended, and he held her in his arms for a few moments longer, smiling mischievously, rubbing his nose against hers—despite knowing it was highly inappropriate—and said, "I hope you can put a cover on my thoughts too!" Then he turned his face away, stifling his laughter.

She smiled slyly, "Yes, I can."

Queen Etliea watched all this calmly while Echor's face was shadowed by darkness.

That long night finally ended, and Achilla promised them a journey they would never forget on the island of Fala.

The History of Fala... And an Uncertain Future!

"And in the end, we know that we loved in order to love and to break."

— *Mahmoud Darwish*

Karl woke up early, feeling his eyelids heavy from the long sleep. He had slept like a log after the party, having not slept well the night before. He stretched out on his bed for a bit, then jumped up to take a hot shower. While he was dressing, he heard a knock on the door. "Come in!"

His companions entered, all ready and energetic as well! Abraham said, "It seems you haven't prepared yet!"

Karl replied, "I'm ready." He fastened the last button on his shirt and began rolling up his sleeves.

Paul said, "I'm hungry. Are we having breakfast here or what?"

A voice from behind answered, "You will have breakfast with Kharissa-Achilla in her private room." Everyone turned towards the voice.

Tarah, with his bright smile, said, "Good morning, gentlemen. You're ready, that's good! Kharissa sent me to escort you to her."

They all headed to Achilla's room. Her door was wide and very tall, unlike theirs. The door opened to reveal a room with light colours, looking like a room above the clouds with white, sky blue, very light grey, and pale yellow. Her suite was spacious, like an apartment, not just a room, and it didn't contain much furniture, just several seats forming a sitting area near the wide balcony door. The sheer sky-blue curtains moved towards those seats as if trying to touch them with their edges, driven by the gentle breeze. A white dining table with twelve chairs was set for breakfast. The rest of the room was filled with various known and unknown musical instruments, paintings, artefacts, and yellow, blue, and white flowers, along with small exotic plants. There was a single yellow chair that allowed one to stretch their legs on it, placed in a corner of the room elevated by two steps. A few meters in front of it was something resembling a large blue screen with strange decorations on its edges. It appeared very thin and was suspended in the air by itself, with nothing holding or supporting it.

The balcony was also filled with flowers, climbing plants, and a rocking chair with a book resting on it and other books scattered around on the floor here and there.

Achilla was seated on one of the white chairs with cushions of grey and sky blue, facing the balcony. She had one hand resting near her mouth, her elbow propped on the couch, and seemed lost in thought, gazing out at the view beyond the balcony on her right. Some strands of her gypsy hair fluttered in the breeze. She had one leg crossed over the other and held a book in her other hand, resting it on her lap. Faint music filled the room, its source unknown to them.

She noticed their entrance and stood up, placing the book on the table beside her empty coffee cup, greeting them warmly: "Good morning, I hope you had a restful night."

They responded affirmatively, and Emily added, "Believe me, I haven't had a more peaceful night than this, in a room that seems straight out of the tales of One Thousand and One Nights. Who wouldn't be content?"

Achilla laughed, "I'm glad to hear that. Please help yourselves with breakfast. I hope you'll excuse me for starting a bit earlier."

As they began their breakfast, Echor entered, his hair tousled in every direction, and said, "Good morning, it seems I'm late! I thought you all would sleep longer."

He took the empty seat next to Achilla, planting a kiss on her forehead, and she patted his face gently.

Emily said, "Welcome, Echor. Will you be joining us today?"

Echor smiled charmingly, causing Emily's cheeks to flush, and said, "If you don't mind, of course!"

Emily flustered, replied shyly, "Oh, we'd be delighted to have you join us," (*Damn, he's so handsome my heart might stop!!*) she thought, becoming even more embarrassed by her own thoughts, fearing he might hear them. She hoped he was blocking her thoughts as Achilla had once told them, and she didn't notice Giovanni's frown due to her thoughts. He didn't seem to have heard anything and turned to whisper with Achilla in a strange language. Achilla nodded as if something was on her mind. Their conversation seemed somewhat serious. Achilla stood up while they were still talking and began preparing two cups of coffee from the cart beside them.

She answered a question that had been lingering in Abraham's mind without him voicing it and which had also started to occupy Giovanni's thoughts. She said, "It's a television."

They didn't understand, so she spoke in a strange language, and the blue panel moved from its place to beside the dining table and then began displaying a channel.

Giovanni commented, "Wow... So, this isn't an ancient, old-fashioned mythical island, huh?"

She laughed lightly as she handed Echor his cup, and he kissed her hand while she still held the cup, then took it from her. She returned to her seat and said, "Yes, we have very advanced technology here. We used technology long before the Earthlings, but we must admit that we benefited from some of their discoveries and works as well."

Paul, looking at the strange television, commented, "These are regular television channels. Where are the channels of the Heavenkin?"

She answered with a broad smile, "Well, that's the domain of the Earthlings only. We don't have channels; we don't broadcast news or produce movies, series, or programs. Our sports events are held in festivals attended by all Heavenkin. We created the television after the Earthlings invented it and developed it as you see, but we had communication and computing devices long before, although our uses for them are different from yours."

Emily said, "That's unfortunate, I would have loved to watch one of your films."

Achilla replied, "Films, theatre acting, and writing stories and novels are all things Heavenkin don't do. They are exclusive to Earthlings, but we enjoy them immensely! We are a people who appreciate the arts, as you know. We practice painting, sculpture, poetry, singing, and playing music. We also perform musical plays that tell our past stories. We limit ourselves to writing books on philosophy, astronomy, poetry, medicine, scientific and historical books, biographies, and stories that happened long ago. For this reason, Earthling writers hold a special place among us."

Emily asked in surprise, "Why don't you do that?"

Achilla shrugged, "We can't do everything. We don't act or make films because of our small numbers, and many responsibilities and tasks don't allow us to. Also, we can't create made-up tales!"

Emily said, "But you write poetry?"

Achilla replied, "But it's not purely fabricated from the imagination only. It's also based on real things that have happened, whatever their nature. And we certainly don't lack the skill of eloquent expression, metaphor, symbolism, parallelism, and other literary devices."

Emily said, "But what about philosophy? Philosophy relies on fertile imagination!"

Achilla answered, "And so do all the other sciences. They all require imagination. But can we say that the imagination used in crafting stories is the same—or even similar—to the imagination required for contemplating and delving into philosophy and other sciences? To be precise, I'm not entirely sure whether Heavenkins are incapable of inventing or creating stories, but it has never happened before."

Emily nodded, thinking about her words, and Achilla returned to her conversation with Echor.

Karl was glancing at them from time to time, disliking the clear closeness and harmony between them. The attention Echor was giving her was too obvious. It was clear that Echor was deeply interested in Achilla *(Of course, he is attracted to her! How could he not be?)* Karl thought to himself.

Echor was always around her, wanting to protect and help her. That was why he had accompanied the three knights and their leader, Abigail when the queen had sent them to protect her, even though he hadn't been very successful in doing so.

She also cared about him and trusted him. Could she be attracted to him too? *(No, she isn't. She definitely doesn't love him. She loves me...*

doesn't she still love me?!) Karl thought, then tried hard to push these thoughts out of his mind.

They finished their breakfast and set off on their tour of the Fala Forest. The first thing that caught their attention was the fragrant scent of the trees scattered everywhere and the vibrant colours of their leaves and plants. Some tree leaves looked like long pins, others like cones, some triangular, and others circular, and some had no shape at all. Some trees resembled banyan trees, others like linden, Asian beech, oak, pine, and camphor, bearing fruits they didn't know the names of. As they walked, they encountered pink water gushing from the ground and rising several meters like high fountains. After two hours of wandering in the magical forest, they reached a long path covered with red soil, shaded by branches of trees resembling oak but bearing beautiful multi-coloured flowers, leading to a white waterfall surrounded by trees that looked like a mix of Sakura and willow. Beside the waterfall's outlet, a wide rug was spread on the golden-red grass, with a basket placed on it.

Achilla was clinging to Karl's arm as she always did, while Echor walked with the rest of the group ahead of them, telling them about the forest and the nature of their land and plants. They listened to him, asking questions here and there.

When they reached the white waterfall's outlet, Achilla said, "We will sit here for a while to relax, then we will head to the source of the three rivers in Mount Fala." The riverbanks were filled with small flowers, some of whose petals had fallen into the water. Bright colours surrounded them from all sides, and the sweet scent kissed their noses. Small, strange-looking animals hopped around, and birds resembling colourful parrots, peacocks, hummingbirds, and swans fluttered around them, some gathering near them due to Achilla's 'magnetic' presence.

They sat on the rug, and the basket contained those fruits they didn't know the names of. Achilla commented with a gentle smile, "I thought you would like to try them."

Beside the basket was a silver pitcher and several cups. She pointed to it and said, "This contains the water from Lithi. It's the white waterfall." She picked up a cup, poured some for Karl, and handed it to him. He drank it, finding it very sweet, somewhat like sugarcane juice but tastier. He grimaced slightly as he drank it, not expecting its taste.

Achilla and Echor laughed while his companions looked at his face, waiting for his assessment. He said, "It's delicious! But very sweet, I didn't expect that." The sorcerers tried it, along with the fruits in the basket, enjoying the challenge of finding Earthly fruits with similar tastes.

Paul shouted, "I'm telling you; it tastes like banana!"

Emily retorted in frustration, "How can someone who eats all the time not tell the difference between the taste of banana and mango?"

Giovanni shrugged and said, "Actually, I think it tastes like cantaloupe!"

Emily slapped her forehead with the palm of her hand and said, "Has everyone lost their sense of taste today?!"

Abraham laughed, "It's okay, Emily. You have to admit; these fruits have a strange and rich flavour, resembling more than one fruit!"

Achilla watched this debate with great enjoyment, loving the warmth and intimacy that surrounded them.

Emily muttered after tasting a fruit that looked like cherries but tasted like chocolate, "Oh, I wish Selene were here." Her voice was filled with longing, even though she had only been away from her for one night. Everyone fell silent, and then Achilla patted Emily's knee and said, "You can take whatever you want for her from here. I'll ask Tarah and Adnos to help you with that."

Emily's eyes lit up, "Really! You would do that?"

Achilla nodded, "That's a promise, dear." Emily jumped up, hugging and thanking her.

A little later, Emily, who was interested in the history of mythical creatures, began asking Achilla about the history of the Heavenkin. "What caused their islands to descend? Why did most of the heaven's folks become extinct? Why are their numbers so few now? Why did they hide from people and keep their existence a secret? The Heavenkin hadn't suffered like the sorcerers; humans revered them. How did they manage to keep the location of their island a secret until now?"

Achilla answered that, in truth, they didn't really know despite the research they had conducted on the cause of their islands' fall. But they were very grateful that the ancients managed to prevent their island from being destroyed like most of the islands at that time. The people of Fala were the most numerous and the strongest in terms of spiritual energies among all the Heavenkin. Numbering around thirteen hundred now—slightly fewer than before.

About fifty thousand years ago, the first island of one of the extinct peoples fell and was destroyed, leading to the death of everyone on it. Heavenkin could not live without their islands, which contained their sacred temples. These temples maintained and provided their spiritual energy. No matter how far a heavenly was from their island, their connection to their sacred temple remains. However, Heavenkin naturally preferred not to stay away from their islands for long periods, as they began to feel something akin to fatigue or exhaustion due to the decrease in their spiritual energy. The other Heavenkin were shocked by this news. They didn't know the reason for the fall, whether it was something the people of that island did or something beyond their control. These questions didn't last long, as the second and third islands fell in succession, and no one still knows, not the Sibyl nor the immortal souls. But the ancients prepared for the worst.

Achilla began to recount the tale of the last immortal soul with unparalleled enthusiasm. She said, "The guardian of the people of Fala at that time was Yusa'as-Aldara, a great woman who became one of the immortal souls because of her deeds. The islands continued to disappear one after another until it was our turn. Yusa'as-Aldara had ordered the people of Fala to form large, scattered circles spread across the entire island and to release their maximum spiritual energies, entering a state of meditative slumber to sharpen and develop their energies and wrap this energy around the entire island of Fala. They were to do this until the time foretold by the immortal souls for the fall of the island. When the time came, they were to give their all to ensure the island's descent was safe and slow, preventing it from crashing and shattering. She and the Sibyl sat protecting the heart of our island (the sacred temple of Urbahra). It wouldn't harm us if the edges or most of the island were destroyed as long as the temple remained standing, so she made sure to protect it herself. They stayed like this for days and weeks, and then the final hour struck. Suddenly, a terrifying earthquake hit the island, announcing the beginning of the fall. I swear I can hardly imagine what the ancients felt as they prepared to face their fate of annihilation. The tablets that recount the story of the fall tell us that never before had the energy of the Fala people been so strong, unified, and harmonious. More than a thousand souls became like one mighty soul, with Yusa'as-Aldara at its heart. The island trembled violently, and the ground and houses cracked, but the temple remained intact. Then, it began to descend quickly at first. For a moment, the people of Fala felt helpless. A great force was pulling the island down, seeking to destroy it. At that moment, Yusa'as-Aldara let out a resounding cry from the heart of Fala, a thunderous cry that rallied the spirits of the Heavenkin, some of whom had faltered under this immense force. She released a great wave of energy with her scream, her voice piercing into the deepest corners of their hearts and minds. They heard her words, shouting inside their heads as if she were holding their very souls, shaking them violently to rouse them, as if she were telling them not to give up, to give everything they had and more until their last breath. She told them, "If we are to die, we will die as brave warriors," then let out a booming laugh. They all saw her through telepathy, sitting cross-legged on the low cliff in front of the Urbahra cave, spreading her great white wings, sparks and determination flashing from her eyes glowing with red light, and a defiant smile dancing on her lips. Every soul that had felt despair and weakness sneered at themselves in the face of this greatness, determination, and challenge and returned to give everything they could and more. And the miracle happened. The island's descent gradually slowed, but the island was high, very high, and the ground was still far away. Yusa'as-Aldara began to chant war hymns and old folk songs that told stories of courage, struggle, and great ones, as well as songs about the people of Fala, to keep their spirits up and ease the horror of the situation. And they all echoed her... they all repeated after her."

"They became nothing but a single body, a single soul, and a heart filled with life that never dies. Slowly, gradually, the island of Fala descended upon the surface of the sea in the heart of the ocean. They felt as if the water was touching the tips of their feet, not the edges of their island. They sensed it settling on the ocean's surface, gently floating, not sinking, not breaking! They had succeeded in saving their island... it did not break!

But it was not yet a time for celebration; they had to ensure their island remained firm in its place, not carried away by the waves nor gradually sinking into the heart of the ocean. Aldara called upon the immortal souls for aid, and they granted her the power to control nature. She made the ocean floor rise, lifting like a great mountain beneath the island, connecting with it from below, surrounding its borders, and anchoring it in place as if a volcano's crater embraced the island's edges with love.

Everyone leapt from their places, cheering at last, despite their extreme exhaustion. Their eyes were drowned in tears; nothing could describe their happiness. They released threads of energy everywhere, filling the sky above them with vibrant colours resembling the aurora. As for Yusa'as-Aldara, she could no longer bear it and fell from the cliff, unconscious, into the Lake of Clotho, disappearing for seven days.

The people of Fala were worried about her. She had expended a great part of her spiritual energy, nearly killing herself. For it is the spiritual energy that makes our hearts beat after all, and the amount of spiritual energy a heavenly body possesses determines its lifespan and the preservation of its body. They wondered if she had exhausted all her spiritual energy to protect the people of Fala.

After seven days, Yusa'as-Aldara emerged from the Lake of Clotho in a radiant form with enchanting spiritual energy. She was surrounded by a brilliant aura emanating from the high spiritual energy within her body, captivating all eyes with its beauty. She bid farewell to the people of Fala, informing them that the immortal souls had called her to join them in the world of Clotho, and she had accepted. She then performed the rituals to transfer the guardianship to her heir, King Evim and returned to Clotho, where she continues to protect the people of Fala to this day.

Since that incident, the immortal souls began granting divine gifts, the 'Dia' to the guardian of the people of Fala according to the needs of the people during their period of protection. Yusa'as-Aldara had great abilities from the start, as she possessed the Wings of Light, which allowed her to revive all the legendary creatures. Can you imagine?

Cadmus, the sea dragon; Behemoth, the land dragon; Aetos, the great golden eagle; Pegasus, the winged horse; Khalykon, the storm birds; and Adria, the giant serpent of darkness. She controlled them all!

They all turned to stone after Yusa'as-Aldara departed to the world of Clotho, and their statues remain in the cave of Urbahra to this day. They never came back to life, as she was the last to possess that ability.

The remaining two islands were able to benefit from our experience after we informed them, but they suffered greater losses due to their smaller numbers. Half of the island of the Demogorgon people was destroyed, while the temple of the Alcibiades people was the only structure that survived, though it sank. The survival of their temple allowed the energy to continue flowing through their bodies, albeit gradually diminishing. They moved to the island of their allies, the Demogorgon, awaiting their slow demise. However, they discovered that they could live off the energy of the Demogorgon temple as well after adapting to it. The sudden cessation of spiritual energy flow in the extinct peoples, due to the destruction of their temples, led to their extinction before they could adapt to other temples like the Alcibiades people."

She also told them that their small numbers were due to their low reproduction rate. A heavens being could not have more than two children, and a female carries for five years before giving birth. Several years had to pass before she could conceive again. A heavenly body did not fully mature until they reached one hundred or one hundred and fifty years old. They might be fifty years old but appear as a fourteen-year-old teenager! They do not consider marriage until they are over five hundred years old. However, their long lifespans, eternal youth, and abilities protected them from extinction and ensured their continuity, even though most tribes have perished.

The Heavenkin kept their islands hidden under walls of spiritual energy, which you could liken to a bubble, keeping them invisible to the eyes of humans and undetectable by modern devices.

"There was a time when we lived among the earthlings and mingled with them easily, but over time, the earthlings began to revere and even worship us because of our abilities. Eventually, they started seeking our help with their personal matters, asking for our assistance when they were sick when their crops were damaged, or when they were wronged, and we did help. However, they began to bother us with their wars, disputes, and killings. Gradually, we distanced ourselves from them. The ancients had enough of their own conflicts with other Heavenkin. All Heavenkin chose to distance themselves from the earthlings until they were forgotten, and time took care of everything. Our stories became mere legends about Greek, Assyrian, and Egyptian gods, among others."

Emily asked, "Did you also fight among yourselves?"

Achilla replied, "Certainly. Each island contains different resources and treasures, and every tribe wanted to extend their dominion over them and benefit from them. But we were always the strongest and most peaceful of the Heavenkin peoples."

Giovanni interrupted the history lesson after accidentally spilling a cup of water on Emily's dress. She chased him with a fork, aiming for his neck! Echor and Paul turned over laughing, followed by Abraham, who laughed but also wanted to save poor Giovanni before Emily could stab him to death.

Achilla laughed so hard that tears streamed down her face while Karl chuckled softly, shaking his head at the spectacle. He looked at Achilla sitting beside him, her laughter making everything around them shine and sparkle. He placed his finger on her cheek, wiping away the tear that had fallen from her laughter. She turned to him, rested her head on his shoulder, and hugged his arm tightly. He placed his cheek on her forehead and said, "How about another walk together?" She nodded in agreement, and they stood up.

They walked along the White River, her arm linked with his, leaving their friends behind. They walked in silence for a while before he finally said what he had been holding back for a long time: "You and Echor seem very close."

She replied with a sly smile, "Oh... so you're jealous?"

She hit the nail on the head, making Karl feel embarrassed and flustered. How could he hide anything from her or even from him? Karl cleared his throat and said, "That isn't my place anymore... I know that, and maybe it never was." He kept looking down, avoiding her gaze. She sighed and said, "Oh Karl, Echor is my friend and cousin. There's nothing between us."

Something danced within his chest, an involuntary joy curling the corners of his lips upward as he said, "But that doesn't mean he's not interested in you!" He added with a hint of pride, knowing that, once upon a time, he had been the one to win her heart.: "Though I can't blame him... poor thing!"

She looked at him with a small, playful frown and a smile, tugging at a lock of his hair and said, "When did you become so mean?"

He laughed heartily.

After his moment of pride subsided, he thought for a moment and said in a serious tone, "But I still think you two are very close, and... I think your feelings for him are strong... why didn't... why didn't anything happen between you?"

She said, "Yes, Echor means a lot to me. He, Dasha, and my aunt Beth-Nahra were the only ones who stood by me after my mother was killed. They put in their efforts, searched for me when I left, and brought me back.

I was very close to them before my mother was killed, but I distanced myself from them afterwards. Despite my isolation, they always held good feelings towards me.

After what happened between you and me, they got closer to me, and Echor, in particular, never abandoned me.

I had changed after you... I no longer found solace in solitude as I once did. It became more intense, and I became more irritable. Echor stayed by my side despite all the bad things I did at times... he understood me... accepted me and accompanied me when I left Fala for the second time after we parted ways.

Our bond only grew stronger. He became someone I respect, someone I trust.

He helped mend, if only slightly, the break in my heart.

He became a true friend to me. Through him, Dasha, and my aunt Beth-Nahra, I was able to feel, even if just a little, like I still had a family.

Nothing happened between us because I don't see him that way and Echor is a very respectful man. He knows how I feel about him, and he never tried to express anything."

Karl commented, "Because you already know how he feels anyway!"

She replied, "Yes, I know... but it's not like that. He struggles to hide it a lot. We can suppress thoughts, as I told you, but it's hard for us to block the emotions that reach us. It depends on the person's ability to conceal them."

After a few steps, Karl said in a low voice, "I think you have deeper feelings for him than you realise."

She replied sarcastically, "What now! Are you playing matchmaker?"

He didn't answer, and after a moment, he added playfully, "Well! I finally understand why you insist on calling me a child. You don't mature until you're a hundred years old, huh?"

She tightened her arms around his, rested her head on his shoulder and said, "Yes, my little child, you were only seventy years old. You were truly a child!"

He joked, shrugging his shoulders, "Many would love to hear that, believe me!"

Cries erupted behind them. Giovanni had thrown himself into the river to prove to Emily that it was okay for her clothes to get a little wet, but he was surprised by the high, sticky density of the water. It was as if he had fallen into a cup of condensed milk slightly diluted with water. His eyes burned, and he choked on the very sweet water. Echor and Paul were still laughing while Emily shouted, obviously concerned for Giovanni, "Give me your hand, you stupid fool! I can't go any further; my dress will get dirty. Abraham, help this idiot, don't just stand there!"

Abraham had his face in his hand, and his other arm crossed over his chest, despairing of his friends. Karl sighed and turned to them, "For the love of—! Giovanni, what's gotten into you, man? Since when have you been this reckless?"

They finally pulled Giovanni out of the Lithi River. He was completely sticky, covered in a milky layer, so they had to return directly to the palace, cutting the tour short.

Emily said, "Oh Giovanni... we couldn't go to the river's source because of you."

Echor said, "Don't worry about it, you didn't miss much. We'll go there later."

Paul asked, "So... what do the other two rivers taste like?"

Emily muttered, "That's what matters to you, you glutton!"

Echor replied, "The blue one tastes like incense water, and the golden one... well, you wouldn't like it. It's bitter but useful in medicinal serums."

Giovanni, unable to open his eyes due to the burning sensation, asked, "Do you get sick?"

Echor answered, "Of course! We are living beings, too. We may not get fatal diseases, and our immunity is strong, with high healing abilities, but we do get sick. Though our illnesses are different from yours, we get injured just like you."

Giovanni added, "We can die in some fatal car accidents and natural disasters!"

Echor laughed, "Yes, I know. We are a bit tougher than you."

They reached the palace, and Giovanni went to his room to shower. The rest gathered in Karl's room, joined by Tarah and Adnos, while Achilla and Echor disappeared.

After Giovanni finished, they took him on a tour around the palace. When it was time for lunch, they went to a large hall with a big, long table that accommodated all the guests. The queen sat at the head, and Achilla was at the opposite end. They sat next to her on the left side, and Echor sat to her right, while Beth-Nahra and Dasha sat to the right and left of Queen Etliea. Echor and Achilla were whispering in their language, having a serious conversation like in the morning. Karl felt something was bothering them. After lunch, they all went to the palace's inner garden, while the guests went to the back garden with the queen.

Karl finally decided to intervene and asked, "Is something wrong?"

Achilla seemed a bit lost in thought, and Karl's question seemed to distract her. She said, "No... I don't really know. We're bothered by the absence of the Demogorgon and Alcibiades tribes from the coronation ceremony despite the queen's invitation! They didn't even send an apology for not attending, which is strange... and rude!"

Karl asked, "What do you think?"

Achilla shrugged indifferently, but Echor answered, "We had a bad relationship with the Demogorgon people in the past, which stopped after our previous help during the island's fall. Without the information we provided, they would have faced extinction. But the relationship remained tense despite that. We still believe they haven't abandoned their aggressive nature."

Achilla said, "Oh, come on, Echor, they can't do anything to us. They're not that foolish!"

Echor, deep in thought, said, "I don't know, I don't like this, Kanaki. I feel something bad."

Achilla commented sarcastically with a broad smile, "It's just your warrior spirit, Prince of Warriors, Ajax."

Echor bared his teeth and scrunched his nose at her, playfully objecting to her words.

Karl muttered, "Prince of Warriors, Ajax?"

Achilla replied, "Yes, Echor is the Prince of the Warriors of Fala. Ajax is one of his titles, meaning the strong warrior."

Karl shook his head, "I can never wrap my head around your titles. One moment, you're Kharissa, then you're Sarai, then Kanaki, and then Alika. I've heard other strange titles, too!"

Achilla explained, "Well, look, Kharissa or Kharis is like saying dear or darling, used out of politeness and respect. Sarai means princess, a formal title or rank used only on official occasions. Alika is a title held by every protector of the people of Fala. The other titles like Kanaki, Inanna, and Khalykon are names or titles given by the Heavenkin to each other, either because of their traits or abilities... Do you understand?"

He nodded, "Yes, but it's still... confusing!"

****

In the evening, they attended a reception for guests from the island of Fala. They welcomed a few guests of scientific standing, then Chief Physician Lashon, followed by the great temple knight Abigael and his three knights. Next came the Prince of the Warriors of Fala, Echor, accompanied by five warriors. They looked splendid in their green attire, which incorporated pieces of black leather, their golden armour, and heavy black cloaks that hung from their shoulders but did not touch the ground, hovering a few inches above it. This was the first time Echor wore his golden ring. Finally, they welcomed the temple seer Sibyl Wert-Hakaou and her two junior Sibyls, one with a tattoo under her right eye and the other with a tattoo on her forehead, identical to Wert-Hakaou's tattoos. One of them would become the high oracle of the sacred temple of Urbahra in the future after completing the remaining three tattoos, each symbolising a specific ability.

The celebration finally ended, but they enjoyed it more than the first one, as it was less tense for them.

Karl went to his room and changed out of the clothes Achilla had chosen for him. He had to admit—he looked remarkably elegant in them. He lay down for a while but didn't feel like sleeping, so he got up and went out to the balcony. He opened the door, took a deep breath, and looked at the curtain of twinkling stars in the sky, his hands in his pockets, the fragrant scent of Fala's trees filling his chest. A voice whispered to his right, "It's beautiful, isn't it?"

He turned quickly, surprised, "Achilla! What are you doing here?"

She was sitting on the edge of his balcony railing, leaning her back against the wall, one knee drawn to her chest with her elbow resting on it and her other leg dangling in the air. She answered softly, looking at the sky, her eyes reflecting the starlight, "I missed you."

He approached her and pulled her inside the balcony, his eyes filled with tenderness and longing, "How long have you been waiting here? Why didn't you knock on the door?"

She replied, burying her head in his chest, "For two hundred years."

He hugged her tightly and said, "Oh, you shouldn't have done that. What if I hadn't come out to the balcony?"

She answered, "It's okay. It was enough for me to feel close to you and watch your dreams... like last night."

His eyes widened in surprise as he tried to look at her face, "Last night?!"

She let out a soft laugh, then turned to look inside his room at the heavenly piano, saying, "Will you play for me?"

He played for her the melody that had echoed in his mind the day he saw her standing by his kitchen window. Then, he played other tunes he remembered she loved. She joined him, her fingers dancing over the keys in harmony with his. And then, she sang.

Her voice was pure, rich with emotion, carrying an aching beauty that wrapped around him, seeping into his very soul. He did not understand the words, yet they filled him—reached deep into his heart, weaving a tapestry of love, longing, sorrow, and pain.

Unconsciously, he stopped playing. Her voice lingered in the air, unbound and haunting. He sat in silence, breathless, listening. Until the final note faded into the night.

With an unsteady voice, he asked, "What do the lyrics mean?"

She answered:

"I exist in nowhere
With a warm cup of coffee, I await our meeting beyond time
A sorrowful date, lost outside of time
No place for us, no time
Does that mean nothingness?

I saw you in a world that is not mine
You always fill that empty chair before me
I loved you with a heart that does not know from what existence it drew its love for you…
You exist only within me
You are nowhere but inside me
And love holds no truth for me except with you

Oh, the sorrow!
A lost scene. my scene
A sad scene, my scene

As I wait for you with a warm cup of coffee
In no place, in no time...

A great and profound sadness grips me
When I find myself standing on the margins of life
No path leads me to it...
No path leads me to you...
How to arrive?

Do all people feel this loneliness?
What is loneliness?
Is it the shoulder you long to rest your head upon without reason, yet never find?
Or is it the one who laughs with you deeply...
Who gazes into your face
And sees the world within you, as you see the world within them... yet never comes?

Is it the distant companion who has forgotten us?
Or the grieving family?
Or... is it yourself?

What is it?

Ah... do we regret the choices we made?
Do we regret choices we do not even remember?
Oh, my God... is it possible to return and undo what we have done before life itself?
I have chosen wrong...

How I long to be a bird…
To soar high, to sing endlessly…
But life does not work that way.
So be it…

But do not abandon me, my God…
For I am deeply sad… unbearably lonely…

Oh, my God, how strong I seem…
Yet I am like a mighty ship with no sea
A train with no track
A body with no heart
A bird with no sky…

For birds, even when they land… their home is the sky.
Their salvation is the sky.
Their freedom and fate lie in the sky.
So what is a bird to do with wings but no sky?
Give me a sky… or take my wings away."

In a low voice, he said, "It's beautiful… and so very sad."

She replied, "Yes, I wrote it a long time ago. It doesn't sound as good after translation." She laughed.

He took her hands and kissed them, then hugged her and planted several more kisses on her forehead and said, "I'm so sorry… sorry for being gone so long… for not remembering."

She said, "What are you apologising for, you fool? It's not your fault… it's not our fault." Her voice broke.

He shed a tear, unable or unwilling to speak. What could he say?

Should he lament fate... Or just their own misfortune? What could he say now when words had already died?

No language could express what he felt...

His only solace was that she knew.

Her torment was that she knew!

How she longed to weep like him; she had needed this for so long but couldn't... Is there anything harder than being unable to cry?

After a while, he said, "Did you know they're planning trips to Mars?"

She laughed deeply and looked up at him, "That's a bit far from the temple of Urbahra!" She wiped his tears, and everything seemed easier after she laughed.

She said, "You need to sleep now. The Clotho Lake rituals will start early."

He said, "You'll be gone for three days."

She nodded. He sighed and commented sarcastically, "Don't they allow companions?"

She kissed the tip of his nose and said, "Goodnight."

He said, "Stay with me... just a little longer... until I fall asleep."

He slept on her lap that night. She watched him as he drifted into a deep sleep, murmuring, "My beautiful baby, oh my little one." She ran her fingers through his hair, memorising every small detail of his face. She hummed softly when he stirred, and when the first light of dawn appeared, she gently placed his head on the pillow and left.

After a few hours of sleep, Karl woke up and looked around for Achilla. She wasn't there, but he could still smell her scent on the pillows, so he hugged them tightly and inhaled deeply. He looked out the window; the sun had just risen, and the sky still held that rosy hue. He quickly changed his clothes and headed to her room, having tried to remember the way.

He stood before the door, hesitating for a moment before slowly pushing it open, hoping he wasn't about to intrude upon the wrong room. A delicate melody drifted to his ears, and he caught a glimpse of the interior. Good—he hadn't made a mistake.

He entered slowly and closed the door behind him, scanning the empty room before moving to look out onto the balcony.

There she was.

Balanced on one leg atop the stone railing, her posture resembled a yoga stance. Her folded foot rested against the knee of her supporting leg, arms pressed together before her chest. She wore loose, flowing white trousers and an oversized white shirt that was buttoned carelessly, fluttering with the breeze. Her hair was tied up in a messy bun.

Seeing her like this reminded him why he always felt a strange sense of nostalgia whenever he saw someone practising yoga or tai chi. He remembered one of the few times he had seen her perform these rituals, right at the first light of dawn, ending when the sun's light spread across the horizon in a pinkish-blue hue.

Yoga wasn't known in his country at that time, and he was amazed by those strange movements. She moved her arms and legs as if speaking to the wind, drawing circles in the air, bending and twisting like a piece of clay as if she had no bones in her body. Then she would stand on one leg for a while, frozen like a statue.

He had asked her back then what she was doing. She had told him it was the Meditation Slumber Ritual—a practice to sharpen spiritual energy, one that some earthling peoples also adopted long ago, having learned it from Heavenkin peoples.

He waited a bit until she emerged from her meditative dormant. She turned to him with a broad smile and said, "Oh, you're here! Good morning." She jumped off the railing, stood in front of him, and rubbed his cheeks, "Did you sleep well?" He replied, "Like a baby!" She laughed and asked, "Coffee?" to which he replied, "Please."

She started preparing two cups of coffee and said, "We need to start getting ready soon. I'm sure Dasha will storm into my room any moment now." He hesitated a bit but decided to ask, "Is there… is there no hope for us? Ever? Is there no way… for us… to…" and he went silent.

She listened quietly while her back was turned to him. She finished preparing the cups, turned to him, and handed him one, her smile was soft, filled with unspoken emotions, but her eyes… her eyes were like the void itself.

She said, "It's too late for such talk, my dear. We each have different paths now. We belong to two different worlds, like parallel lines. There's no place for one of us in the other's world. They say that if the lines were to meet, it would mean destruction… a disruption of nature's order. I would have given everything for you… except your life!

I loved you and will always love you, but that won't change reality…."

She fell silent for a moment, then her smile widened, though it did not reach her eyes.

"You have a beautiful family now," she said softly. "A family you cannot live without… a family you would never abandon or hurt… Live, Karl… live, and be happy."

Her last words silenced him. He had never been a selfish man, but was his love for her, his desire to have her in his life, truly selfish? Why had he even asked a question he already knew the answer to? It was futile—pointless... but what could a helpless person do?

Doesn't a fish thrash on the deck of a boat, fighting death until the last moment, despite the futility? Doesn't a sheep kick after being slaughtered, despite the futility? Why did he still cling to hope, knowing it was futile?

The door swung open: "Rise and shine, beautiful! Today, I'm in charge of your hairstyle... Good morning, Karl."

Dasha entered energetically, showing no surprise at Karl's presence. He did not realise that she had chosen this moment specifically to end the sad conversation between them. It was coronation day; there was no room for a bad mood today!

Achilla shook her head in annoyance and sat on the white chairs and said, "For heaven's sake, leave me alone."

Dasha didn't care. She stood opposite the table, placing one hand on her chin and the other crossed over her chest, putting her weight on one leg, and tilted her head, studying her. "Hmm... let's see... I think an updo would be very suitable," she said. Suddenly, Achilla's hair began to move in the air by itself, as if an invisible person was undoing, lifting, twisting, and tying it.

Achilla shook her head slightly, "Ah... stop that... not now!" Her hair fell back onto her shoulders. Dasha plopped onto the edge of the seat, her posture straight and hands resting on her knees, her impatience barely contained.

Achilla pretended to ignore her until Dasha started tapping her foot on the ground. Achilla commented, "Oh, Dasha! At least wait until Kashirta arrives!" Dasha fidgeted in her seat, then leaned back, resigned.

Karl was still standing, sipping his coffee slowly. He didn't feel that their conversation was over. There were still words stuck in his throat, things he wanted to say, but the timing was wrong.

Would it be too late if he said them later? But too late for what? That foolish feeling called hope —did it not know logic? What did he really want to say after all? Was there anything left to say to her? Or was it just a pathetic desire to hold on to her, to stay near her for as long as he could?

His train of thought was interrupted by the door opening again. A very small woman, like a doll, entered. She was one of the Borrowers and looked very charming with her hair styled in high layers resembling Victorian-era hairstyles. She clapped her hands and said in her very high-pitched voice, "Good morning, everyone! To work, to work! We have a long day and a lot of work... no time!"

Achila sighed in boredom, while Dasha jumped up with excitement. Karl cleared his throat, "I'm afraid I have to leave now, ladies," he said, stepping forward and placing the cup on the table. "I'll see you soon." He smiled at them and left.

****

The sky seemed slightly cloudy this morning. Karl gazed at it for a while, wondering, *Has her mood darkened, or is this just a coincidence?*

He didn't know that Fala's climate was always mild and that it never rained there naturally due to the energy surrounding the island, which repelled clouds, rain, and storms. Only an unnatural force could attract them!

He looked ahead at the sacred temple of Urbahra. Finally, they were able to stand there in reality. It looked exactly as they had seen it in their memories, and standing there felt awe-inspiring.

They were all dressed in white. Karl's eyes fell on Echor, whose chest was visibly rising and falling with his breaths. Was he nervous? Why?

Queen Etliea emerged, and the attendees performed the same greeting they had seen before, murmuring "Bissilia," as did the sorcerers. She wore a white silk dress and spoke in a language that all the guests could understand, out of respect for them. When she settled in her stance with a gentle smile, she said, "Dear guests and the great people of Fala, today we witness one of our most important rituals, the ceremony of appointing the successor to the Guardian of Fala. The people of Fala have performed these rituals for thousands of years, and our traditions that have preserved our existence for centuries continue. Today, we continue the journey, writing a new chapter in the glorious history of Fala."

She stepped aside slightly, extending her arm towards the cave's entrance behind her as if summoning someone from within.

"Let us pray," she continued, "for a prosperous future that preserves our glory, rituals, and laws and propels us forward. Let us pray for ourselves and for the generations yet to come, to whom we owe the sacred duty of passing down Fala's civilisation, values, and history, just as they were passed down to us by those who came before us."

Achilla emerged wearing a sky-blue silk dress with hints of dark blue cascading from a thin, intricately engraved golden armour that covered her upper body except for her arms. Long, open sleeves extended from under the armour, revealing her arms and reaching the ground. Her hair was swept up in an elaborate, wavy style, with loose strands—both short and long—framing her face, and a circlet with a sparkling gem was fixed on her forehead.

Her expression was emotionless, just like her grandmother's.

She was followed by the temple Sibyl, Wert-Hakaou, who sat cross-legged in front of the cave's entrance. She placed the staff she carried in front of her, clasped her hands in front of her chest, bowed her head, and closed her eyes.

Achilla stood facing the queen. Above them, the clouds thickened.

For a brief moment, they exchanged glances, as if a silent conversation was passing between them. Then, Queen Etliea raised her hands and placed her fingertips on Achilla's head, and the chanting began.

The queen, the Sibyl, and the attendees all chanted together. Everyone clasped their hands like the Sibyl, the guests hesitated at first but soon followed the people of Fala—albeit without chanting.

Achilla remained still, her gaze fixed on the queen, who met her stare unwaveringly.

After a while, the Sibyl Wert-Hakaou grasped the staff in front of her and struck its rounded head on the ground with moderate force.

Everyone stopped and opened their eyes. The queen lowered her right hand and made a fist with her left, directing it towards Achilla. She wore a strange ring, large and rectangular, black with raised engravings. Achilla murmured in a voice only the queen could hear, "You will regret this one day..." and lifted the corner of her mouth in a mocking, defiant smile.

Everyone recited a short phrase in unison, loud and clear, unlike the previous chants. When they finished, the queen placed the ring on Achilla's neck, right where the queen herself bore a rectangular tattoo upon her own neck.

As she did, Achilla's face contorted, and the sound of muffled thunder rumbled through the heavens.

The queen held the ring there for several seconds before lifting it, leaving Achilla's neck marked with the same tattoo as the queen's. Achilla murmured again, "My reign will change everything you fought to preserve in yours."

The queen, with the unwavering confidence of a proud grandmother, whispered, "You will do everything in the best interest of the people of Fala." Achilla gave her an inscrutable look.

The surface of Lake Clotho began to ripple and grow more turbulent. The queen stepped aside to stand next to the Sibyl, who had risen to her feet. Achila turned to face the audience and stood at the edge of the cliff. Then the souls emerged from Lake Clotho, this time in the form of spectral orbs, spiralling upwards until they surrounded Achilla, swirling around her. More souls emerged, and an aura of energy enveloped Achilla. Her arms extended, raised to shoulder level, her head tilted back, and she began to rise gradually from the cliff, lifted by the souls. The aura around her grew stronger and stronger as she ascended. The threads of energy around her started to coalesce, forming a shape around her body.

The shape that would appear would represent one of the immortal souls, indicating that it would grant her its special "Dia" and remain bound to her throughout her guardianship of the people of Fala.

Then something unimaginable happened! A blinding light shone, forcing everyone to shield their eyes. When the light dimmed and the scene became clear, they saw two enormous, radiant wings of light behind Achilla. She lowered her arms and returned her head to its natural position, and a red light glowed in her eyes.

Achilla truly embodied everything mythical in this scene; a magnificent aura, enormous wings, light radiating everywhere, hovering in the air, sparkling and dazzling.

The audience felt the weight of this formidable soul, and the guests fell to their knees instinctively. Half of the people of Fala gaped in disbelief at the soul that had appeared. Those who comprehended began the gesture of reverence: three fingers on their bowed foreheads, a semicircle to their hearts, and a strike to the chest with their fists. Then they extended their palms towards Achilla, releasing threads of energy and chanting:

"Yusa'as-Aldara."

Everyone followed suit—the attendees, the knights and their leader, the warriors, the Sibyl, and the queen—all without exception, turning the sky above them into an aurora.

Achilla closed her glowing red eyes and bowed her head, gradually descending into Lake Clotho. She entered the lake slowly—her legs, then her torso, then her chest and neck, until she was entirely submerged beneath Clotho's surface... and the aura vanished.

Echor turned the pages of the book that had been placed on the rocking chair he was sitting on in the wide balcony filled with flowers. It was a poetry book containing the complete works of the poet Farouk Gouida. The pages had become worn from frequent reading; she must have memorised it by heart by now, yet she continued to read it.

The soft music still played in the room. Echor smiled to himself (*only Achilla would leave the music playing in her room even when she was away*). He leaned back on the wooden chair and recalled a conversation they had long ago when he saw her holding the old book, a deep sadness in her eyes.

He said, "I don't understand! Of all the poets in the world, and all the types of poetry you've read, why do you like free verse?"

She looked at him and gave him her enchanting, sarcastic smile, her eyes holding back sorrow, and said, "Because it's free."

He nodded, smiling, then asked, "Alright... but why this poet in particular?"

She turned her face away, looking at the horizon, hugging the book to her chest. After a while, she murmured:

And I remain alone, suffocating my longing
In my chest, only to be saved by nostalgia…
And there are thousands of miles between us,
And destinies that wished to separate us…
Then it ended… whatever was between us
And I remained alone,
Gathering memories, fragile threads
And I saw my days slipping away,

Not knowing what they were.
And you left, O my world, a wound that time will never heal,
And deep within, I folded a heart that once beat... with yearning.
Had I known that I would melt in longing,
Had I known that I would become something of nothing,
I would have remained alone,
Singing poems in a distant world...
I didn't realise that I would become a lost soul,
With sorrow in my heart,
And wounds deep within my body...
Tell those who will come after me:
This was fate's decree,
A destiny that wanted our meeting,
Then it ended, whatever was between us,
And I remained alone, for suffering.

She paused for a moment, then recited another poem:

And your lips stuttered, O my mother, and words turned against them
And I saw your voice seep deep into my soul, flowing... in melancholy
And tears scarred your eyes over remnants... from a time
The last words I heard with goodbye:
God bless your steps, my son,
God be with you, my son,
And our voices embraced in tears
As the sun gathered its light at sunset, between the hills...
I went, O my mother, a stranger in life,
How the yearning for you pulled me during prayer...
We used to pray it together,

O Mother...
The first thing I knew about life
Was to offer people peace,
But now, I am here, O my mother,
Alone, a stranger... amidst the crowd...
And I grew, O my mother... and embraced love,
And knew all the shades of love...
But my heart's pulses shattered one day,
When love itself died.

Her voice cracked, and she fell silent, struggling to contain the emotions rising within her. After a while, she whispered, "How could I not love a poet like this?"

He opened his eyes and resumed flipping through the poetry collection, reading whatever caught his eye. Did Farouk Gouida know her? Or was he just as unfortunate? Doesn't sorrow, in the end, resemble itself?

Her sorrow for her mother, her sorrow for her love, and his sorrow for her... and for his love for her.

Oh, how much he loved her! And for how long has he loved her?

Since the moment he first laid eyes on her, the day she opened her eyes to this life for the first time, he was always around her, watching her, protecting her, making her happy, and loving her.

Who among them truly suffered the agony of love? Which was more tormenting to the heart; a love that was impossible, or a love that is one-sided?

He sighed deeply, recalling the events of the previous morning. For Achilla to possess the power of Yusa'as-Aldara is a significant matter! And what does it mean for her to have this power? Are the old tales true, that the Dia will be according to the needs of the people of Fala in the future?

Today was Achilla's second day in the world of Clotho. She would stay there for five days, not three, for a strong and rare Dia like this would not conclude its rituals in three days like ordinary Dia. Something was bothering Echor... a bad feeling had been haunting him for days, and he didn't know its nature. His feeling worsened after seeing Achilla's Dia... but why?

Queen Etliea...

*"Inside me is a balcony,
Through which no one passes to greet me."*

— Mahmoud Darwish

Etliea wandered aimlessly through the palace corridors; something troubled her since the immortal soul that accompanied her had left to guide Achilla through the rituals of the world of Clotho, and she didn't know why.

(Oh, my dear Achilla... I always knew you would be someone of great importance, possessing much, and giving much to the people of Fala. I am certain you will achieve what I could not. The fate of the great is to be unhappy, isn't that what history has taught us? They give and do not take, and I took from you without giving, but fate took from me as well. It took my beloved child and by my own hands...

How could I explain to you? What should and should not be... The customs, the laws... None of this concerns you... I hoped you would understand one day, but you did not, and you will not. You still see the world only through your own eyes; you have your own sense and your own way of everything...

I know you will break many laws and customs; you are meant for that! Not everyone has the destiny or the ability to set or abolish laws, to establish or eliminate rules and foundations, and to create a path for life that others will follow. Only the great can do that... and yesterday confirmed my belief.

That's why I was so keen on your return, despite your hatred for me... How hard it is to see hatred in your eyes for me, but... it was my duty, dear, to make you understand; the meaning of mistakes, their consequences and the meaning of being a protector... a guardian, To place others before yourself, your desires, your comfort, and your emotions...

To harm yourself, to shield them from harm...

That is the duty of a guardian...

If only you knew... how my home became my prison after your mother's death... after I killed my daughter...

If only you knew... How it kills me slowly every day to feel that I sent my daughter... my beautiful daughter... my tender, loving daughter...... into a world of eternal abyss... by my own hands...

If only you knew...

But there is no regret... no regret...)

The echo of sorrowful thoughts resonated behind that icy face as she watched the Urbahra Temple from one of the palace windows overlooking it. Despite all this pain, Etliea never regretted any decision she made for Fala and its people.

She stood there for a while, gazing at the temple, feeling an inexplicable urge to go there. She decided to follow it.

Etliea walked briskly. Beth-Nahra saw her and called out, wanting to ask about some preparations needed after Achilla's return from Clotho. But Etliea was too preoccupied to hear her! Something mysterious was pulling her strongly towards the Urbahra Temple. Beth-Nahra was puzzled and followed her; with Dasha by her side; she kept calling out, "Bissilia... Bissilia...", but there was no response!

Echor heard his mother's worried voice as they passed by Achilla's room, calling for the queen. He placed the book on the rocking chair and left the room, finding his mother and sister hurrying after the queen, who was ahead of them. They quickened their pace, and the bad feeling inside him intensified, so he hurried to follow them.

Etliea exited the palace's back garden with quick steps, almost running, but she managed to control herself, although with difficulty. She passed by the sorcerers who were accompanying the elders of the sorcerers, exchanging conversations with them, along with some other guests spending the afternoon there.

One of the guests jumped from his seat, wanting to address the queen, "Your Majesty..." he called, but she did not respond and hurried on. The guest stood bewildered by her behaviour, watching Beth-Nahra and Dasha following her with worried faces, and then Echor, too! What was the reason for this tension surrounding them all, and where were they rushing off to?

Karl jumped from his place, "Echor, what's going on?"

Echor waved his hand without looking at him, in an incomprehensible gesture, and Karl followed him instinctively, along with the sorcerers, the elders, and the guests followed as well!

A crowd of people was now hurrying through the forest, none of them knowing why. From the path they were taking, it was clear they were heading toward the Urbahra Temple... but why?

Was it right for them to follow without knowing the reason? Perhaps it was a personal matter? But no one stopped them, and curiosity surrounded them all!

Etliea stopped several meters from Lake Clotho, her breathing quickening with rising anxiety. She looked at Wert-Hakaou, who stood at the edge of the cliff, gazing down at the lake with glowing eyes. Etliea's worry and tension increased, and she watched Lake Clotho, knowing that something was about to happen.

The small crowd gathered behind the queen, hesitant, questioning, and anticipating. Then the surface of Lake Clotho began to ripple, trembling more and more, until it seemed to be boiling.

Suddenly, something enormous leaped from it with the speed and force of a projectile, landing in front of them with a loud crash, in the space between them and the lake.

Betrayal... Betrayal!!

"I walked alone, a wanderer, my steps shattered,
My breath trembles within me, my glances fill me with fear.
Like a fugitive, lost—knowing not whence he came nor where he goes.
Doubt... fog... ruin—pieces of me tearing one another apart.

I asked my mind, and it listened, then whispered: 'No… you shall not see her.'
But my heart cried out: 'I see her… and I shall love none but her.'
Oh, heart, tell me—are you the curse of my love?
Are you my fate's affliction? How long will you remain my heart?"

— *Kamel El-Shenawy*

Achilla knelt before them on her left knee, her fists on the ground, her body curled up so tightly that her right knee almost touched her face.

She unfurled her great white wings, which had initially wrapped around her, revealing them like two towering walls. She appeared in a new, strange, and dazzling attire: black leather pants, over which was a golden, fish-scale-like armour covering her thighs. Above, she wore a broad, thick golden breastplate, intricately and deeply engraved, flaring slightly at the edges of her waist and shoulders with sharp angles. The collar of the armour was slightly high around her neck, allowing the edge of her rectangular tattoo to show. Her arms were bare, with a large tattoo on her right arm reaching halfway to her elbow.

Her body trembled, and she panted as if she had just finished a marathon. She stretched her neck and raised her head, her wild hair flying around her, revealing her bright red eyes.

She bared her teeth, showing her sharp, gleaming fangs. Anger marked her face, and she let out a thunderous cry as she lifted her head to the sky... a war cry!

From behind her, Wert-Hakaou shouted, "They are coming... curse the traitors... curse the traitors... Demogorgon and Alcibiades want Fala... they are very close!"

The guests understood only three words: Demogorgon, Alcibiades, and Fala, which were enough for Karl.

Suddenly, from where the guests could not know, the temple knights and fifty warriors appeared.

Echor leapt from behind the queen and knelt before Achilla in the same stance she had been in, but Achilla was now standing. The sorcerers did not understand how Echor's clothes had changed! Just moments ago, he had been wearing ordinary attire, but now he was clad in the same green and black outfit with a golden armour that they had seen him wear on the second day of the guests' reception.

Echor raised his head to look at Achilla, his eyes glowing yellow like molten lava. He furrowed his brows in anger, bared his fangs, and spoke through clenched teeth, his voice hissing like a snake. He spoke in their language, which the guests did not understand, but his words seemed like a short question. Achilla nodded in response.

Echor stood up, sparks flying from his eyes. Only then did the sorcerers and guests truly grasp his immense size and towering presence. It was as if, in that moment of wrath, he had suddenly expanded, grown larger, though the truth was they were only now seeing him for what he truly was—feeling the sheer force and power concealed beneath his usual gentle demeanour, his carefree face, and his moderate temperament, which had not allowed them to see him fully until that moment.

Echor growled at the warriors who had surrounded the temple from all sides, scanning them with his eyes. He stretched out his arm and pointed with his open hand, the back of which, covered by part of his golden armour, gestured toward a direction behind the guests without speaking a word—and the warriors vanished. His gaze then shifted to the three knights standing before Lake Clotho, then to their leader, Abigael, who stood atop the hill beside Wert-Hakaou.

And then, Echor disappeared.

The people of Fala began to gather around them, all of them furious and agitated, their teeth bared, eyes gleaming, scanning their surroundings as they assumed combat stances, as if ready to pounce on the enemy at any moment. Within seconds, they were prepared for war!

This swift and sudden movement was bewildering for all the guests, who stood in their places, wavering and unsure of what to do, not understanding what was happening!

Except for Karl, who rushed towards Achilla at the same moment the queen did. Out of the corner of his eye, Karl noticed that the queen was now also wearing a red outfit and golden armour. He deduced that these strange armours and garments were linked to their spiritual energy, not crafted by their hands but by their power! It was like a transformation from one state to another, from one phase to another.

He stood beside the queen, two steps behind her, while she began to speak in what seemed to him like directives to the knights and the people of Fala. The Falans dispersed here and there, some moving away to some unknown destination, and the guests drew closer to each other.

Achilla was looking over the queen's shoulder, seemingly unaware of what was happening around her, not seeing them, but gazing into the distance as if observing what was happening beyond the forest.

Then she let out a growl from deep within her chest and bent her knees, preparing to leap. Terrifying sounds echoed from the wide mouth of the cave, accompanied by earth-shaking footsteps. Two great dragons emerged one after the other, one as black as night with large horns and long fangs and the other as blue as the sea, its head, back, and wings covered in sharp spikes like armour. Both had gleaming red eyes. They spread their wings and took flight, followed by a golden eagle, its body seemingly covered in gold feathers, almost as large as the dragons, with red eyes and a large, hooked beak. It spread its mighty wings, covering the sky above them. Behind it were five large birds, smaller than the eagle, with red feathers on their backs and black feathers on their bellies, each with a horn on its forehead and long, sharp beaks. Their red eyes gleamed as they flew behind it.

Along with them emerged a radiant white-winged horse with golden hooves and two backward-curving horns. It was twice the size of a normal horse. It landed beside Achilla, folding its wings. It neighed loudly, filling the place with its sound as it stood on its hind legs, shaking its long, wavy white mane. Then it placed its front legs back on the ground and looked at Achilla with its red eyes. She leapt onto its back, not sitting but standing, holding its golden reins and bending her knees slightly. The horse struck the ground beneath it and spread its wings, taking off and stirring the air around it powerfully. To an observer from afar, they appeared as one massive creature with four wings, moving very fast and very strong.

All of this happened in a rapid, explosive sequence in just a few seconds!

From the darkness of the cave, two large red eyes glowed, moving slowly. Then, the majestic head of a silver serpent, streaked with black, emerged, rising five meters above the ground. Its head nearly blocked the cave's entrance as it slithered out, causing the small ledge beneath it to groan under its weight. Its length seemed endless!

Everyone watched in breathless silence. Karl stiffened as he moved away from the serpent's face, which passed between him and the queen. He raised his head, trying to see the top of its body, which appeared like a wall erected before him.

Everything happened quickly. He hadn't even had the chance to speak to Achilla. The serpent continued to slither slowly beside him when he heard the sound of massive explosions coming from the shore behind them. The queen let out a high-pitched scream and took flight, followed by some of the people of Fala, Karl followed suit, barely aware of his companions trailing behind him.

They reached a vast shore with crimson sand and white rocks. The place had indeed turned into a battlefield. Blue and red fireballs were being hurled at them from seven massive, armoured black ships. Some warriors stood on the shore while most flew in the sky with Echor, hurling green and blue energy orbs from their hands. These spheres grew larger as they surged toward the enemy vessels. Echor wielded a very large, long black sword that radiated a green aura, standing in the air as if observing.

The dragons, Cadmus and Behemoth, circled above the ships, spewing black flames. Aetos, the golden eagle, tore through their sails and struck down any attackers who flew towards him with his wings. The mighty Khalycon birds flapped their wings, creating fiery whirlwinds that headed towards the giant ships. Pegasus soared high above the ships, emitting waves from its horn that caused illusions and visual distortions. Achilla stood atop it, commanding these legendary beasts, orchestrating destruction upon the invading fleet with unwavering control.

The sky began to fill with clouds, a strong wind howling, and lightning and thunder rumbling here and there. The scene suggested that Achilla alone could break the enemy's might and repel this attack. Karl felt that these foolish invaders, who seemed to have no idea what they were facing, stood no chance. They certainly hadn't expected to confront these legendary creatures, and this must have crushed them completely!

(But why did the queen seem so worried?) Karl thought as he looked at Etliea's face. This question dissipated moments later with what happened next.

Suddenly, massive whirlwinds of darkness began to form and move towards Fala. The fireballs from the ships increased, as did the counterattacks from Fala.

The queen began her assault, unleashing immense energy. She brought her hands together, forming a real fireball, then widened her hands, causing the ball to grow until it resembled a miniature sun with molten lava swirling on its surface. She launched it towards the leading ship, shattering its bow in flames. However, a large group of invaders had already reached the shore, and the greatest shock was what they carried in their hands—each wielding a staff topped with a pointed amethyst stone.

They had come with the intent to commit a great massacre. They were neither weak, as Karl had thought, nor foolish. They fully understood the strength of the people of Fala, even if they were surprised by the mythical creatures.

But these were fierce and formidable warriors—brutal to the extreme. They had come with no intention of retreating. It was victory or death, as their island's resources had dwindled, and their temple's energy was not like that of the Urbahra Temple. The people of Demogorgon would never accept living under the guardianship of the people of Fala, as the people of Alcibiades had.

No! They intended to seize the Urbahra Temple and annihilate the Falan people, having always coveted their land.

Echor struck one of the ships with his sword, releasing a powerful energy that split it in half, then moved on to destroy the remaining ships. Meanwhile, the invaders charged—toward him, toward the warriors, toward the shore where the queen stood, hurling fireballs at them.

From above, Achilla shot forward like a lightning bolt, leaping from Pegasus and landing on the sand with such force that she skidded a short distance, leaving twin furrows in the ground beneath her feet. She stood beside the queen, placing her hand calmly on her shoulder without looking at her, her gaze fixed on the ships ahead. The queen's focus wavered as she looked at Achilla, then lowered her arms, stood upright, nodded to her, and quickly returned to the Urbahra Temple.

Meanwhile, the serpent Adria arrived.

The battle raged everywhere, on land and in the sky. The clouds turned black, and lightning struck the enemy from all directions, hitting some and causing them to fall unconscious into the sea for a while. The invaders' healers emitted healing auras to help their wounded recover faster, as did the Falan healers.

However, there was one danger they couldn't avoid—the amethyst stones. They avoided the invaders' spear attacks as best they could, and some warriors disarmed the enemy of their spears and used them against them. Echor, along with five warriors, tried to break through the enemy's army, striking left and right, aiming to reach and eliminate the healers, but the defenders' circle around them was strong.

Achilla slowly raised her hands from below, as if lifting two invisible iron balls. The air began to gather around her, forming two great whirlwinds on either side. She unleashed them upon the dark whirlwinds that were devouring everything and heading towards the island, dispersing and pushing them away. She succeeded, but more black whirlwinds formed, and the Khalycon birds released their whirlwinds as well. The whirlwinds clashed, some destroying the dark whirlwinds, while others were swallowed by the darkness. The enemy's numbers were vast, and some managed to bypass the warriors, only to be confronted by the people of Fala.

One of the invaders managed to stab a man of Fala in the thigh. The latter avoided having the amethyst stone pierce his heart, but the pain from the stone was excruciating and burning, causing him to cry out like a wounded bird, a pain felt by all the people of Fala.

Achilla turned her face ablaze with anger, looking like a mother defending her young. She let out a scream that made the mythical creatures fiercer, the whirlwinds stronger, the sky thunder with more and stronger lightning, and the ground shake and tremble.

She shouted at the Falan people, ordering them to retreat except for the warriors.

Then her eyes fell on Karl. He was fighting!

He and his group were casting spells here and there. Unleashing their magic amidst the chaos.

A sharp pang of dread seized her chest. Had she forgotten them?!

She saw him leap towards the one who had stabbed the man of Fala, pushing him away and pulling the spear from the wounded man's leg, then trying to stab the attacker with it. Could he face him? Was he mad?!

Karl saw the attacker leap towards him, about to pounce, when suddenly something invisible hurled him away into the air as if struck by a giant unseen hand. His gaze fell on Achilla; it must have been her. Her face was contorted with pain and anger.

Suddenly, Karl felt a force pushing him back, one he couldn't resist. He and his friends were gathered into one spot by this force, and then a barrier of energy formed around them like a bubble. Achilla said through clenched teeth, "This is not your battle... You must leave... now."

The bubble began to rise slowly from the ground. Karl shouted, "Achilla!! Don't do this... Don't exclude me again...!! I can protect myself!!!"

Achilla turned her face away from them. He saw her starting to form fiery whirlwinds, standing firmly as her hair blew wildly like flames. At the same time, she pushed back all the enemies who had breached the warriors' barrier, hurling them into the air away from the island. She unleashed the two fiery whirlwinds, which swept away anyone who came near. Dozens of whirlwinds were before her in the sea—fiery, watery, and airy, along with the Khalycon storms and the dark whirlwinds.

From the heart of these storms, a glowing black figure emerged, cutting through them violently and heading towards Achilla like a bullet. Karl saw Achilla spread her wings and leap towards it with great force.

That was the last thing he saw as the bubble reached a high altitude and then shot off at incredible speed, making everything around them blur into lines and disappear. Karl clung to the barrier, screaming at the top of his lungs.

Two Parallel Lines...

"I'm always searching for you, always looking for your image
On the opposite sidewalk, or through the window of a narrow passage—
Even though I know you won't be there.

If wishes could come true, I'd wish to be by your side.
Then, there would be nothing beyond my reach.
I would risk everything just to hold you,
If it meant escaping loneliness.

That night, when the stars were about to fall,
I couldn't bear to be alone.
Don't fade from existence again.
I want to relive those moments,
When we wandered together without a care.

I'm always searching for you, always looking for your image
At the crossroads of my dreams—
Even though I know you won't be there."

— *A Japanese song by* ***Masayoshi Yamazaki***.

Karl arrived home within an hour inside that bubble, unable to break through it despite his multiple attempts. His friends tried to calm him down but failed, so Abraham forced him to calm down. When Abraham lifted his power from Karl, he remained still, suppressing all his anger and not uttering a word until they arrived. The bubble dissipated as they landed, and Karl took off alone, running away from the house like before, heading to that rocky shore.

Selene was sitting on the rocking chair behind the glass wall, holding a book and a chocolate bar, with steam rising from a cup of coffee beside her. When they arrived, she jumped up in surprise. They had returned three days early! She saw Karl rushing away, angry and grim. What had happened? She had hoped he would return in better spirits, but now he seemed worse!

She hurried to the door and was met by Emily as she opened it. She asked anxiously, "What's going on? Why is Karl angry? And why do you all look like you've been in a fight?"

Emily, pushing her back inside, said, "It's okay, we'll explain everything. Come on in."

****

The sorcerers sat in the living room on the second floor, having all showered and changed their clothes. Selene brought them light snacks and cups of coffee, placing them on the table before sitting down herself. She said as she looked at them: "Oh my God, I can't believe it... Did a war really break out in Fala?"

A low growl rumbled from Paul, wishing he had been there to fight the invaders. Emily groaned, "I wonder what happened to them. Did they manage to defeat the enemy or are they... oh!" She buried her face in her hands, and Giovanni gently rubbed her back, reassuring her in a soothing voice, "Don't worry, I'm sure they can defeat the enemy. Didn't you see Achilla's power, Echor's, and the warriors'? They are all very strong and have more hidden strength. They will win, I'm sure they've already won."

Emily looked at him with tear-filled eyes, bringing her face close to his and clutching his collar and asked, "Are you sure? Can you predict this?" His heart skipped a beat due to her closeness, and he stammered, shaking his head, "No, I can't predict their fate, but I feel it... I have a strong feeling they will win."

She began to cry on his chest while he wrapped his arms around her. She asked, "You're not just saying this to comfort me, right?" He shook his head, resting his cheek on her hair, feeling a strange warmth flood his heart.

Selene watched Emily with some surprise, noticing how deeply she seemed to be affected by their situation. Emily had always been an emotional girl, but this was a bit more than Selene had expected.

Everyone seemed affected. When Emily calmed down, she began to recount all the wonders she had seen in Fala. Everyone listened quietly as they ate. When she reached the part about the fruits, her voice choked up as she remembered Achilla's promise to let her take some for Selene to try. Giovanni patted her back again, and she composed herself, commenting on the battle events she had previously described: "I swear I've never seen anything so terrifying. Our abilities seemed so weak compared to theirs." Then she remembered something and added, "What do you think happened to the other guests?" Abraham shrugged, "They must have sent them home like they did with us."

****

Karl returned the next morning, completely exhausted, and isolated himself for days, either in his room or the library. Selene wanted to get close to him and talk, but she didn't. She felt a huge barrier had grown between them. She wished they hadn't gone, as Karl's condition had worsened, and he had become someone she didn't recognise.

After a few days, he started to mingle with them a bit, but he treated her like the others, just like another family member, nothing more. She held herself together, her pride preventing her from showing anything. Only one person knew of their emotional struggles, and even he kept it to himself.

****

Everyone noticed Giovanni's changed behaviour towards Emily. He became much kinder to her and allowed her to get angry at him without saying a word. He even started changing his taste in clothes to match hers, letting her choose them for him! Once, while they were having dinner, Paul made a joke with a hidden meaning that Giovanni understood. He said, "I see you've become a well-behaved poodle now, huh!" and ruffled Giovanni's hair. Giovanni's face turned red as he pretended not to care about Paul's words and quietly moved his head away.

What Giovanni didn't expect was for Emily to throw a forkful of spaghetti at Paul's face, shouting in his defence, "Don't call him a poodle!"

Echor...

"Years upon years have passed from my life,
I've seen much, and only a few were lovers.
Some complain of their fate to themselves,
While others weep for the songs they sing.
The people of love, indeed, are poor souls.
How many times love called upon my heart, but it gave no reply,
How many times longing tried to coax me, and I told it, 'Go, torment.'
How many eyes distracted me, but none truly possessed me,
Except for your eyes—only they captured me, and in your love, they commanded me.
They commanded me to love, and I found myself loving,
Dissolving in love, morning and night, at its doorstep."

— *Morsi Gameel Aziz*

Paul protested, looking at his shirt stained with food, which the fork had hit instead of his face, "Hey, you were the one who called him that, remember?!"

She replied, "That was in the past, pumpkin head, and no one has the right to insult him but me, got it?" Giovanni's face broke into a goofy smile!

****

Two months had passed since the battle...

Karl idly flipped through a book on the history of World War I, seated in the rocking chair tucked into the corner of the house behind the glass wall. His eyes skimmed over the words without truly absorbing them, hoping—perhaps in vain—that they might offer him some solace, something to pull him away from his thoughts. He knew that grim chapter of human history all too well, but maybe—just maybe—distraction lay in its pages. Anything to silence the ghosts in his mind.

How he wished he could rip his heart from his chest, that worn-out, useless thing, and sell it off at a junkyard. Though, come to think of it, even a junkyard might refuse to take it.

As he continued turning the pages, more out of habit than curiosity, a sharp gasp from outside reached him through the open glass doors, followed by a single word:

"Achilla!!!"

His heart stopped at the sound of that name.

Slowly—painfully slowly—he lifted his head, turning his gaze toward the left, where the voice had come from. His eyes landed on

Emily and Giovanni emerging hand in hand from the small grove of trees he had planted, his own little forest.

Emily's face was alight with astonishment. Her free hand hovered near her mouth, and her eyes were wide as she stared upward at something—something directly in front of Karl yet high above him.

He flicked his gaze to Giovanni's face, noting the slight unease in his features as his eyes darted between Karl and whatever it was that had caught Emily's attention.

Karl turned his head ever so slowly.

He saw nothing.

So, he lifted his gaze.

And there she was—Achilla—sitting cross-legged high in the air, her palms resting lightly on her knees as though she were deep in meditation. In this freezing weather, she wore nothing more than a pair of extremely short denim shorts and a red plaid shirt with its sleeves rolled up, utterly unfazed by the cold. Her usual wide grin stretched across her face while her wild, gypsy-like hair danced with the wind.

She was looking at Emily, her voice as cheerful as ever: "Hello, Emily! Hello, Giovanni! I didn't forget my promise—you'll find the crates by the door."

Emily's eyes glistened with emotion. "Oh, thank goodness—you're okay!"

Achilla laughed, raising a fist in the air to flex her arm muscles playfully. *"As a horse!"* she declared.

She then turned her face and looked at Karl with the same broad smile, waving at him like a child without speaking. He could see a faint scar on her right eyebrow, which looked very old. If he didn't know her so well, he might have thought it was a scar from years ago.

But what was she doing now? And she keeps doing it every time?!

She returned suddenly after worry and thoughts had consumed him after he had lost hope of her return as if nothing had happened, as if they had just seen each other yesterday!

Karl hurled the book at the glass barrier between them. She grimaced slightly, "Enough! This is enough!" he shouted. "Now you think about us... Now you think about me... Now, after all this time, you remember to assure us that you're okay! Not even a single message, not a letter, nothing!

And on top of that... your damn behaviour! Every time, you push me away, like I'm some helpless, worthless child. I don't need you to protect me.

Do you know what?! You're exactly like that old hag you despise so much! Yes! You're a perfect copy of her! You do whatever you want, no matter what others need or feel... You do what you think is right and don't care what anyone else thinks! How are you any different from her, huh?!

Go! Just go! Don't come back! I'm tired of your arrogance! Tired of your contempt for me!"

"Karl!" Emily shouted, rushing toward them. He turned to her instinctively, his outburst cut short. She said, her voice trembling, "Have you lost your mind? How could you say such things?! You know it's not true. Achilla just wanted to protect us!"

Achilla had extended her legs and began to descend slowly as Karl shouted at her. Suddenly, her face lost all its cheerfulness, replaced by something different, strange, perhaps like an echo of a break in the heart.

She was completely calm as she stood before him behind the glass wall, looking at him. She turned her head towards Emily and forced herself to smile slightly, her eyes shimmering but not like usual—they shimmered with sadness.

She murmured very softly, perhaps they heard it, perhaps not: "It's okay, I deserve this… Goodbye."

Achilla turned to leave, her steps quick and resolute. Emily jumped on her, hugging her arm tightly and crying, resting her head on Achilla's shoulder. Achilla was a head taller than Emily. Achilla spoke in a voice like a loving mother bidding her children a final farewell while stroking Emily's hair with her other hand: "Why are you crying, dear?"

Emily replied in a choked voice as she looked at her, "He didn't mean any of what he said… he's just angry."

Achilla hugged her, saying: "I know that, but it doesn't change the truth of his words. He's right." She hugged Emily tightly, kissed her hair, and then quickly let go. She took two quick steps, stomped the ground with her foot, and took off into the air.

Karl paced back and forth, pressing his hands against his temples, then dropping them, repeating the motion over and over. He looked as if he were on the brink of madness—trembling, angry, sorrowful, and suffocating, his thoughts scattered and incomprehensible. He paused for a moment when he saw Emily crying on Achilla's shoulder and began to recall the words he had said. Slowly, he started to grasp their meaning. Just as Achilla stomped her foot on the ground to take off, the echo of his own voice rang in his ears, shouting at her: "Go away."

He shouted after her, pounding his fists on the glass wall, then ran towards the door, chasing after her like a madman, apologising. But she was gone from his sight, leaving his words to the wind.

He fell to his knees, his companions following behind him, who heard him muttering the same phrase repeatedly with tear-filled, vacant eyes: "She won't come back again."

What happened in Clotho...

"Greetings, O worlds of the soul, I have grown weary of this wicked world.
Life has caused me pain in this existence—can you guide me to your realm?
You are purer in spirit, more radiant in soul, so choose me from among them, and take me with you."

— *Ahmad Rami*

Achilla stood surrounded by thirty vibrant souls, their voices echoing around her like a distant hum, like prayers. She saw herself wearing a long, flowing white robe with wide sleeves, her hair cascading over her face, shoulders, and back, and she was barefoot.

A deep, broad voice came from in front of her. She squinted, searching among the souls, and felt it was the one that had taken the form of a large, broad man with a thick, long beard, the largest of the souls. He said, "No time, you must hurry. Your people are in danger."

Achilla whispered in confusion, "What?"

Another voice came from her left, soft and high-pitched: "Tomorrow... you must complete the rituals tomorrow... you must give it your all."

Hissing rose around her from all directions: "Tomorrow... your people are in danger... tomorrow... tomorrow... danger... battle!"

Achilla was bewildered, looking left and right, not understanding, wanting to understand, but unable to.

A deep, resonant, powerful, and clear voice of a woman said, "Enough! You are confusing her." The souls parted slightly, and a radiant, magnificent soul with great wings appeared. Achilla murmured, "Yusa'as-Aldara."

Achilla felt a sense of reverence and calm fill her. Yusa'as-Aldara said, "Tomorrow, the Demogorgon and Alcibiades will attack the people of Fala." Achilla, alarmed, said, "What?!"

A voice from behind said, "They took advantage of your distraction with the coronation and our preoccupation with the ceremonies. They hid their plans well, but we were able to predict it, though too late."

Aldara spoke: "Tomorrow they will arrive... on seven giant ships... crossing the far ocean swiftly, two thousand people from both tribes... they will arrive tomorrow. You must give it your all, complete the preparation rituals, and receive my Dia before sunset tomorrow. You must be ready tomorrow."

Achilla, with wide eyes, repeated after her: "Tomorrow!"

The spirits whispered: "Tomorrow... tomorrow... tomorrow."

Achilla was overwhelmed with tension, looking around as if lost. Her breathing quickened: "But how... how?! It takes five days to contain and control a powerful Dia like Aldara's, while an ordinary Dia takes three days. Can I complete the rituals for such a Dia in one day?" She looked at their faces, waiting for a response. Aldara said, "Your people will perish... you must try."

Achilla felt she would perish from the immense energy she was expending trying to contain and control the Dia. She sat cross-legged, her palms on her knees, eyes closed, in a dark, desolate, airless place. The souls hovered around her, illuminating the space with their aura, chanting prayers and hymns. In front of her, Aldara sat cross-legged as well, transferring the Dia.

It was incredibly painful, immense amounts of energy flowing from Aldara into her. She felt it like electricity coursing through her veins, filling her heart, filling her body, almost bursting it. She writhed in place, straining until her face turned purple, and all the veins in her face and body stood out. Her breath was ragged, as if she had climbed a thousand mountains without stopping and still had a thousand more to go, as if she had been swimming across the ocean for a thousand years, with a thousand more years ahead. She struggled to catch her breath. The pain continued for hours and hours, never stopping, never easing, but she kept trying.

The transfer of the Dia is usually not painful, though it is exhausting and bearable if done correctly and within the appropriate time frame. The wings typically took three days to emerge, but now, after only a few hours, something was trying to tear through her back to come out. It was painful, sharp, like dagger stabs. She wished she could reach back and tear her own back open. Her sweating intensified, her hair sticking to her face and neck, her breaths coming in gasps. She was straining herself violently, like a woman about to give birth... like a woman about to give birth to an elephant!

She slammed her palms hard into the ground, anchoring herself there, folding her legs beneath her, her back arching in response to the unbearable pain.

Her breath grew erratic and uneven.

She felt a sharp buzzing in her ears.

Dizziness overcame her.

Her heartbeat slowed.

Everything around her turned cloudy and blurred.

She could hear nothing anymore.

Her breath stopped.

She felt a cold drop of sweat emerge from her hair, slowly travelling over her ear, curving along her cheekbone, crossing her jawline, and reaching the tip of her chin before falling and hitting the ground. She heard the sound of it hitting the ground.

Then, two large white wings burst from her back with great force and speed, making a loud sound. As they emerged, she gasped deeply, and the wings tore through her robe as they extended and finally came out. The robe ripped from her back and shoulders, and she remained hunched over, struggling to catch her breath.

Aldara asked, "Are you alright? Can you continue?"

Achilla took another deep breath through her nose, closed her eyes, and exhaled through her mouth. Then she opened her eyes and slowly raised her head, holding her robe over her chest, wanting to look into Aldara's ghostly face. She said with a tired but defiant smile, "I don't give up without a fight," baring her teeth in a broad grin. "And this is just the beginning."

Hours passed after that, but Achilla grew stronger and more resilient. It was still arduous but less painful than before. The white robe fell around her like a tattered rag, and she returned to her original position, sitting cross-legged with her palms on her knees, now in her new form.

The souls whispered, "Well done… you are strong… yes, she is very strong… keep going… just a little more… they are about to arrive."

Achilla opened her eyes, glowing with a red light, and her lips curled into a dancing smile.

****

She cut her way through Clotho with immense speed. The souls had warned her that the enemy was at the gates. Emerging from Clotho, she let out a resounding cry, summoning the mythical creatures back to life. She could see them approaching, very close to the shore.

Now at the forefront, she attacked them with her fifty-one warriors. She felt something tear through her body; one of her people had been struck hard. She went mad with rage, and then she saw him—her beloved, fighting alongside them. How could she have forgotten him? No, she wouldn't let him intervene. This wasn't his battle... it wasn't his responsibility. She couldn't bear to lose him or have anyone hurt because of her. They must leave.

A terrifying, swift black shadow attacked her, aiming a sharp, gleaming object at her heart. She lunged towards it, and they began to duel in the sky. With a swift move, it thrust its spear towards her. She bent her back sharply, and it passed swiftly over her, missing her heart but slashing her right eyebrow. It was a burning, stinging, annoying wound. Something warm, sticky, and dark red, almost black, flowed—it was her blood. The golden eagle ambushed her attacker, snatching the spear from its hand and tossing it to her. Within a second, the spear was in her attacker's heart.

The battle raged on, fierce and unyielding. Parts of the island near the battlefield lay in ruins, not only because of the enemy but also due to the sheer, uncontrolled power of Achilla, which she had yet to fully master. It was enough for her to focus slightly on something, and lightning would strike it, the ground would tremble beneath it, and mythical creatures would attack it.

She was utterly exhausted from the Dia rituals, but she continued to fight fiercely. Hundreds of enemies fell, but many of the Falan people were seriously injured. The enemy couldn't kill any of them because of Achilla. Telepathically, she monitored everyone—thirteen hundred souls. The moment the enemy was about to pierce someone's heart, she made the surrounding air push them forcefully as if struck by an invisible giant hand. Achilla was expending tremendous energy, watching a thousand enemy fighters simultaneously, fighting and killing some, dodging others' blows, controlling the mythical creatures to avoid destroying the island, and controlling her anger to avoid destroying the island herself.

A few reached the Temple of Urbahra, where the knights and the queen took care of them. Hundreds were killed, and there were hundreds of quartz statues scattered around. The enemy weakened, and their resolve shattered after hours of battle, and the rest surrendered.

Achilla walked heavily through the dark, devastated forest, her breaths laboured, her body filled with serious injuries, and she had lost a great deal of her energy. Heavy rain poured down, extinguishing the fires that had erupted here and there. The mythical creatures calmed and headed to the highest mountains of Fala.

She left the prisoners behind under the guard of Echor and the warriors, making her way to the Urbahra Temple. Her eyes scanned those around her—the tribe, the knights, the Sibyl, the queen. The matter of the prisoners now belonged to the queen.

She headed to the cave, threw herself onto the cold stone floor, and fell into a deep slumber.

Two weeks after the battle, Achilla emerged from her slumber. Her wounds had healed, and her spiritual energy had improved. Beside her were Wert-Hakaou, the other two Sibyls, and Chief Physician Lashon, all surrounding her, doing everything they could to heal her energy and body. A little further away, the queen was praying.

She opened her eyes, feeling her body stiff and heavy. She moved her limbs—she was fine. She could not feel her wings; she must have returned to her normal state. Her gaze swept over those around her before she asked, "The tribe?"

Wert-Hakaou answered with a smile of satisfaction and gratitude, "They are fine, all of them. You have made a tremendous effort, Kharissa... No, Alika—Achilla."

The queen moved closer to her with expressions on her face that Achilla had never seen before. She said with clear relief, "Achilla... thank the god... well done, my dear."

The queen quickly composed herself, her features returning to their usual calm: "You saved everyone. No losses in lives. You... did well."

Ignoring the queen, Achilla sat up from her recline. Lashon asked, "How do you feel?" She replied sarcastically, touching the scar on her eyebrow, "Just perfect!"

They heard a strong landing and the fluttering of multiple wings. Achilla turned to look over her shoulder, and through the dark opening of the cave, lit only by a few scattered flames, she saw her mythical creatures gathering their massive bodies at the cave entrance, nudging each other's heads, wanting to look inside, to see their mistress, their beloved Achilla.

Achilla let out a low laugh at the sight—mythical creatures behaving like little puppies searching for their mother. She said as she stood up, "I missed you, too, little ones!"

Behemoth, the black earth dragon, made a sound as he raised his head and shook it, resembling a laugh! Cadmus also shook his head and blew smoky air from his nostrils. Pegasus neighed cheerfully, the birds flapped their wings and made happy sounds, and Adria, who had just arrived, simply stuck out her tongue and hissed.

Wert-Hakaou commented, "They really seem to have missed you. We didn't see them throughout your slumber. It seems they only come near when you're around."

Achilla was the only one who could communicate with them and read their thoughts, and they could also feel her, understand her, and read her thoughts.

She said cheerfully as she approached them, "Well, little ones, how about a tour around the island?"

Lashon, concerned, said, "Kharissa, why don't you do that tomorrow? You've just come out of slumber. Aren't you even hungry?"

Achilla's stomach growled at his words, and she held her belly and said, "Oh, speaking of that," she trailed off for a moment, then continued cheerfully as she walked and called out, "Tarah! Adnos! Where are those fools when I need them… what kind of assistants are they?!"

Within seconds, Tarah and Adnos were beside the cave. She had mounted Pegasus, but Tarah came rushing and jumped on her, hugging her, causing both of them to fall off Pegasus. Tarah exclaimed with overwhelming joy, "Kharissa, oh Kharissa… I swear my heart almost stopped. You're alright… thank the god!"

He was still hugging her despite them being on the ground, her right arm on his chest, and he was squeezing her left arm with his. It was a messy, tilted, and annoying hug. She slapped him in the eye while he showered her head with kisses and said, "You fool, stop it. You're about to break one of my ribs!"

As he helped her up, he said, "Oh, I'm sorry, Kharissa, but I'm so happy, I even missed your slaps."

She laughed and embraced him in a more appropriate, calm manner, then did the same with Adnos. Turning to Tarah, she said, "How about you feed me then? I'm starving." He replied, "Right away!"

As she climbed back onto Pegasus, she added, "Alright, I'm heading into the forest. Follow me there." Then, suddenly remembering something, she asked with apparent curiosity, not concern, "Oh! What happened to the Demogorgon and Alcibiades tribes?"

Adnos replied, "The queen made them swear a sacred oath. After you defeated their guardians, they felt very weak and thought we would annihilate them. But the queen decided instead to place them under our protection since they have no guardian now until a new guardian appears. She didn't want to destroy the remaining few of the last of Heavenkin despite what they did. They felt immense gratitude for the queen's mercy and swore a solemn oath never to repeat their aggression, neither they nor their future generations, and to serve us whenever we need them. They inscribed the oath on tablets and returned to their island."

Achilla shrugged indifferently and went on with her mythical creatures.

The queen exhaled through her nose and shook her head in disapproval, and muttered, "Just when I thought she had changed a little."

Achilla reached the forest near the shore, the area that had sustained the most damage on the island. The rest of the places fared a little better, but still, the destruction was evident. She looked around sadly at the shattered and burned trees, the dead birds and animals, and the cracked ground. She dismounted Pegasus when she reached the centre of the wreckage, stood still for a moment, and then sat cross-legged in meditation, releasing healing energy.

The forest and the entire island of Fala thrived on energy, just like its inhabitants and animals. The Urbahra's energy would heal the island, but this healing would take time; it wouldn't be quick. The people of Fala had likely been busy treating their wounded over the past two weeks, and only a few days ago had the last of them healed, leaving them no time to tend to the island.

Slowly, the trees around her began to grow again, flowers bloomed, and leaves regained their vibrant colours. It was like a circle expanding gradually, with Achilla at its centre, spreading life wherever it passed. Her beloved creatures sat around her, watching. It wasn't just Achilla's high spiritual energy that helped heal the forest, but also her ability to control nature. This, too, required great effort from her, as she still lacked her full strength, but she continued, nonetheless.

She felt a hand on her shoulder. She opened her eyes and looked up, seeing the person who had blocked the sunlight behind him. It was Echor, with his gentle, sweet smile.

"What do you think about eating first... then we can do this together?" he asked, placing a basket in front of her.

Laughter, like that of children!

"For twenty years, I have painted your eyes
On the walls of my prison,
And if darkness comes between me and your eyes,
Your face appears in my illusion,
And I weep... and I sing!"

— *Samih Al-Qasim*

Twenty years had passed...

Yet, that memory still pained him. He still felt that strange iron ball in his chest whenever the memory resurfaced against his will, despite his efforts to avoid it.

Since she left, he never tried to think about her, at least not willingly. Her image would suddenly invade his mind when the sun set and rose, when the birds sang, when the gentle breeze blew, and when the snow fell... and in his dreams.

Sometimes, he could almost swear he heard her laughter echoing from somewhere. He would suddenly look around, eyes wide open, only to come back to his senses when his friends asked him what was wrong.

Perhaps she invaded his imagination very often, against his will! But he made every effort not to think about her. He had lost her, and it was over. She would never return, and he would never find her, no matter how hard he searched. Even if he did find her, she was not his, never was, and never will be.

The first two years were the hardest. After that, he gradually returned to his old self. His relationship with Selene somewhat returned to its former state, but neither of them was the same. Despite Selene's efforts to help him in every way she could and love him always, even more than before, she always wondered: when she saw him staring off into the distance, was he thinking about her? She always felt she was second best, even though Karl never showed her anything, never made her feel any different once he got better and they resumed their relationship. Yet, she felt him more distant, the barrier still standing. When would it break?

But over the past twenty years, she had learned to ignore that barrier, insisting on acting as if nothing had ever happened.

****

The place was extremely crowded, with loud music and drumbeats everywhere. The weather was very hot, and people around them were dressed in strange outfits. They were in an alley of a popular neighbourhood, a stone alley surrounded by some old buildings, with people hanging from balconies and windows.

Karl and his family were at a festival. They had unintentionally entered the heart of this parade while trying to take a shortcut to the city centre. They were in a foreign country, spending their summer vacation. Selene was holding his arm, and all their friends were behind him. Emily was cursing; she had always hated narrow, crowded, and hot places. Giovanni tried to calm her down. She said, "For heaven's sake, how are we going to celebrate our tenth wedding anniversary looking like this? Look at my dress, it's completely wrinkled, and my smell… damn it, I smell like I just came out of a cow barn."

Giovanni replied, "No matter what, you are stunningly beautiful, and you smell like flowers."

She said, "Oh, don't try to flatter me. Look, my hair has turned into straw because of the humidity. I am not going into that fancy restaurant looking like this, I'm telling you."

Selene, looking back and addressing Emily like a mother, said, "Don't exaggerate, Emily. You look fine. Don't ruin Giovanni's surprise for you because of this."

Emily grumbled a bit, but as soon as they got out of the suffocating crowd and breathed the fresh air, her mood quickly improved, and she planted a kiss on her husband's cheek, apologising.

They had entered a large, wide street where the celebrants dispersed. To their left was a wide circular square with a thick stone column resembling an obelisk in the middle. Most of the celebrants were heading to that square, which was filled with music and dancers. To their right was their destination, where they intended to celebrate Emily and Giovanni's wedding anniversary.

The square wasn't far from them; they could see inside it. Karl's eyes fell on someone standing on something elevated, making her stand out above the heads. She was spinning and dancing, gathering people around her, holding a small tambourine with jingles, playfully tapping it. He couldn't make out her features, but he froze in place, staring at her from a distance. Selene tugged at him while chatting with Abraham, but he remained rooted, gazing at the brown woman with black hair. Selene turned to him and asked, "What's the matter?"

His heart raced without knowing why. He blinked, trying to gather his thoughts, and said, pointing to the square, "I'll catch up with you in a bit. Go ahead. There's something I want to look at in that square… I'll be back in a few minutes."

Confusion spread across Selene's face, but before she could respond or ask any questions, he hurried off.

He rushed forward, something pulling him there. He felt as if he had plunged into a magical world without realising it. The sounds around him faded, his heartbeat grew louder, and everything seemed to move in slow motion.

He pushed through the small crowd gathered around her. The woman was dancing on a short stone barrier surrounding the column in the middle of the square. She swayed joyfully, her wide white skirt flowing down to her knees, topped with a tight lace blouse.

The woman had her back to him, then turned slightly, giving him a side view. She brushed away her gypsy hair that cascaded around her and danced with the breeze. He saw her broad smile, her light dimples, and heard her beautiful, resonant laughter.

He stopped in his tracks, lost in thought, as if in a dream, not thinking about anything but just watching her, his heart pounding.

Someone placed a hand on his shoulder, breaking his reverie. He looked at the tall, handsome man who had one hand in his pants pocket, his amber eyes fixed on the girl dancing in front of them.

The man commented, "She's beautiful, isn't she?"

Karl blinked and then turned his face away, looking at her again and muttered, "She always is."

The man asked, "How have you been? It's been a long time since we last met."

Karl replied, "I'm fine, I guess… And you? How are you? And… how is she?"

Achilla noticed the person standing next to Echor. Their eyes met, and she stopped dancing, her smile fading slightly. She jumped off the barrier and handed the tambourine to the person next to her with a sweet smile, and the small crowd dispersed a bit. She approached them, biting her lip lightly as if reluctant to go. She kept a distance between them, placing her hands on her hips while Echor moved to stand beside her, his shoulder behind hers. She glanced at Echor briefly, then crossed her arms over her chest, shifting restlessly in place.

Finally, she said, "Hello, Karl!"

Karl muttered, "Hello... Achilla."

They were silent for a moment before Achilla added, "Well then... don't forget to greet your family for me... goodbye."

She said this as she wrapped her arms around Echor's elbow and pulled him away from Karl, waving to him as she walked quickly, almost running.

Karl stood frozen in place, his voice caught in his throat, unable to come out. He felt a sharp pain in his chest, a mix of disappointment and shame. He had asked her to stay away from him, and now... what did he want to say after that?

No, he had to apologise, at least, for his rudeness, his foolishness, his hurtful words. He had compared her to the person she hated the most, the one who had hurt her and taken away what she cherished most. He needed to apologise.

He quickened his pace, calling after her, while she ignored him until he caught up and grabbed her by the arm. He said, "Achilla, please, listen to me. I know I don't deserve this, but please."

His eyes were tormented and sad, his face pale with sorrow and pleading. She looked at him hesitantly, then glanced at Echor, who was looking away, staring ahead. A small frown creased his brows, which he tried to hide. He said in a calm voice, "I'll wait for you at the hotel."

She squeezed his arm slightly before letting go, and before he left, he planted a small kiss on her hair, avoiding looking at her at the same time.

They walked side by side for a long time without speaking. He knew a nearby place with a high hill, away from the noise of the bustling city. They sat on that hill under the shade of a weeping willow tree beside them.

He said, "I'm... very sorry. I overreacted. I was feeling incredibly helpless and anxious, but that doesn't justify what I said to you."

She replied, "It's alright, I know. I'm not angry or even upset with you; there is no need to apologise. You did tell the truth in the end. I am like her."

He said, "No, you're not like her at all. Maybe you're both as stubborn as bulls and as hard-headed as walls, but there's a world of difference between you two."

She smiled at his words and commented, "I think I didn't know her well. In the past twenty years, I've had the chance to know her better. I avoided her for a long time before that and never thought of getting close to her. I think I... wronged her."

He looked at her in surprise, his eyes questioning.

She continued, "Don't get me wrong, I haven't forgiven her and never will for what she did to my mother. There are no excuses for her actions in my eyes. But I've recently realised that she didn't kill her in cold blood as I thought. Behind that icy face were deep emotions she hid well. She was a master at concealing her feelings from everyone."

She sighed and paused for a second before continuing, "One day, I entered her room for the first time since my mother's incident. She never allowed anyone in, but... you know me. I barged in without a care. I was shocked when I saw my mother's statue... there in the corner of the room, surrounded by candles and wreaths of flowers. I had long thought she had destroyed it and gotten rid of it. That foolish old woman prayed every day for her soul, hoping she would find the way to Mata…"

Her voice choked, and a tear almost escaped her eye, but she held it back, and the clouds thickened a bit. Karl instinctively hugged her and said, "No… no… no rain, that would be very strange in the middle of this summer here, it might even make the local news headlines."

She let out a small laugh, enough to make the clouds disperse and reveal the beautiful sunset once again.

She looked at the setting sun and continued after taking a deep breath, "Who tortures themselves like that! Every day, she faces her actions, never allowing herself to forget. Then she puts on that icy mask and shows herself to us. What a woman! In a way… your comparison of me to her made me understand her in some way… even if she still remains elusive to me. But we both do what we think is right, even if it hurts us or others."

She fell silent, and several minutes passed in silence… until Karl broke it.

He exclaimed with emotion, "How do you do it? How do you spend your days like this… laughing as if there are no sorrows filling your heart as if nothing happened? How do you forget?"

She replied, "I don't forget… I keep everything inside a small, closed box in my heart."

He asked, "What does that mean?"

She explained, "For example… you! I place you in a small box of your own… and I keep you there… always with me. It's like when you hold onto a collection of cherished memories in a bag in your closet.

You may never look through it, never flip through its contents, but it reassures you to know it's there... not gone, not vanished... waiting for you whenever you wish to revisit it, to bring back those beautiful memories.

As for me, I never open the box... It might be hard to accept at first, but once you get used to its presence... like a piece of furniture in your home, you see it every day... closed. You don't see what's inside, even though you know what it holds... until its presence becomes natural.

Sometimes, brushing against it might bring back some memories and feelings... for you don't forget.

Instead, you keep them in a box inside your heart, and you accept it... but you never open it."

He said, "It sounds like a strange philosophy. How is it different from forgetting?"

She replied, "Completely different. Forgetting means the weakening of memory and the fading of pain. Gradually, your feelings toward something fade, and you forget... then, when what reminded you of what you've forgotten returns, the memory no longer holds that sharp ache, that old sorrow. Perhaps there is some nostalgia and remnants of sadness."

With a touch of solemnity in his voice, he asked, "And the box...?"

She said, "The box keeps everything as it is, unchanged... it doesn't diminish its glow, doesn't hide its features or distort them. If you opened it, you'd be able to feel every minute detail of what you've kept inside. And perhaps, you would no longer be able to close it again."

Some time passed in silence as he pondered her words, their truth, and their worth.

She interrupted his thoughts, looking directly into his eyes: "Do that, too."

He met her gaze questioningly. She continued, placing the tip of her finger on his heart: "Place me in a small, closed box, and reserve a small corner inside your heart for me instead of trying to force me out...

This way, you will accept the reality more... This way, my place won't overshadow the other corners of your heart and take up space that others deserve...

This way, you can laugh deeply again, as if nothing ever happened..."

She looked away from him and continued, "We won't forget, and forcing ourselves, forcing our hearts to do something we can't control will be exhausting, painful, and very sad. We won't succeed in doing it at all... But embracing it, accepting it, and keeping it—that's different... It's enough to know that you're breathing somewhere and maybe happy... for me to carry that box inside me with joy."

He cried despite himself; tears flowed from his eyes, and he made no effort to stop them; he fixed his gaze on the last ray of the sun about to disappear.

It was like what he was trying to do, but in a different, more chaotic way—perhaps even a wrong one. He wasn't trying to forget her, but he was trying to avoid thinking about her, attempting to push her out of his heart, which was filled with her so that he could breathe properly. He hadn't tried to embrace her inside his heart willingly, to peacefully reserve a space for her there, to accept her presence there by his own choice and not out of necessity, and that she would always remain a part of him, despite the circumstances and distances.

He wondered to himself, how could she see things this way, from this angle! She made her choices, created boxes, placed them in a corner of her heart, and then moved on with them, laughing deeply.

To continue, to hold it together in life, to always face obstacles with your head held high, to resist until the very end—was one thing. But to be able to laugh deeply despite all the sorrow that had befallen you, like a small child... as if nothing had ever happened—was something entirely different!

Was it the wisdom of years? He really was a little child in front of her!

He looked at her with his tear-filled eyelashes and smiled sadly, "You see, you're nothing like that old woman."

She laughed cheerfully and commented, raising her index finger in the air, "Except for her stubbornness."

He repeated quietly, "Except for her stubbornness…"

He turned his face away from her, "So, it's goodbye then."

And she smiled at the last light of the sun that had departed.

Thirty souls... thirty-one souls!

"Swiftly walk o'er the western wave,
Spirit of Night!
Out of the misty eastern cave,
Where, all the long and lone daylight,
Thou wovest dreams of joy and fear,
...
Thy brother Death came, and cried,
Wouldst thou me?
Thy sweet child Sleep, the filmy-eyed,
Murmured like a noontide bee,
Shall I nestle near thy side?
Wouldst thou me?
...
Of neither would I ask the boon
I ask of thee, belovèd Night
Swift be thine approaching flight,
Come soon, soon!"

—*Percy Bysshe Shelley*

Achilla wandered the streets, intoxicated by her thoughts, unaware of where her steps would lead her. She needed some time alone. A not-so-distant memory crossed her mind less than a year ago.

Echor had stormed into her room, agitated and unable to control himself. He cast a quick glance around the room; Achilla wasn't there. He headed straight to the balcony where she always sat. She was on the rocking chair, holding a book in her hand, reading. Her cheek rested on her other hand, and she had her legs folded over the chair. Despite the agitation she felt from Echor, she asked him with a kind of indifference as soon as he stood at the balcony door, still looking at the book: "What's the matter, Echor?"

He yelled: "What's the matter!!" He approached her and grabbed her arm, pulling her from the chair. She stood up, eyes wide with astonishment at his violent behaviour. He had never acted this way with her before; he had never acted this way with anyone before! She looked into his eyes, her bewildered gaze darting between them in a quick motion, trying to fathom his depths. After a moment, she said: "Oh, so you spoke with the old woman then."

She turned her face away from him and sighed: "My God, she really has become a gossipy old woman! And I really don't understand her… I expected her to strongly support my departure."

She tried to pull her arm away from his grip instinctively, but instead, he grabbed her other arm too and began shaking her forcefully between his hands. With a burst of emotion, he shouted: "Why are you hiding this from me and everyone else? Do you plan to leave suddenly!! Do you plan to kill me? Tell me. What exactly are you planning? Since when do you care about spirits, traditions, honour, and all this nonsense? Why now do you want to join the immortal souls? Why are you accepting their offer? I know all this nonsense doesn't mean anything to you, so why are you leaving?!"

She shouted at him: "Calm down!! What's wrong with you? Let go of my arms... This matter is mine alone!"

He yelled back, "No, it's not just your concern! Never just yours alone. Are you blind or pretending to be?

You know my feelings for you all these years. There's not a child in Fala who doesn't know my feelings for you, and now you say it doesn't concern me!

I never interfered in your life... never opposed your desires and madness... All that mattered to me was your happiness, just being by your side. I know you don't feel the same way about me... but I swear, Achilla, this is too much!

How can you be so heartless? How can you do this to me... and for what? So, your soul can remain forever in Clotho, the intermediate world!! The world of nothingness?!! Do you realise what you're planning to do? And don't you dare say honour... I know that nonsense means nothing to you. You won't even be happy with this, so why are you doing it?!"

Achilla was silent for a moment, contemplating Echor's face, which was covered in pain beyond pain. She had never seen him so tormented before, and the emotions he unleashed were no longer suppressed as he always did; she could feel them just as he felt them—deep, mighty, painful, and very sad feeling.

Oh, how much he had suffered because of her, how much he had endured for her, silently and patiently. He never spoke, never complained, never objected. He was always concerned about her happiness... *her* happiness alone! Was there a sacrifice like this? A devotion, a selflessness... a love like this?

Her expression changed from angry to sad, then tender. She smiled a gentle smile, raising her hands to place them on his face. His grip on her arms softened as she did so, and his features softened immediately. How easily she could affect him!

She said: "Oh, Echor... Oh, my dear Echor... No one really knows the fate of the immortal souls. I don't believe they will stay there forever. When the end comes, which it surely will one day, when the last soul departs to Mata, they will go too... after completing their mission, right? That's logical. And the god is not cruel to reward their good deeds with eternal exile! I know you'll tell me these are assumptions that can't be relied upon. Well... I'm not very interested in Mata! It doesn't intrigue me... What would I do there anyway?! I have no one there I long to meet."

A mocking smile curled on her lips, sadness gleamed in her voice, and a vast emptiness in her eyes as she spoke the last sentence.

Echor gritted his teeth and clenched his jaw, lifting his head and gaze as if he wanted to curse, to pull his face away from her hands, but he didn't. Instead, he tightened his grip on her arms again and spoke through clenched teeth: "Damn it, Achilla, damn it... Do you hear yourself? Why do you want to go to Clotho in the first place? What drives you to do this?!"

She sighed slightly and then said: "I know my words will sound stupid or strange to you, but... I don't feel a sense of belonging to anything here. Years have passed, and I've been searching for something that makes me cling to this place and truly belong there. I haven't found it.

I've always felt empty. I've travelled the world... tried everything, read all the books, eaten what I desired, even loved, and done what I wanted, well, to some extent! But I always returned with the same feeling... that my place is not here... that I don't belong to anything... There, in the world of Clotho... despite the short and painful time I spent there, somehow, I felt that was my place, among the thirty souls that surrounded me there...

I felt they were... my family... that I belonged to them! Do you understand me, Echor?"

She asked him, furrowing her brows like a math teacher explaining how to extract the coefficient of (x) to a seven-year-old child!

As for Echor, it was very difficult to describe the expressions that covered his face. The strongest were confusion, lack of understanding, and disappointment. Thoughts battled in his head for a while, not knowing what to say. After moments of exchanged glances, he found himself muttering to her like a small, pleading child: "Don't go... don't go... please... for my sake... I've never asked you for anything, but this time... don't go..."

She felt her heart shatter. How many times can a person's heartbreak?

Echor had always been loyal and devoted to her. He loved her deeply, and now she could truly feel the depth of that love and the immense difficulty he had endured over the centuries, holding back that love from her.

How could she have hurt him this much? And unintentionally, too. He never asked for her love nor her attention; all he asked for was her presence... just that!

As she was about to speak, Echor surprised her with a kiss. It was a passionate kiss filled with a whirlwind of emotions. He held her tightly in his arms and kissed her. She felt her heart leap into her throat; the shock was her initial reaction. But she didn't push him away, didn't resist, and didn't want to resist. The feeling that washed over her surprised her; she felt she wanted him just as much as he wanted her. Was Karl right? Had he seen something in her that she couldn't see herself?

Was Achilla really attracted to Echor... did she love him?!!

At that moment, she didn't know the answer to any of these questions. All she knew or felt, to be precise, was that she wasn't repelled by him, and she didn't hate his kiss; in fact, she returned the passionate kiss.

Echor felt his heart would explode. Was this a dream, an illusion, a fantasy? Was he really... finally kissing her? And was she really... truly kissing him back?

When he realised she was responding to him, he lifted her in his arms and carried her into her room.

Several hours later, they lay together on the longest of the white sofas, large enough to seat three people. It wasn't the most comfortable arrangement, but he wouldn't have complained, nor did he even notice. He was utterly happy; it was undoubtedly the best day of his entire life.

Yes, in the nine hundred years he had lived, he had never experienced such a feeling or such joy. How could he complain or even notice the narrowness of the couch? It was enough that his body was pressed against hers now, enough that she was in his arms as he had always wanted, as he had always dreamed.

The feelings he had in these few hours of joy and happiness made him doubt if any dream could be this beautiful or this powerful. No one's imagination could conjure feelings like those he had just experienced or felt — SO IT MUST BE REAL. *Real...* he thought to himself as he buried his face between her hair and face and wrapped his arms around her tightly as if she were a liquid that might slip away like mercury at any moment if he loosened his grip.

After a while, a thought crossed his mind; he didn't keep it to himself and whispered close to her ear: "Are you regretting what happened?"

She said, with a hint of incredulity in her voice that made him feel at ease: "Why would I regret it... No, I'm not regretful at all. In fact," she let out a short laugh, "I think I feel strangely good, in a way I don't understand!"

He didn't comment, didn't ask her what she meant. He just wanted to cling to the glimmer of hope in her words. Inside his chest, her words were etched onto the tablet of his heart... even those past hours were engraved in detail.

All he did in response to her comment was to pull her closer and hold her tighter. She let out a small laugh; he had squeezed the breath out of her, but she didn't object. She understood well what these moments meant to him, and she was completely content with what was happening, experiencing a new, beautiful feeling she never thought she would feel. It was somewhat similar to her feelings towards Karl, yet it was different, too!

After a long silence, she whispered: "Why did you never try to confess your love to me?"

He said, while still holding his position: "I told you thousands of times, but you weren't listening... you didn't care..." Then he lifted his face to be directly in front of hers and continued:

"Well, let me recall that line of poetry... umm, oh...

(A sentence starts out like a lone traveller heading into a blizzard at midnight, tilting into the wind, one arm shielding his face, the tails of his thin coat flapping behind him. There are easier ways of making sense, the connoisseurship of gesture, for example. You hold a girl's face in your hands like a vase. You lift a gun from the glove compartment and toss it out the window into the desert heat. These cool moments are blazing with silence.)[1]

She made a playful grimace and said: "What poetry to quote!"

He smiled, the vitality evident in his eyes and on his lips, and said: "I told you a thousand times, no, thousands of times that I love you... silently... because no words could truly convey the depth of my feelings for you. And you knew very well that I adored you... Silence spoke louder, clearer... You didn't need to hear it from me to know that, but you simply ignored it... ignored me, and I respected your wishes..."

A tinge of sadness coloured his last words. He fell silent, gazing into her grey eyes. Had they always been this beautiful, or was it his happiness that made them shine so?

She, in turn, looked into his amber eyes, those enchanting eyes. How had she not fallen in love with them? Or did she love them without knowing? Echor was a wonderful man in every sense of the word. Why had she never noticed him as she did today? Why had she

---

[1] Billy Collins, Winter Syntax Poem.

never given him a chance? Isn't love strange and twisted in its ways, or is it fate? Who knows!

Didn't his love seem obvious, easy, and natural? Hadn't he always stood by her side, supporting her, helping her, loving her?

Or was it because she was used to his presence? Because she had opened her eyes to him, grown up with him, never understanding the true nature of her feelings towards him? Because she treated him like family only, knowing he was always there, anytime and anywhere, ready to fulfil whatever she wanted! She had never experienced or understood the feeling of losing him or being apart from him; maybe that's why she didn't know the truth of what she felt now!

She whispered: "Why... why didn't you ever try? You never tried to fight or get closer, nor did you try to distance yourself either?"

He said: "My love for you is a strange thing... Despite my intense desire to be with you, to have you with me and for myself... my primary concern has always been your happiness, even if it meant you being with someone else... Well, I'm not that Platonic! But I never felt that you loved me, I mean, in the way I love you, or that there was any hope that you would love me.

How miserable! I accepted my reality! In a sick and strange way, I accepted it! But I was too weak to let go of you completely.

I settled or was content with having you in my life as a friend, as a family member, as long as I could see you, as long as I could be by your side.

Even though, as you surely remember, I had my failed relationships "—he laughed at the last sentence and shook his head, then continued—" Nothing worked out. I went through many relationships, some wonderful, some boring and annoying. Whatever their state, I didn't care, I didn't really want them, I didn't love any of them as I loved you.

There wasn't a soul on earth who didn't know I loved you, and that was one of the reasons for my failed relationships, obviously. After that, I gave up on them, or they gave up on me; whichever is more accurate, it doesn't matter. The important thing is that I became a hopeless case, as they say."

He said this and then buried his face between her cheek and hair, inhaling her scent. She pressed her cheek against his, ran her fingers through his hair, and said sadly: "I didn't know things were this bad for you... I'm sorry."

He replied in a joking tone: "It's okay. I've gotten used to your neglect, coldness, foolishness, and emotional numbness."

She gasped in mock protest, slapped his shoulder, and muttered: "You rascal," and tried to push him away. He chuckled in her ear and didn't let her move. She mumbled, stifling her laughter: "Idiot!"

He whispered to her after a moment, in a pleading tone, "Stay... don't leave, please... stay with me, even if just for a trial period."

He said it spontaneously without any thought, then suddenly felt it was a good idea. He lifted his head and propped himself up on his elbow, his eyes shining with hope and joy, filled with vitality. He continued with clear enthusiasm and a broad smile: "Yes, just for a while, try life with me. You said I never tried to fight for you; here I am doing it. Please stay, even if... even if just for a year. You know you still have a long time before your first prophecy appears! Let's travel the world together. Let's do everything we want to do and more. Let's explore it as lovers, not just as friends. You haven't tried life with me...

maybe after that, you'll change your mind, maybe after that, you'll feel... a sense of belonging."

She looked at him with sorrow; she never wanted to break his heart, to take away that joy and hope that filled him. She had broken his heart enough already. Didn't he deserve her to respond to him, to help him as he always helped her, to try to repay even a small part of his love, sacrifice, and generosity? To fulfil his one and perhaps last request from her? But was this the right thing to do? What is the right thing to do in this situation?

To agree or refuse? Which is worse?

She mumbled after a short silence: "What if I don't? What if I don't change my mind after that?! Their offer isn't new... I made my decision after long years of thinking!"

His smile faded slightly, but he looked at her seriously and said: "Then I will respect your decision."

She asked: "Won't that be worse for you? Won't it increase your pain? If we go through all this together and then...?"

She didn't finish her sentence, but he replied, his eyes filled with determination and resolve: "I can take care of myself. Do this for me, and I will be grateful, no matter what your decision is afterwards... believe me."

After a moment of thought, she replied with a small smile, "A year, then?"

His smile widened, and his eyes sparkled as he said: "Yes!"

She said: "And you'll respect my decision, whatever it may be afterwards?"

He nodded. She said: "Promise me?" He replied: "I promise."

Then he leaned in and kissed her. That night was undoubtedly the happiest night of his life.

Can a person love two? Two people at the same time? Many have spoken about this—authors, psychologists, and who knows who else! What's the answer? How can the heart hold space for two people? To have the same intensity of love and feelings for them? And if given a choice between them, if circumstances allowed for no obstacles in the decision, and both were equally wonderful, would it be possible to choose? Would it be possible to favour one over the other? Could or should the strength of feelings be equal toward both, or would one inevitably surpass the other, even by a small degree?

That night, Echor revealed the truth of Achilla's feelings towards him. Yes, she loved him, yes, deeply and profoundly, more than she had imagined or expected.

The more time she spent with him, the more she surprised herself with the depth of her feelings for him, to the point where she began to compare her feelings for him with those for Karl!

Both were strong and deep, but they were also different. She had never shared the same kind of relationship with Karl that she shared with Echor. She had never crossed the line of pure platonic friendship with Karl. She had never allowed her emotions to be free with him, to express them openly, to tell him what was in her heart, and for him to do the same. There was always a barrier, always a fear for his fate, for his life.

As for Echor, it was entirely different—no worries, no fears, no suppression, freedom to express and do what she wanted. She finally felt she could soar freely in the skies of love!

If she loved Echor this much, how had she never felt it before? Or rather, how had she never understood the truth of her feelings? Was her love for him sudden? No, it wasn't. His love had been growing inside her over the years, slowly, bit by bit. It wasn't something overwhelming and crushing that struck her at first sight, as it had with Karl. Karl was something different in her life; he resembled her greatly in his loneliness and isolation despite having a family, in his lack of belonging to anything or anyone, and in his nature. This was the strongest factor and the main reason that drew her to him. On that day, under the oak tree, if she hadn't listened to his loud, sad thoughts, if she hadn't intervened in his life, each would have gone their separate ways. Perhaps they would have met by chance on some narrow or wide path without it meaning anything to either of them.

What happened to him after she erased his memory and he forgot her —might have happened to her as well. He eventually found his belonging and created his own family. Had their meeting done nothing but cause chaos in each other's lives?

Perhaps if it hadn't happened, she would have eventually come to this inevitable conclusion: falling in love with Echor, finding her belonging after all, with him, with Echor alone, not a heart divided between two... one of them in a box.

But the box was no longer closed!

And what does it matter if it's not closed? The relationship is impossible. It won't happen, no matter what. But Echor, he's real, tangible, easy, and beautiful!

So, why the struggle? What's so difficult about this?

Or is it because... no one belongs to two people at the same time?

(And what about this matter of belonging? What?

What if I don't feel a sense of belonging to anything or anyone?
I belong to Echor... yes... why not?!
Why am I trying to convince myself against my will!!
Don't I love him? Yes.
Don't I desire him? Yes.
Aren't I happy with him? Yes.
Don't I belong to him?!...
Damn it, why don't I belong to him?!
What does the feeling of belonging mean?!
What does this nonsense of belonging really mean!!

Is it connection, love, protection, home, the desire to stay, the motivation to stay, the feeling of completeness, the feeling of WHAT?!

Is what I'm searching for really belonging?!
Why do I feel that I need reasons to stay?
Why has my existence here become difficult for me after the offer from the immortal souls?
Why do I want to leave... so much? Why can't I just live simply like everyone else here?
Why has my heart become so heavy!!
All this is exhausting... all this is too much... and I no longer have the desire for all this chaos...
I can't find the point behind it...
I can't understand...).

She sighed at the echo of her thoughts as she walked back to the hotel. She walked for a long time, and midnight had passed. She let her feet take her along the road, turning over her thoughts after this unexpected, fateful, unfortunate meeting! She didn't know what to call it, but it certainly came at a crucial time.

The year she had agreed upon with Echor was nearing its end, and it had undoubtedly been one of the best years of her life! But would this affect her decision?

She felt the weight of her thoughts pressing down on her head and shoulders, like tiny, bothersome green imps jumping, playing, shouting, and annoying her for hours until fatigue finally overcame her.

She felt as though her eyes were swollen, though she hadn't cried, and her body felt heavy and stiff, even though she hadn't exerted herself. Something was squeezing her stomach—was it her heart? Or perhaps her lungs? Breathing was difficult!

She took a deep, strong breath, filling her lungs, held it for a moment, and lifted her head to the sky. Only a few stars were visible in the illuminated city sky. She looked at them and then slowly exhaled the held breath through her mouth, muttering Karl's last sentence to herself as she watched the stars: "So, it's goodbye then."

His words were more accurate than he could have imagined.

Finally, she stood before the door of their suite in the hotel, still turning over in her mind how to tell him, searching for the best, easiest, and least painful way. He had promised her he would accept her decision, whatever it was, that he would understand.

Should she tell him now? No, this was not the right time at all. She had just met Karl; he would think it was related to him, which it wasn't. The meeting might have added to the confusion and worsened the situation, but it certainly wasn't about him, or Echor, or anyone else, though they were both part of it. The main reason was related to her alone and that strange, annoying, inexplicable feeling.

The year wasn't over yet. The condition still stood!

Echor sensed her presence and opened the door without her knocking, a look of surprise on his face: "Why are you standing like that?"

She smiled at him with a broad, lively grin and walked in.

Shall I meet you tomorrow?[2]

"Who would believe winter if it said, 'Spring is in my heart'?"

—*Khalil Gibran*

---

[2] The title of a poem by the poet Al-Hadi Adam.

Karl smiled to himself when the last memory of her returned to him after several months. He had followed her advice, and somehow, it worked!

That day, he walked alone on the road, and when he arrived at the restaurant late, he had placed her in a closed box in a corner of his heart. He managed to smile at them with some vitality when they asked where he had disappeared. He apologised sincerely and said he had met an old friend. Only Giovanni knew his little secret, but he kept it anyway.

He felt lighter as if his old spirit was being restored to him. He hadn't distanced himself from her, he told himself. She was still with him in his comings and goings; she hadn't disappeared or gone far. "Always with me," as she had said.

He couldn't accept her departure, and now she never left him. He carried her inside his heart in that small box. "Always with me," he repeated to himself, making everything seem better.

While he was lost in his thoughts, something landed with great force in his front yard, stirring up dust around it. Karl jumped from his seat, watching what had struck the ground so hard. When the dust cleared, he could see it.

Echor was kneeling on one knee, his face pale with sorrow and anger, his eyes carrying sharp, intense looks that were hard to understand. Small tremors ran through his body from the emotion. He seemed as if he had been forced to come, and the truth was that if Echor hadn't reached the depths of despair if he had known another solution or idea, he wouldn't have hesitated for a moment to pursue it. For her, and only for her, he would do anything!

Karl stood frozen in place, not comprehending what was happening. Emily gasped in surprise: "Echor!" It had been many years since their last meeting with him. Emily's voice made Karl move from his spot. Selene wondered: "Is he okay? He doesn't look well!"

Karl said as he headed towards the door: "Alright, leave it to me. I'll see what he wants."

Karl went out to him, and Echor stood up his body tense. The sorcerers gathered at the door of the house, and Karl approached him calmly, and said: "Hello, Echor, what good wind brought you to us?"

Karl stood directly in front of him, his face marked with confusion. Echor didn't answer, instead gritting his teeth as he looked at him. It seemed an internal struggle was raging within him at that moment. Echor averted his gaze from Karl's puzzled face and looked at his family members, then muttered: "I need to talk to you"—he returned his gaze to Karl and added after a moment—"away from here."

There was something in Echor's face that prevented Karl from refusing. He agreed quickly, having never seen Echor like this before. It must be bad... very bad. Karl suddenly felt his heart pounding as he thought about how bad the matter must be for Echor to come. Yes, it was bad. That was clear. *Is Achilla alright?* Karl thought. He turned directly to his family, waving his hand: "I'm going with Echor to discuss something," and without waiting for a response or signal from them, he turned and began walking with him.

They delved into the nearby forest with quick steps, Echor not uttering a word as he walked ahead of Karl, who followed closely behind. With a sudden movement, Echor turned and stopped in front of him, almost causing Karl to bump into him, as he had been lost in his thoughts, his anxiety gradually rising. Echor spoke in a strained, emotional voice: "Do you remember the story of the immortal souls?"

Karl was surprised by the question! Surely, Echor hadn't appeared out of nowhere, in this state, to take him to the middle of the forest to tell him legends and stories of Fala! What was he getting at? Karl blinked and answered hesitantly: "Y-yes... which story exactly do you mean?"

Echor said: "The one about their request from Aldara to join them and the request for any great soul to join them in the world of Clotho!"

Karl didn't understand anything, but for some reason, he felt his legs failing him as if a deep, bottomless black abyss had opened where he stood. He was somehow hovering or suspended above it, ready to fall into it at any moment, to fall forever without reaching its bottom. He nodded to Echor while swallowing hard.

Echor felt all the turmoil, emotions, and thoughts that passed through Karl, even though he didn't understand anything. But Karl knew that what was about to be said was very bad... for both of them.

Echor's features calmed slightly, sadness becoming apparent and overwhelming. He said, averting his gaze from Karl: "The immortal souls have offered Achilla to join them in the world of Clotho, and Achilla agreed to it despite the queen's objection and mine. Today, in a few hours, she will perform the rituals to join them. You understand what this means, right? It means she will leave here to stay with them in the intermediate world. She will stay there forever, unable even to go to Mata"—he paused for a moment, then added in a low voice, as if telling himself or convincing himself or consoling himself or wishing—"as far as we know."

Karl felt everything around him stop moving—the branches, the leaves, the air, the squirrels, the rabbits, the insects, and the birds. All sounds ceased, a dreadful silence, a strange stillness. The light disappeared, and everything around him vanished. There was only that grieving man standing before him. The deep pit had swallowed him—swallowed both of them. They were falling together into it, falling slowly or quickly, who knows? They were falling endlessly.

Echor looked at that stunned face from which the last breath of life had been stolen, pale and ashen. How quickly he despaired! How quickly he surrendered to the news! Why didn't he scream as Echor had when he first learned? Why didn't he ask, inquire about the matter, about what happened? Could he perhaps do something, as Echor had thought, or was it just wishful thinking? Perhaps coming to Karl was nothing but a desperate, hopeless idea —one that refused to surrender, that fought weakly against the fate that had already been sealed.

Echor placed his hand on Karl's shoulder as if summoning him from the world of the dead he had entered. A faint light of hope and expectation shone in his eyes through his sorrowful, pained face. He said: "Karl… you are my last resort. I have done everything I could to prevent her from doing this. For a year, I did everything I could, and I thought she was truly happy, that she had changed her mind, that she was convinced, that she…"

Echor's expression changed, some anger returning to his features. He glared at Karl and continued: "Anyway, I thought I was close to succeeding in my endeavour… if it weren't for you… if you hadn't appeared suddenly that day a few months ago, I'm sure that…" Echor fell silent, pressing the palm of his hand to his forehead, then ran his fingers through his hair. He let out a strong sigh, suppressing his anger, which faded from his face: "I'm sorry, I shouldn't say that. Anyway… you need to come with me to Fala. We need to stop her from doing this. Maybe… we can influence her, maybe we can get her to postpone the rituals at least, for a few days, and we can try to convince her of the foolishness of her actions, of what she is about to do!"

Echor then shook Karl's shoulder forcefully, speaking with urgency and passion: "Imagine that even the queen thinks Achilla's decision is wrong… the queen! The one who reveres all the old customs, traditions, and beliefs. Despite the greatness of this matter and the belief of the people of Fala that it is a great honour, she refused it. She was shouting at Achilla… the queen was shouting! I swear it was the first time we saw her so agitated. Her voice echoed roughly throughout the palace while Achilla stood before her like a stone statue and left simply without saying a word. But even the queen eventually gave up and said that nothing would change her mind, that it was no use.

I don't believe that… I will try… we will try, we won't give up, right?"

Echor stopped speaking, staring at Karl, while the latter still stood with his mouth open, looking stunned.

Echor dropped his hand to his side, looked at Karl for a moment, then turned away, pressing his palms to his temples as his anger resurfaced. He clenched his jaw and said through gritted teeth:

"Damn it, there's no use! Here, he stands like a fool, understanding nothing. This was a stupid, desperate idea."

He then quickened his steps to leave when he heard a voice booming behind him: "No... no!! Take me to her... take me now... now!!!"

Echor turned to him, his eyes widening. Finally, Karl spoke. Karl rushed towards him, grabbed his hand, and shouted: "Now!" Echor gripped Karl's hand tightly and said: "Get ready."

Karl felt something pulling him forcefully and swiftly from behind, just like the first time he experienced instant travel, but this time, it was stronger, more violent, and faster. His eyes were open, and the colours around him suddenly mixed and intertwined, making him feel dizzy. Then, he found himself above Fala, descending rapidly to the same stone circle where they had landed the first time.

Everything was strangely still, as if no one was there. Echor stood in front of him, anxiously scanning the surroundings and glancing towards the palace as if searching for something, as if listening for something. Then he let out a muffled cry: "No! No! They've started the rituals early, taking advantage of my absence!"

Suddenly, Echor grabbed Karl by the collar and shot through the air, carrying him like a bag. Karl couldn't see or comprehend anything; all he knew was that within a second, he had moved from that square to the heart of the Urbahra Temple.

Echor and Karl landed forcefully in front of the gathered crowd, just a few meters from the Clotho Lake. Echor stood, angry and tense, his breathing erratic, his chest rising and falling heavily, his fists trembling. Karl, thrown off balance by the speed and force of the landing, was on his knees, his face filled with sorrow, pain, and confusion. Both saw what they had dreaded.

The thirty souls stood in a circle around the Clotho Lake, while Achilla stood at the edge of the small cliff. It was a majestic and beautiful scene at the same time.

The immortal souls glowed and shimmered with their clear limbs and misty faces while Achilla stood there with her magnificent wings spread wide, dressed in the same attire Karl had seen her in when she emerged from the Clotho Lake during the coronation days. She looked stunningly beautiful and majestic, and around them, the chants echoed everywhere.

A hint of surprise appeared on Achilla's face when her eyes fell on Karl and Echor, quickly turning into a look of sorrow.

Echor shouted something Karl couldn't understand, and Karl felt his tongue tied, standing before this scene that was nearing its end.

Echor lunged forward, but before he could take more than two steps, the temple knights and their leader leapt on him.

Echor was on the ground, screaming at the top of his lungs, calling out to Achilla. He almost freed himself from the four giants holding him, but more warriors joined in to restrain him. This was a sacred ritual that could not be interrupted or stopped. A few of the crowd stopped chanting to watch what was happening while the rest continued.

Achilla looked at this swift, final scene of Echor and Karl with deep sorrow. This was not how she wanted to leave, not how she wanted to treat Echor, that stubborn one who would never give up.

She cast a quick glance at Karl, which didn't last long, while Karl remained rooted in place, unmoving, silent, not breathing, his eyes fixed on her.

Achilla crossed her arms over her chest in an X shape and folded her outstretched wings. The souls moved in a spiralling, fluid motion from the edges of the lake towards Achilla, surrounding her from all sides as they hovered and circled her. Slowly, Achilla's limbs began to turn to stone… and bit by bit, she would turn completely!

Echor's screams grew louder, and he kicked, struck, and resisted fiercely, but he was firmly pinned to the ground, surrounded by the crowd, barely able to lift his head to look at her.

Achilla continued to gaze at the two standing before her, the two dearest to her heart. This was the last time she would see them, and what a state they were in!

Broken, sad, shattered—one like a hollow statue, the other like a volcano. What would become of them? Would they ever forgive her? Would they understand her decision?

Achilla shed a tear as she watched them, her second tear in public, and on her cheek, that tear turned to stone. She had now become a complete stone statue… with a tear that would accompany her evermore!

They saw her radiant, shimmering, beautiful soul leave that stone and move fluidly with the other thirty souls. They rose together, swirling like a luminous, tall column of mist above the Clotho Lake, like a strange dance, with Achilla at the top of that column. Then, after rising, they descended swiftly into Clotho Lake, followed by the souls, and they all disappeared into it. The chants ceased.

Achilla's stone statue rose into the air, lifted by the power of Wert-Hakaou, slowly flying to join the other stone statues of the immortal souls and the legendary beasts that had turned to stone with their masters inside the sacred Urbahra Cave.

The queen stood pensive among the crowd, with Beth-Nahra and Dasha silently weeping behind her, their eyes fixed on the stone. All three of them were consumed by thoughts of the shared fate of Hanila and her only daughter. Both had been exiled from Mata as if a curse had befallen Hanila and her lineage.

Echor's face was pressed against the ground. No one was holding him in place. They had all left him as soon as Achilla turned to stone. He remained there for a while, not crying, not speaking, just lying quietly. Meanwhile, Karl was still kneeling, his eyes overflowing with tears. After a long silence, he muttered, "It's no use."

The difference between Karl and Echor was that Karl had lost Achilla gradually over time.

When his eyes had fallen upon her, he saw the farewell etched on her face. "No use", as the queen had said. There was no use in screaming, protesting, or objecting. She had made her decision, and everything was over. When had Achilla ever gone back on her decisions? When had anything ever deterred her from her intentions? Nothing! He knew this—had known it from the beginning. That was why he was silent, motionless, dazed, not looking for anything, resigned to it all. No use. Yet, he still wished to be there, to see her, no matter how painful… for the last time.

As for Echor, that wretched soul, he had waited a long time, a lifetime, to be with her finally. He couldn't accept losing her, couldn't accept her departure. Even the promise to respect her decision, whatever it was —"Damn promises!" he had said, or rather shouted, when Achilla reminded him of it, after a year had passed. What did that year mean in the span of time? It was like a day and a night.

He remembered that recent day well. It was a beautiful, happy day like all the days of that year, but better. They had been strolling together in the streets, and he recalled how he laughed until he cried when Achilla took the microphone from a street performer. She asked the band of three young men, no older than nineteen, to play a song for her, and they gladly agreed. She sang to Echor, performing some dance moves, circling him, sometimes bumping her shoulder against his, sometimes pulling him by his tie.

While he chuckled at her public flirtation, his face flushed with both shyness and joy, a small crowd gathered around them. They watched the elegant couple dressed in formal attire as the sophisticated lady in her fancy clothes sang and danced in the street. They had just left a restaurant after a lovely evening. He remembered how he had lifted her in his arms and spun her around after she finished her "comedic" song and kissed her. He hadn't noticed the small crowd until he heard their applause and cheers. They were a beautiful, attractive, and happy couple, drawing attention wherever they went.

Echor saw an elderly couple standing a bit away from the crowd, watching them. The old woman sighed as she wrapped her arm around her husband's and rested her head on his shoulder. She whispered, "Oh, do you remember, my dear, when we were like them, full of energy and vitality? How I miss those days." The old man placed his free hand on his wife's cheek and replied in a tender, raspy voice, "When did those days ever leave us, my love? We may have aged, our joints may ache, our legs may no longer support us, and we suffer from rheumatism, but nothing has changed in our hearts... they are still young!" The woman laughed at her husband's comment, a soft light shining in her eyes. They exchanged deep looks, sealed with a gentle kiss, and continued their walk.

Echor saw himself and Achilla in that elderly couple, or so he wished! But not all wishes come true. His hopes didn't last long, for that day, he received her decision.

I won't describe how he raged and fumed, how he pleaded, how he asked for more time, how he cursed the promises, how he smashed the belongings in the cottage they had rented by the sea. You all know how Echor is now, but what is worth mentioning is what happened at the end of that argument.

Achilla remained calm throughout, accepting all his outbursts and trying to soothe him. Her voice finally broke when he asked, kneeling before her with his hands on her knees while she sat on the chair, "Didn't you love me... even a little, to change your mind?"

She answered, holding his face in her hands, "I loved you very much, so very much... but unfortunately, this has nothing to do with that. I know I'm hurting you deeply, and that kills and torments me the most because you, my love, don't deserve this. After everything you've done for me, and this year... the best year of my life... it deserves to be the ending. And what an ending! This is how I want to leave. I know you don't understand. I honestly tried to convince myself to stay, but it's far beyond that now. My place isn't here, no matter what this world is like or who I'm with, I don't belong here. That's exactly why the immortal souls have called me... I only realised this recently."

Tenderness, sweetness, and sorrow overflowed from her eyes. He felt himself collapsing in her hands, his strength failing him, and he laid his head in her lap… and cried! For the first time, he cried in her arms like a small child. She had never seen him cry before.

Karl placed his hand on Echor's back, who was still lying motionless on the ground, looking like a corpse, still and rigid, his eyes staring blankly, his face pale and features dull. No one tried to approach him, not even his mother or sister. They all understood what he was going through, the pain he was in, and yet everyone had left him, leaving him and Karl almost alone in that place. They knew how proud he was and how he refused anyone's comfort or pity. They knew he didn't want anyone to see him in that state. Echor was never a weak man, nor one to show his emotions, but everything changed in her presence. She was his exception.

Karl's hand on his back brought him out of the memory. He slowly lifted himself off the ground and sat up. He looked at Karl, the last hope for which he had restrained his jealousy and pride. Strangely, Karl's face bore a touch of sad calmness and a dignified look that hinted at despair.

For a second, Echor wanted to scream at him, to blame him, asking why he hadn't tried to stop her, to convince her. But he held back, knowing it was useless. Everything was over now, and he found the answer in Karl's thoughts. Karl had known what would happen, having experienced losing her more than once. He had suffered before, was closer to reality, and more accepting of it than Echor.

Echor asked him, his voice coming from the depths of pain, his eyes distant from life: "How can you do it? How can you accept it… endure it?"

Karl smiled, the saddest smile one could ever see, while the tears flowed from his eyes unceasingly. He felt as though his voice was choking him, but he forced himself to speak. With a broken voice, he replied, "I carry it in a box... inside my heart."

He ended his words there, unable to say more, and there was no need for more. The memories he had just recalled from that final meeting had already reached Echor.

****

Echor opened the door to the room quietly, and the sound of music reached his ears. He smiled bitterly and muttered to himself, "Only Achilla would leave music playing in her room, even when she's not here." He wandered through the room, among her musical instruments and other belongings. Everything was the same, unchanged, despite the time that had passed. He moved toward the balcony, her favourite spot. The curtains danced gently as always. He gazed at the chair, books still scattered around it, with Farouk Gouida's poetry collection on it. He picked it up and sat down in the chair, holding the book to his chest. It was the first time he had entered her room since her departure.

The music changed, now playing an old Arabic song. He knew it, but what was the name of it? It escaped him for a moment! Rarely did songs play in her room; it was usually just music. He listened closely:

"Oh, my heart, do not ask where love is... it was a palace of illusion, and it fell.

Drink to its ruins and quench your thirst from it... and tell my story as long as tears are telling.

...

Give me my freedom, release my hands... for I have given all, leaving nothing behind.

Oh, your chains had bled my wrist... why I keep it, when it's kept nothing of me left

What is holding onto vows that were not kept... and why the captivity, when I have the whole life?

...

O sleepless one, you slumber... remember the vow and awake.

And when a wound heals... a new will appear by remembering

Learn how to forget... and learn how to erase.

My beloved, everything is by fate... we were born unfortunate, not by our hands.

Perhaps our destinies will bring us together... one day, after so long.

Then, if a lover denies his lover... and we meet like strangers.

And each went to his own way... do not say we willed it, for fate had its will".[3]

The long song ended, and Echor shed a solitary tear as he gazed at the horizon, clutching the book of poems.

---

[3] *The Ruins*, song by Umm Kulthum, lyrics by the poet Ibrahim Naji.

In Your Eyes, My Home...[4]

"In the direct middle of the flowing season
I suddenly think of the length of the day
In the midst of these busy days
I draw a dream of you and me
Sending thoughts on the March breeze
...
Standing at the entrance of a new world
The thing I realised is I'm not alone
If I close my eyes
You're still there on the other side (of my eyelids)
I wonder how strong you've become
And I want to be that same way to you

From here on, side by side
With a gentle smile."

—*A Japanese song by Remioromen*

---

[4] The title of a poem by the poet Farouk Gouida.

Echor strolled leisurely through the palace, one hand in his pocket, greeting everyone he passed with his broad, mischievous smile.

A dwarf carrying ten large tomes atop his head greeted him, "Good morning, Kharis-Echor!"

Echor nodded, "Good morning, Kaldo. I see you're still stuffing your room with volumes. Why not move to the library, Kharis? It would be easier for you!"

Kaldo smiled, nearly tripping over his long beard as he walked, "They kicked me out because my loud snoring disturbed them. It seems you can't sleep in libraries! Nor eat, nor conduct experiments, nor practice astrology…" Kaldo's voice faded as he listed the prohibitions while walking away.

Echor continued his light walk, shaking his head with a wide smile, and muttered, "It seems my idea is outdated!"

One of the handmaidens greeted him and sighed wistfully as he walked away. Isn't it sad that such a handsome and distinguished man is alone? What a waste!

Echor finally stopped in front of a wide black door. He stood there for a second without knocking, and a deep voice from inside called out, "Come in!"

The door opened on its own, and he stepped inside. This room was different from the rest of the palace, with dark colours and dim lighting illuminated by flickering flames. Near the centre of the room stood a massive round black stone table, surrounded by chairs with very tall backs covered in black and burnt brown leather. The walls were made of stone bricks.

As Echor entered, he said, "Good morning, Bissilia." The queen, who was contemplating an old painting depicting one of the first guardians of Fala, replied, "Good morning, Kharis-Echor." She then moved to the large table and sat on one of the chairs, followed by Echor who sat beside her.

Echor's face radiated confidence, comfort, and something else indescribable, while the queen's face remained as expressionless as ever. She said, "The Sibyl Wert-Hakaou has informed me of your condition or 'desire' to be precise. She considered your request somewhat… impudent!" The queen seemed to ponder a bit before uttering the last word.

Echor replied sarcastically, "Oh, that's good. I thought she would consider my request forbidden! So, are we alright?"

The queen listened to his response with dead eyes, paused for a moment, then shook her head impatiently and muttered, "You are all fools! Useless! What a corrupt, irresponsible, and disrespectful generation you are!"

She rose from her seat, still muttering similar phrases, and began to pace slowly around the meeting room. Echor, maintaining his calm demeanour and still wearing his smile, remarked, "I believe we've discussed this matter before, Bissilia, a long time ago. My decision is final. No matter what you or the seer may think of our generation, it won't change my resolve."

The queen turned towards him, a faint frown appearing on her marble-like forehead, and said in a calm yet firm tone, "Do you truly understand the meaning of your request? And what its consequences might be? Do you know that the souls might consider your interference in their affairs an affront to their wisdom and insight?"

Echor replied nonchalantly, "Well… I believe the souls chose me, knowing my nature well!"

The queen's voice showed some irritation as she said, "Such recklessness! Such impudence! Is this how you repay the souls for their honour and trust in you?"

No sign of concern or interest appeared on Echor's face. He simply shrugged, then stood up, walking toward the queen to stand directly before her. He brought his face close to hers, locking his eyes with hers. In that moment, determination and strength clearly shone in his gaze. With deliberate precision, he said, pressing each word slowly, his head moving gently as he spoke, "If you want me to become the heir to the throne, if they want me to become the heir to the throne, they should speak to me first… It's a simple matter."

Now, the queen's icy features bore a hint of disgust. She turned her face away and walked away from him and replied in a sharp voice, "Go to Wert-Hakaou, she is the one who decides this matter."

Echor left the room without saying another word and headed to the sacred cave of the Urbahra Temple, walking leisurely. He entered the cave's mouth and let his eyes adjust to the darkness of the vast, deep cavern. He walked as if he knew his way to a specific spot, despite not having visited that part of the cave often. It was a strange, suffocating, and unsettling thing to do, despite all the time that had passed.

He stopped in front of a stone statue standing among several others, gazing at it for a while. Then he raised his hand and placed the tip of his finger on the petrified tear on the statue's cheek as if trying to wipe it away. A deep sorrow and longing gripped his heart. Nothing had changed except that the love in his heart had grown steadily with the longing. Isn't it said that out of sight is out of mind? Then why was she never far from his heart? Why was she still there, enthroned within his heart? Why?!

A deep voice came from behind him, "You realise it has been nine hundred years, don't you? Kharis-Echor!"

Echor whispered as if speaking to himself, still lost in the statue of Achilla, "Yes... She has been crying for a long time!" Then he turned towards the voice and greeted her with his beautiful smile, "Hello, Sibyl Wert-Hakaou!"

She replied with her small smile and ever-bright eyes, "Oh, you know that's not what I meant, you rascal! Anyway, it's good to see you, Kharis. It's been some time since I last saw you. At first, I thought you were starting to take on her traits and love for disappearing... but over time, you've become even worse!"

Echor replied sarcastically, fidgeting and putting his hands in his pockets, scrunching his face, "Eh... You certainly didn't summon me here, Sibyl Wert-Hakaou, just to scold me for my behaviour!"

She answered with her glowing eyes, "Certainly not, though you deserve some of it! You've kept the souls waiting for a long time to perform the coronation rites."

Echor commented, "That wasn't my intention. Bissilia was strongly opposed to my request, but I think she finally realised that I wouldn't change my mind. I hope you won't be as stubborn as she is, Sibyl!" He added the last sentence, raising his eyebrow and smiling broadly, revealing his molars.

The Sibyl stood, observing him, wondering how a man as tough and resilient as Echor could bend and wither, even perish, for the sake of love. Anyone with a heart would feel some pity and sympathy for him despite the recklessness of his actions. Yet, a hidden voice urged this wise Sibyl to empathise with him, to grant his request and to show mercy. More than four hundred years had passed since the signs appeared on him, and throughout these years, he had not wavered in his decision or his stubborn desire to meet and speak with the immortal souls first. There was no other solution but to allow him, even if the true motive was out of mercy for him.

Echor ignored the thoughts of pity and sympathy that crossed Wert-Hakaou's mind. If this was what would grant him his wish, he didn't care. Many around him secretly pitied him, even though there was nothing outwardly pitiable about him. But his isolation, his withdrawal, his unwillingness to replace Achilla with anyone else, and his acceptance of solitude were what called for it.

The Sibyl turned and began to walk into the depths of the dark cave, with Echor following her. She said, "You know your request is impudent."

He replied, stifling a laugh, "Yes, the queen told me that."

She continued, "You know we only summon the immortal souls in rare and extremely important cases?"

He answered, "Yes."

She turned to face him and said, "And you know that what you intend to do is a blatant interference in matters you have no right to?"

This time, Echor stood silent and did not answer her. The Sibyl exchanged glances with him before turning to continue walking. She added, "Let's hope the souls find your request more amusing than infuriating. Personally, I'm curious about this matter… and that's the only reason I'll grant your request." Echor didn't comment, only offering a small smile.

They approached a place with stronger lighting than the rest of the cave, located at the very end of the deep cavern. The lower Sibyls sat facing each other there, their hoods pulled over their heads just like Wert-Hakaou. She joined them, sitting beside them. After standing there for a while, unsure of what to do, Echor was signalled to sit in front of her, forming a group as if to play cards. They placed their hands in front of their chests, bowed their heads, and closed their eyes. Echor did the same, and Wert-Hakaou began chanting, followed by the lower Sibyls.

After some time, Echor felt a strange presence, or as if he had been transported to another place with a strange presence. Everything felt cloudy at first, but as the chanting grew quieter, he felt as if he was drifting farther away from it. A heavy weight pressed against his chest with such force, a tremendous energy, making it hard to breathe. Signs of discomfort appeared on Echor's face… Was this normal? What was happening to him?

The pressure on his chest increased, and the air around him became dense and still, as if the place's humidity had increased to the point of suffocating him.

He felt unable to inhale and was suffocating. He clasped his hands to his chest, raised his head high, and opened his eyes wide, trying to take a deep breath through his mouth, but it didn't help much. Darkness surrounded him from all sides, with only a faint glow emanating from him in the oppressive darkness. He struggled to breathe, sweat beads forming on his forehead. He felt extreme fatigue, and his vision blurred. Then, he began to see a faint light appearing around him like points of light, gradually glowing brighter and more radiant.

The lights approached him slowly, and as they did, his exhaustion increased, and the force of their presence crushed him until he was almost pressed to the ground. He bent his legs beneath him, leaned on his left hand, and his right was on his chest, his breath quickening as he struggled to maintain his composure. (So, this is what the presence of the immortal souls feels like!) he thought, trying with difficulty to focus his blurred vision on the approaching souls, searching for a specific one in particular!

The souls gathered around him in a tight circle, increasing the pressure on him. They did not try to ease their presence, treating him harshly due to his recklessness and indifference. A voice came from an unknown source said: "Do you mock us?" Another voice followed: "Do you think this is a game?" A third voice added: "Do you not understand the magnitude and importance of the responsibility we entrusted to you?" The disapproving voices came at him from all directions as he looked around in despair, trying to find the sources of the voices among the glowing spectres around him.

Echor struggled to breathe and spoke in a weak, desperate, trembling voice, "What… is wrong… with my… request… I… want… Achilla… to be… the soul… accompanying… me… if… you… want…"

A thick, gruff voice interrupted him, and this time, he could identify the source. It was the tall, broad with a thick beard standing before him, saying, "Do you think this is a choice? Do you think we choose the souls arbitrarily or randomly? If it were that simple, we would let all the guardians choose the spirit that suits them! This is no place for childish folly!"

Echor felt a crushing force on his chest as the gruff voice scolded him, causing him intense pain. He began to cough violently, spitting blood from his mouth. The voices around him echoed, "Did we make a mistake in choosing... Yes, we made a mistake... This is nonsense... Recklessness... This is not the time for love... Guardians must be wise... Nonsense... We made a mistake..."

The voices continued to speak, disapproving and agitated, and Echor's condition worsened. He felt he was about to lose consciousness from the suffocating pressure. Just as he thought he could bear no more, a booming voice rang out from around them: *"Stop!"*

From among the souls emerged a beautiful, delicate, radiant figure. It approached him eagerly and placed a light touch on his shoulder. As it did, it felt as though a massive, heavy stone had been lifted from his chest. He gasped, drawing a deep breath, as his eyes fixed on the face of the worried, smiling soul before him. He cried out, "Achilla!!!"

Calmness filled his heart, and his heartbeat quickened after having slowed. He began to breathe deeply, finally looking into her eyes. Nothing happening around him mattered anymore—not the immortal spirits, not this strange place, not the crushing weight he had been under, not the nonsense they were speaking, nor the sacred summoning he made them perform for her... just to see her again... for another look into her eyes.

He had wondered for a long time what it would be like to look into her eyes again now that she was a soul without a body. Would it feel the same? Would he still see that sparkle and glow, the radiant hair, those rosy lips, and gleaming teeth?

Amazingly, it felt the same but even stronger. This time, he could see the beauty of her spirit clearly. Those eyes still sparkled in that ethereal face. He was overwhelmed with deep happiness and contentment, and his eyes shone with longing and eagerness. A tired, sad smile spread across his lips. He raised his hand, wanting to touch her cheek, murmuring to himself, "Those eyes are still the same..." But as he placed his hand on her cheek, it felt like touching a thick bubble or rushing air, just like placing your hand in front of a fan. The touch was disappointing, and his eyes reflected his disappointment.

He tried to grasp her more firmly, hoping the sensation would improve, but to no avail. Achilla remained smiling despite this, placed her other hand over his with the same light touch, and said in a sweet, concerned voice, "You are a fool."

In a tired voice, he said, "That's a given."

She asked, "What do you hope to gain from this?"

He replied, "To see your eyes."

"Then what?" she inquired.

"Then I shall lose myself in them... or find my resting place... I cannot say exactly, for I am a fool." he said with a broad smile.

She bit her lip to stifle her laughter and turned her face away from him, glancing at those around them whom he had forgotten or no longer cared about. Her expression turned serious and stern as she said, "That's enough. Echor hasn't committed a heinous crime. I think you're overreacting a bit. Please ease your presence so he can stand on his feet and speak with you. I believe there's no harm in letting him talk."

Silence fell for a moment before the thick-bearded soul spoke again, "His actions show extreme recklessness and impulsiveness. Guardians must be wiser and more rational. How can a man like him allow his emotions to lead him and act with such childish impulsiveness?"

Achilla stood and walked to face the thick-bearded soul, placing her hand on her hip with her usual careless demeanour, her dancing smile unchanged. Despite being in another realm and another life, she hadn't changed. She remained the same, with the same traits, behaviours, smile, and eyes.

She said sarcastically, "Really, Kharis-Atti? It's as if you're describing me!" She looked at him defiantly. Then a deep voice came from behind the souls, "I believe Achilla is right. How is Echor different from her in this? In fact, we all know that she was far more reckless and impulsive than him, yet here she is among us now, an immortal spirit."

Echor turned towards the voice that had now come to his left, at the forefront of the souls. It was Aldara, and Echor couldn't help but notice the similarity between her demeanour and Achilla's. Both possessed that free, rebellious, and bold spirit. Aldara continued, "Stand, Kharis-Echor… stand and speak." Echor felt a wave of relief and lightness as Aldara spoke those words. He felt the burden lighten, and he could finally stand on his feet, which he did.

Sweat still covered his forehead, and he still felt some fatigue, but he wiped his forehead with the palm of his hand and sighed deeply before speaking, "I know I have no right to ask this… in fact, I don't know if I have the right or not!"

He shrugged indifferently, and Achilla pursed her lips to suppress her smile. It seemed his penchant for defiance hadn't diminished over the centuries. He continued, "But I know it may seem reckless, and for that, I apologise… I don't mean any disrespect toward your decisions, your wisdom, or your power. My request is entirely personal, and I know that's something none of you are unaware of. Yes, yes, I know… it's not 'professional,' if I may say so! But I… I am desperate."

Silence fell, and Echor's expression took on a solemn air, his eyes filled with sorrow and loss. What could the souls say to such a sorrowful man? A man who decided to break all the rules and disregard the sacred for the sake of love! He cared not for duty, responsibility, honour, glory, protection, traditions, or the Falan people before her, before her eyes!

Achilla couldn't bear the pain in his eyes and the strange tone in his voice when he uttered the last word. She averted her eyes from him, feeling a crushing guilt and shame! She lowered her head. If souls could cry… perhaps she would have wept at that moment.

Echor, who hadn't taken his eyes off her, continued, "To be more accurate, I am a lover to the point of despair. Let me tell you, gentlemen, despite all the absurdity my position may seem to hold right now, despite all the indifference, disrespect, and childishness… and whatever names you wish to give to my actions and words. I am neither ashamed nor regretful of this. And here I stand, telling you— whether with or without my deepest apologies— that I will not accept your selection of me as the future protector of Fala unless Achilla is the soul that accompanies me."

He paused, a sweet and tormented smile on his lips. Throughout his speech, he addressed no one but her, the one who almost hid her face in her hands out of sheer misery and compassion for him. Finally, she raised her eyes to him, filled with evident longing and tenderness.

The spirits remained silent for a while until Aldara finally spoke, "Very well! And while this may be unprecedented, I see no harm in it. There is nothing that forbids one of the guardians from choosing a companion from the immortal souls. As far as we know, there is no danger to the future of Fala in this request. Thus, some exceptions may occasionally be allowed. I believe, dear spirits, the decision lies with our own Achilla... what do you think?"

The souls murmured, "This is nonsense... No harm... Yes, the decision is Achilla's... This is chaos! ... No, it is not chaos, dear. It is a bold precedent... No harm... This is absurd... No harm... Yes... I don't know... This is unacceptable... The decision is Achilla's..."

The voices fell silent after their mixed reactions, both opposing and supporting. Finally, all eyes turned to the oldest and first immortal soul, Atti, who was fiddling with his thick, long beard and looking away. He was silent and lost in thought, his features extremely serious. Atti was a soul of evident high dignity and great energy. At last, he looked at Echor and, after a moment, burst into a booming laugh that spread astonishment among the souls!

He laughed so hard that his head fell back, and his shoulders and chest shook. Then he said, "You poor soul... hahaha... such a wretched lover... hahaha... you remind me of my youth... hahaha... such love is rare these days... hahaha... the matter is up to Achilla... hahaha..." He turned away, still laughing and repeating, "The matter of that poor soul is up to Achilla!"

Achilla looked at Atti in amazement. He had always been a very serious man, and she had never seen him laugh once during her time in Clotho. He had once said that he had forgotten how to laugh over time, with all he had seen and amidst all those heavy responsibilities. He had simply forgotten how to laugh. And in Echor's pitiful state, what made him remember? It seemed like a kind of dark comedy, as they say.

Atti walked away, followed by some of the immortal souls, while others remained, awaiting Achilla's decision. She approached Echor, who seemed unaffected by everything that had happened. She placed her hands in his, and he felt that strange, light, and annoying touch. He missed the old touch, and now he was trying to come to terms with this new, unsatisfying touch. It would be even more disappointing in the mortal world, as he wouldn't be able to hold her if she agreed to accompany him!

She said sorrowfully, "Why do you insist on torturing yourself? You shouldn't have done this... You won't gain anything by having me accompany you. It will only make things worse for you. You need to forget to move on from the past. Haven't you learned anything from what happened? I regret agreeing to..."

Echor interrupted her, "Don't you dare... don't you dare say it. I have never regretted my old request. That year was the best of my entire life. I don't think there is any happiness like the one I experienced with you. I managed to endure all these years after you with that memory, content."

She said sadly, "That's exactly what I mean! Why waste yourself in ruins? What's the point of what you're doing now? Why force yourself to live alone forever when what you should do is move on with your life and…"

He interrupted her again, "And what? Lock you in a closed box inside my heart and move on? In truth, my whole heart is a box that holds only one thing… You know I tried before, and I'm not one to repeat my mistakes."

She shook her head, looked away, and drew a small smile, saying, "I see you've talked to Karl!"

He replied with a hint of sarcasm, trying to touch her hair with his fingertips, "Yes, the Earthlings say that group therapy sessions for alcoholics or those who have experienced similar emotional crises are helpful!"

He looked back into her eyes and said tenderly, "He has become a father to two wonderful children… Nora and David. David was a very troublesome child; in fact, he still is!"

Achilla gasped softly and said, "Really! How wonderful… He has children now! Oh… he must be a great father!"

She fell silent for a moment, trying to imagine Karl as a father with his children, then whispered, "So he finally married Selene!"

Echor, searching her eyes for the meaning of her words, said, "Yes, they finally got married."

He found nothing in her eyes. She didn't appear troubled at all; in fact, she seemed quite at ease with the news. He said, "Had you not made that foolish mistake, you would have known this old news in its time and perhaps even attended their wedding instead of staying in this desolate place, cut off from the world."

She smiled sideways and said, "Not completely cut off. We can track anyone within Fala. I've followed your news for years, but you often leave Fala."

They exchanged glances in silence, and then she asked hesitantly, "Is he happy?"

He whispered, "Yes."

Her face lit up at this confirmation, and Echor didn't know whether to be sad or happy about her reaction. Would his sadness or happiness change his reality? What was the use of everything he felt… and what was the use of his request, after all… other than more suffering for himself?

He was suffering, anyway! But suffering from her ghostly presence was a thousand times better than suffering from her absence. That was how he saw it.

He had lived long enough after her and finally understood what it meant to lose the world's colours around him, reduced to black and white. He understood what it meant for coffee to be unbearably bitter, no matter how much sugar he added. He learned the meaning of the sunrise and sunset becoming equal in his eyes, the meaning of life's taste fading so that music now sounded like the cries of wounded birds, books like incomprehensible scribbles by children, and paintings nothing more than ugly, scattered lines.

He came to understand what it meant for people's faces to become intolerably ugly, impossible to look at, their conversations sounding like the blaring of alarm sirens, and their laughter! That strange sound called laughter! How it had turned into something foreign, incomprehensible to everyone but her, the one who possessed the most beautiful laugh in the world in his eyes. The one whose laughter made everything around her shine and bloom. Laughter had become a living creature that died with her departure... and now, all others carried only a poor imitation of it, a broken version. How could he make her realise that? How could he make her understand?

Breaking the silence, he said, "Come back with me, accompany me. Everything has become ugly since you left. Nothing has any meaning after your departure. The world has become an emptiness within an emptiness. How I long to laugh until I cry again, to dance to music, to enjoy poetry and singing. Accompany me and know that you would be bringing a dead man back to life if you did."

She cupped his face in her hands and said, "This will only make things worse for you..."

He replied like a poor child begging for a piece of bread from passersby, "Nothing could be worse than my current state!"

There is no feeling worse or more bitter than what Achilla felt as she looked at Echor's face at that moment. How could anyone with a heart refuse any request from someone who bore such a face that had endured so much? Achilla gazed at that face for a moment, and then... she drew the same old smile she had when she agreed to his request long ago.

She let out a small, nervous laugh and said, "You fool! Who loves like this nowadays... You really are an old-fashioned man!"

He tried to press his forehead against hers, almost bursting with laughter from excessive happiness, a small vein forming between his eyebrows: "I am now eighteen hundred years old... I must be somewhat outdated!"

How he wished he could hold her tightly at that moment.

****

Echor stood among the musical instruments in the white room, watching Achilla as she wandered through her old room. He had imagined and longed to see her there again thousands of times.

Her voice whispered inside his head as she turned towards him, "Everything is the same!" She then closed her eyes in delight as she listened to the music that still filled the room and added, "How I've missed this!" He replied with his beautiful smile, "I didn't let anything change in your absence. I knew you would return here someday. This place was my refuge, the straw that confirmed your existence was real and that you were never just a figment of my imagination."

No one but him could see or hear her, for the accompanying soul only reveals itself to its companion. Her words were like whispers inside his head, and she appeared to him as a ghostly figure. When he went to the world of Clotho to complete the rituals, and when he saw her that time before the rituals, her presence and form were clearer. But in the earthly world, the image was more transparent, for this was not a world for spirits!

She went to the balcony and placed her fingertips on the book that was still on the rocking chair. It had become more tattered than before despite the obvious attempts to restore and preserve it. She could feel the touch but couldn't hold it or turn its pages. Echor approached her and stood facing her, looking at her for a while with hungry longing in his eyes. He instinctively reached out, as he always did, and tried to place his hand on her cheek, but his hand simply passed through her face as if nothing was there... She blinked.

He let his hand fall by his side, his smile still on his face. Her mere presence was enough for him. He had always been content with little from her in everything, and it seemed fate had withheld more from him.

She lifted her fingertips to his face, and he closed his eyes. He felt something cold brush his cheek gently, like a feather caressing his skin or a cool breeze. He smiled broadly, opened his eyes, tears glistening in them, and said in a hoarse voice, "Welcome back!"

She met his smile with a wider one, and he could see in her ghostly face, her old face, her mischievous smile, her carefree and funny features, and her sparkling eyes. She said, "It's been a long time since I heard you play the violin! I've missed your playing... I've missed you so much!" Her voice trembled slightly at the last sentence.

Echor remarked playfully, raising his hands in the air, "Then, we must not keep my fair lady waiting any longer." He quickly moved toward the room, grabbed the heavenly violin—almost identical to the earthly one, but with more strings and a longer neck—and returned to her. She had seated herself on the edge of the stone balcony, clapping for him enthusiastically like a child when he returned with the violin. He placed it on his shoulder, cleared his throat, and bowed his head to her, saying, "My lady..." He placed the bow on the strings, closed his eyes, paused for a moment, and then began to play a melody that Achilla adored passionately—The winter sonata, *Only You*.

A melody that resembled them, a sad and sweet tune—a tune telling the story of two strange, lonely souls in a harsh, absurd world who had created a new and special world for themselves, a world far from reality. A world that stood entirely on that distant balcony, where the rays of the rising sun fell upon it, as he played that melody for their new world.

The End.

Made in the USA
Monee, IL
17 April 2025